MW00567598

Elimination

When Veronica Newman and her mother are both found dead by their housekeeper in London's Terrace Vale district, Detective Inspector Harry Timberlake is brought in to investigate. Timberlake senses deep trouble. Why does the mother appear to have died from natural causes when Veronica has been brutally murdered? And where is Charles Henry Newman, Veronica's estranged husband?

Inquiries soon reveal that Newman has a criminal record for violent behaviour. Timberlake tracks him down to the seedy underworld of Marseilles, and after their meeting, his suspicions intensify. It's Newman's aura. Timberlake's street-sharpened instinct tells him something . . . But it appears that Newman can't be guilty – he has a watertight alibi.

Timberlake is taken off the case to concentrate on a local corruption investigation. Then, in neighbouring Southington, a fifty-five-year-old woman is found stabbed to death. Soon afterwards, a sixty-year-old widow is murdered – and the forensic team confirms that the same person is responsible. Is there a serial killer on the loose?

Despite all evidence to the contrary, Timberlake's conviction of Newman's guilt remains undented. Could this be Timberlake's first big mistake. . . ? But with his personal life in crisis and a murder squad stretched to breaking point – and beyond – Timberlake cannot afford to make mistakes . . .

By the same author:

VENGEANCE

ELIMINATION

Max Marquis

MACMILLAN
LONDON

First published 1993 by Macmillan London Limited

a division of Pan Macmillan Publishers Limited
Cavaye Place London SW10 9PG
and Basingstoke

Associated companies throughout the world

ISBN 0–333–57096–0

Copyright © Max Marquis 1993

The right of Max Marquis to be identified as the
author of this work has been asserted by her in accordance
with the Copyright, Designs and Patents Act 1988.

All rights reserved. No reproduction, copy or transmission
of this publication may be made without written permission.
No paragraph of this publication may be reproduced, copied or
transmitted save with written permission or in accordance with
the provisions of the Copyright Act 1956 (as amended). Any
person who does any unauthorised act in relation to
this publication may be liable to criminal prosecution
and civil claims for damages.

9 8 7 6 5 4 3 2 1

A CIP catalogue record for this book is available from
the British Library

Phototypeset by Intype, London
Printed by Mackays of Chatham PLC, Chatham, Kent

For Margaret

Chapter 1

The moment she walked into the bedroom Lily Coker knew Mrs Ann Pascoe was dead because she wasn't snoring. Every morning when Lily brought in Mrs Pascoe's tea at nine-thirty on the dot her employer was snoring. Just to make sure, Lily Coker touched Mrs Pascoe on her hand. It was as cold as her character.

Lily didn't squawk or scream at finding the body; she was quite used to death. Four afternoons a week she worked in a funeral parlour, with an air-conditioned Chapel of Rest. In hot weather she preferred to sit in the cool with the corpses and read the *Sun*. Mrs Coker was a versatile, self-employed woman.

She sighed, and put the small tray with morning tea and the *Daily Telegraph* on a bedside table. She would have to break the news to Mrs Pascoe's daughter, Veronica Newman.

Lily crossed the corridor and knocked on the door of Veronica's bedroom, with its *en suite* bathroom. *All* the bedrooms on this floor had *en suite* bathrooms.

'Mrs Newman?' she called after a moment, and knocked again. There was no answer. Then she opened the door.

This time she did squawk, and loudly. Several times.

She had seen a lot of corpses, but never one that had looked so ghastly. Until then Lily Coker had never seen someone who had been strangled. And certainly not in *that* position.

The Metropolitan Police Terrace Vale Area runs from Hill Park in the south to a winding, overloaded main road to the north which finally joins up with a motorway further to the north-east. The journey from the south side of Terrace Vale to the northern boundaries begins in conspicuous affluence, moves through middle-class, tenaciously held respectability, and ends in a text-book example of urban decay. Most of the abundant graffiti at the

1

northern end have something rude, if not downright obscene, to say about the government. Sex comes a bad second.

The south of Terrace Vale boasts expensive houses and medium-sized hotels; the centre has modest houses and flats. The area finally descends into a grimy, half-industrial, half-residential section of badly rundown houses which were once large, elegant homes but now are rabbit warrens of bedsitters and 'studio flats'. The front doors have more bell buttons than a Mighty Wurlitzer organ has stops.

In addition to the expensive private homes and the old houses which have been divided, subdivided and sub-subdivided by anonymous absentee landlords, the area has a few minor embassies and consulates, luxury hotels and seedy boarding houses, upholstered gambling clubs and brazen clip joints, high-class call girls and back-of-the-car whores, four-star restaurants and Chinese takeaways, gardens and ghettos... There are long-standing residents and overnight transients, international criminals and junkie bag-snatchers... a teeming, multiracial community in a self-contained area where something is always going on – usually illegal.

So, Terrace Vale is as complete a melting pot of urban living as you could hope – or fear – to find. Detective Inspector Harry Timberlake sometimes called it, without meaning to be pretentious, a gallimaufry. His colleagues have become sufficiently accustomed to him to know that he's not simply trying to be clever: he is clever, but they forgive him.

In the south-east corner of Terrace Vale just off the main road is a building that never sleeps and never closes its doors. Staffed by a team of men and women it operates 24 hours a day, 365 days a year, like a hospital. And like the people who work in a hospital, the staff have to struggle to preserve some sort of sensibility and not have calloused souls as they deal with people who would rather not be there.

Terrace Vale Police Station, otherwise known as The Factory or The Nick, and sometimes The Terrace Vale Hilton, was built in the last century. Someone once said that it had originally been designed as a workhouse but had never been used for that purpose because it was too gloomy. A couple of hours in there dents the resistance of the cockiest criminal.

*

Detective Chief Inspector Ted Greening sat at his desk and swore as he mopped his face with a handkerchief that looked as if it had come out of a grubby schoolboy's pocket. Both the door and window of his office were open, and an aged fan whined resentment at being forced to try to produce a current of cool air.

Mornings were never his best part of the day. It wasn't merely that it took him a couple of hours for the effects of the excesses of the previous night to wear off. Mornings were when he got up and had to face his wife across the breakfast table. Marjorie Greening was forty-eight, and looked as if she had been for the past ten years. Her mouth was a thin, pallid line set in a permanent inverted V of disapproval. She hadn't always been like that, and if she hadn't been strictly religious, she would have divorced Ted Greening decades earlier. Instead she accepted him as Her Cross.

Marjorie dutifully bore her husband two children early in their marriage then developed a permanent bedtime headache that had lasted for a good twenty-six years. For twenty-four of them Greening hadn't cared.

Greening was just over fifty, but he, too, looked older. He was putting on weight faster than he was replacing his wardrobe. He was a glad-hander, back-slapper, knowing winker and a bad dirty storyteller. All he wanted now was a life with no waves. His eye was firmly fixed on his retirement. The pity of it all was that once he was a first-class copper, a successful thief-taker. He had several commendations for his work and his bravery, but the last one was a long time ago.

'I hate the fucking summer,' he said for the third time that morning to no one in particular. Come about November, he regularly declared that he hated the fucking winter. He didn't have a good word for spring or autumn, either.

But things were just about to get worse for Ted Greening.

'Ted, got something for you.'

He looked up. It was the desk sergeant, Anthony C. Rumsden. In the hierarchy at Terrace Vale sergeants usually called Greening 'guv', and sometimes 'sir', just to be on the safe side. The barometer of Greening's moods usually swung between 'Wet and windy' and 'Stormy', depending on the state of his head and his liver, with only very rare intervals of 'Fair'. Rumsden, however, was something of an institution at Terrace Vale and was tacitly granted an intimacy denied other officers.

3

Greening recognized the tone, and wished he could pretend he hadn't heard, but there was no bolt-hole for him. 'Morning, Tony.'

'Central have passed on a nine nine nine call. Looks like a murder in The Sycamores Avenue. A couple of our own mobiles have already responded.'

'Oh, shit,' Greening grumbled. When it came to imaginative invective, he was hardly in the John Osborne class.

Rumsden continued unperturbed. 'We've informed the SOCOs and the doc. They're on the way. D'you want a car?'

Greening avoided his eye. He indicated a stack of files on his desk. 'I'd like to,' he lied, 'but I've got this lot to cope with.' Lie number two. Nearly all the files were window-dressing to give the impression that he was being overwhelmed with work. 'Anyway, it's a DI's thing. I'm just a desk copper now,' he said with hypocritical dejection. He was glad to be off the streets.

He moved into the corridor and opened the door of Harry Timberlake's office. It was empty.

'Sod it,' he said, as articulate as ever. He crossed to the CID main office. The newly promoted Detective Sergeant Darren Webb, Woman Detective Constable Sarah Lewis, a.k.a. the Welsh Rarebit to her colleagues, and a couple of other detective constables were there.

'Anyone seen Harry Timberlake this morning?' Greening asked.

Sarah Lewis had seen him a couple of hours earlier but thought it imprudent to mention the fact. She and Harry were managing the enormous trick of keeping secret the intimate relationship which had begun when she was responsible for nicking the highly successful burglar who was known as 'Phantom Flannelfoot'.

'I think he mentioned something last night about seeing someone on the council corruption case. He said he'd be in about half-past ten.'

'What about Bob Farmer?'

'At the Bailey, giving evidence in that building society holdup.'

'Oh, bloody hell.' Greening looked at Sergeant Webb with a marked lack of sympathy and encouragement. 'You'd better get over there, Darren, and hold the fort until Harry arrives, I suppose,' he grumbled. 'You won't be able to bugger things up before the SOCOs and the doc have got out of the way.'

Twenty minutes after Webb had left, Harry Timberlake, as spruce as if he'd had eight hours' sleep and a hearty breakfast, breezed into the CID office.

*

4

Detective Inspector Harry Timberlake, the son of a general labourer and a hospital cleaner, was born in the docklands area of east London. The birth took place at home, the Timberlakes' council house, otherwise his parents would have sworn that there had been a mixup of babies in the hospital.

He was a complete enigma to Herbert and Daisy Timberlake – and for that matter to their family and neighbours – for he had almost nothing in common with either of them. The only things he seemed to have inherited were his father's muscularity and his mother's Virgoan nit-picking fastidiousness.

As Harry matured he grew increasingly unlike them: Herbert and Daisy Timberlake were as ordinary as rice pudding, while the teenage Harry had a face with strong planes and deepset eyes under thick eyebrows. A street fight against odds rearranged the shape of his nose, modifying his Roman-emperor profile into something even more intimidating.

Young Harry's physical appearance was only half the story. He sailed through all examinations. When he left school and started looking for a job Harry joined the police. It was an instinctive decision, not a reasoned one. And right.

His promotion was rapid, and would have been even more so had it not been for his tendency not to take fools and time-servers lightly, even his superiors. His colleagues sometimes called him 'The Whiz Kid' or 'H.T.', as in 'high tension'. Significantly, no one ever called him 'Flash Harry'.

'Morning, troops,' he said cheerfully. 'Any messages?'

'Ted Greening was looking for you,' Sarah Lewis said flatly. 'Darren has gone out on a murder.'

'It's in The Sycamores Avenue,' Greening said as Harry entered his office two minutes later. He looked at Timberlake resentfully. Although it was not yet eleven o'clock the heat and humidity were making Greening sticky and irritable. Timberlake looked cool and equable, which made the other man even more peeved. Greening decided to slip out to the pub as soon as Timberlake had gone. A couple of pints of cold lager would cool him down. If not, three might do the trick.

He handed over a slip of paper with the address. 'Darren should be there by now. The doc and SOCOs are on site.'

Timberlake hurried downstairs to the station car park and got into his Citroen BX GTI. He could be generous with many of his possessions, but he never let anyone drive his car. He wouldn't let even Ayrton Senna drive it. *Especially* Ayrton Senna.

Most murder scenes are sordid: back alleys, crumbling houses, unkempt flats or rubbish-strewn waste ground. There are exceptions, of course, but murder victims, more often than not, are misfits or criminals.

Harry Timberlake didn't realize, or simply wouldn't admit to himself, that once he was into a case the intellectual challenge of solving a murder and tracking the criminal stirred his blood like nothing else. For him the end of the case was the arrest of the criminal. His melancholy after that was a simple reaction to the sudden ending of the excitement and nervous tension.

As Harry drove to The Sycamores Avenue he was aware that there was the occasional murder that had a better class of victim in what would otherwise be called comfortable circumstances. These were often eternal triangle crimes. 'Perhaps this one won't be too grisly,' he mused.

The Sycamores Avenue doubly lived up to its name, which was unusual for Terrace Vale. It was a sycamore-tree-lined, wide road that was definitely an avenue. In France it would have been a boulevard. All the houses had large, well-kept front gardens. As the name *The* Sycamores Avenue loudly hinted, it was an even posher area than the nearby Elm Park Square, where the life of Howard Foulds QC had come to an abrupt end with an axe in his skull.* Everybody called it *The* Sycamores Avenue. Visitors who left off the definite article were sharply corrected by the residents.

The houses all bristled with burglar alarms, and quite a number had security TV cameras as well. The well-kept front gardens were big enough for five-a-side football. The odour of money was barely kept at bay by the scent of the flowers and flowering shrubs.

Elm Park Square was reckoned to be as upmarket as you could go without having a nose bleed, but The Sycamores Avenue would not have tolerated anyone like Elm Park Square's actors, television personalities and pop stars, although living in The Sycamores Avenue was one very discreet call-lady who was telephoned by the Foreign Office from time to time when certain foreign dignitaries were in town.

* See *Vengeance*, the first Harry Timberlake story.

Parking space was hard to come by in The Sycamores even though nearly all the houses had two-car garages. Residents left their shiny new Rollers, S-series Mercs and Bentley Mulsannes outside so the neighbours could see them. They hid Porsches in the garages.

On the apex of the crescent-shaped avenue Harry could see four police cars and a couple of vans, their busily flashing hazard warning and blue lights slowly running down their batteries. Double-parked near by were a TV-News brake and half a dozen or more cars with 'Press' stickers. Photographers were trying to get near the Pascoe-Newman home, but uniformed police were keeping them outside blue and white tapes strung from the walls of Number 31 to sycamore trees by the kerbside. In a poorer area people would be peering out through twitching lace or voile curtains. Here the residents were standing about on the other side of the street, openly watching nothing in particular happen. One or two journalists were interviewing the neighbours. They couldn't help much, and wouldn't have done if they could.

Harry guessed that one of the residents had tipped off the newsmen, or one of the papers had been listening in to police radio messages. They were bound to find out sooner or later, anyway, he thought.

Harry tucked his car in beside one of the police vehicles and moved towards the house.

'What's the situation, Harry?' asked a veteran journalist who had seen Timberlake a number of times before.

'You tell me. I've only just got here.'

Chapter 2

Harry Timberlake could hear the SOCO's vacuum cleaner whooshing loudly upstairs as he walked in. A uniformed PC was in the hall, barely managing to contain his self-importance and his desire to make a good impression. He was vibrating almost like a tuning fork with excitement. As Harry approached him he half expected the young man to give off a slight hum like an electric transformer.

'The SOCOs are still working upstairs, sir,' he said unnecessarily. 'The others are in there.' He indicated a front room.

'Thank you . . . Nigel, isn't it?'

The PC glowed. 'Yes, sir. PC Nigel Larkin.'

It was what estate agents would call 'v. spacious 30ft recept.': the sort that appears in shiny magazine photographs under the title 'My Favourite Room', with the celebrity owner draped on a chair and trying not to look too smug or self-conscious. It overwhelmed the occupants with Good Taste: expensive leather sofa and chairs that had cost the slaughter of a small herd of cows, expensive rugs which had ruined a Turkish family's eyesight, expensive velvet curtains, and an expensive grand piano covered with expensive silver-framed photographs. The complete set of expensive status symbols were all in place.

Lily Coker was standing beside a round glass-topped table with slim brass legs. On it was a tea tray, the twin of the one she had taken up earlier. Detective Sergeant Darren Webb was seated on one of the leather chairs. He started to struggle to his feet from the chair's deep embrace when Harry Timberlake entered, but Harry waved to him to stay seated.

'Hello, guv. This is Mrs Coker,' Webb announced. 'She's the housekeeper. She found the bodies and called us.'

Harry turned to Lily Coker. 'Good morning, madam. My name

8

is Detective Inspector Timberlake. It must have been very unpleasant for you. Are you all right?'

'Yes, thank you,' she replied in an even voice. 'Would you like some tea?' Her accent was middle-class London which sounded acquired rather than natural.

'In a moment, perhaps, thank you.' Timberlake regarded her with interest. She was about forty, good-looking and not quite buxom. She was conservatively dressed in a dark grey dress. There was something about her that he couldn't quite define, yet. She returned his gaze directly, almost challengingly.

Timberlake asked the standard opening questions. Although he wasn't trying to make a point, there was no doubt he was the guv'nor. She gave him her full name and address, said she was the widow of a superintendent of a Thames Water pumping station who was drowned six years ago. Darren Webb looked startled. 'On holiday, at Tenerife,' she explained.

'I've got all Mrs Coker's details,' Webb said, holding up his notebook.

'Well done.' In fact it was routine, but Harry wanted to make the younger man feel good. 'Now tell me about this morning.'

Lily Coker licked her lips and thought. 'It was the same as always . . . until I . . .' She paused, and pulled herself together. 'I got here at nine o'clock. I picked up the morning post and newspapers, and then made tea. I—'

'Wait a minute. How did you get in?'

'I have a key. I made tea—'

'What about the burglar alarm? I noticed there's one on the front of the house.'

'Oh, yes. Sorry. I'm not quite . . . you know. It was turned off.'

'Is that usual?'

'No. I thought it was funny at the time. It's the first time I've come to work and it's not been on. You've got about thirty seconds to switch it off after you open the door, so I always get the key ready before I come in.'

'Have you got the key now?'

Lily Coker picked up a handbag from near her chair. It was an expensive lizard-skin model that must have cost getting on for a couple of hundred pounds. Timberlake didn't comment. She took out a key ring with four keys. There was an ordinary Yale key, a rather more impressive-looking key of the same type for a more sophisticated snap-shut lock, and one for a burglar-proof Bramah, which was a deadlock; or in other words, the key had to be turned in the lock for it to shut. These were all for the front door. There was a fourth oddly shaped key. 'It's that one.'

'Show me the alarm, please.'

Lily Coker got up and led the two detectives to a small cupboard in the hallway housing the control box for the alarm. It was a good-quality, well-known make.

'Darren, tell the SOCOs to have a good scout round in here, see if there are any signs of tampering.' Timberlake thought for a moment. 'Are there any panic buttons for the alarm?'

'There's one by each of the beds,' Mrs Coker said.

'What time was the alarm usually turned on at night, do you know?'

'Mrs Pascoe told me that either she or her daughter switched it on before going to bed.'

They all went back into the spacious reception room.

'Who else has got the key to the alarm?'

'Just Mrs Pascoe.'

'Darren, see if you can find the key when they've finished upstairs, then get on to the manufacturers and have them check the number of keys that've been supplied.' He turned back to Lily Coker.

'What time did you finish last night?'

'About seven.' She anticipated his next question. 'I went straight home and didn't go out again.' Then she added, 'I'm extremely careful with the keys, Inspector.' Timberlake believed her.

'I know you haven't had a chance to have a good look round yet, but is there anything obviously missing? Has anything been disturbed?'

'Not that I've noticed.'

'You'll let me know when you've been through the house?'

'Of course, Inspector.'

'Do you know what time they would have had their last meal?' Timberlake didn't explain the reason for his question, but he guessed that Mrs Coker would know.

'If they weren't going out, it was always at nine; and as far as I know they intended to stay at home last night.'

'Guv?' Darren Webb said diffidently. Webb was about twenty-five years old and was a medium man: medium height, medium weight, medium colouring. His off-the-peg suits were thirty-six medium. His apparent ordinariness made most people – particularly villains – underestimate him, which he successfully exploited.

Only in two respects was Darren Webb not medium. He had a face which Harry Timberlake once described as looking like a depraved Botticelli child with a hangover, and he was very bright. He admired Harry Timberlake, and was slightly in awe of him. Timberlake nodded to him to go ahead.

'Mrs Coker, it's a big house. Do you get any help?' Webb asked.

'There're two or three local women who come in on a casual basis.'

'Do they have keys to the alarm, or the house?'

'Neither.'

Webb nodded. 'I'll get their names and addresses from you later.'

Harry took over. 'Now, about your employers, the mother and daughter. They were both married?'

'Mrs Pascoe was a widow. Her husband died about ten years ago. He was a stockbroker. Mrs Newman, the daughter, was married but she was separated from her husband. I mean, they didn't live together any more.'

'Any other relatives?' Webb interposed.

'I don't think so. No, I'm sure there weren't.'

'How long had Mrs Newman been married?' Timberlake asked.

'Two or three years. But he was away a lot.'

'Business?'

Mrs Coker shrugged. 'Not *business* business, if you get what I mean.'

Timberlake did. 'How long had they been separated?'

'About a year.'

'When did she last see her husband, do you know?'

'He came here two days ago. Tuesday.'

'Really. How long did he stay?'

'Couple of hours. Then he left to go back to France. Or at least, I heard him say that's where he was going.'

'What sort of meeting was it? Do you have any idea?'

Mrs Coker shrugged again. 'I didn't listen at the keyhole, if that's what you're suggesting.'

'I'm not. Was it an angry meeting, or what?'

'There wasn't any shouting. Not this time.'

11

'You mean they did shout at each other sometimes?' Webb asked the obvious question.

'Yes, when he was living here. Often, actually.'

'Violence?' prompted Timberlake.

'Not that I know of. I never saw Mrs Newman with any bruises, a cut lip, anything like that. I don't think she would have stood for it.'

'I see.' He paused. 'What about money? What does Mr Newman do for a living?'

'Sponges. He's a waster. That's all he married her for, her money.' She sounded as bitter as if she herself had been a victim of the husband.

Timberlake studied her curiously for a moment, wondering what was behind her malice. 'Have you got Mr Newman's address anywhere?'

'No. He lives in France. Down south somewhere. Marseille, I think. I expect she'll have it in her address book. She was very finicky about keeping her records in order and all that. She has a sort of office upstairs. Her study, she called it.'

'Darren, have a go through Mrs Newman's papers when the SOCOs have finished in there.'

'Right, guv.'

'Was she well off herself, or did her mother have all the money?'

'You'll have to ask their solicitor. I expect the address is in her book. It's a Sir Tarquin Sparrowcroft.'

'Who?' asked Timberlake incredulously.

'I've heard of him, guv,' Darren Webb said unexpectedly. 'Senior partner of a big firm near Holborn. One of their people was burgled when I was at Southington nick. Very heavy outfit.' Timberlake looked at him. 'I mean, a big practice with important clients.'

Timberlake turned back to Mrs Coker. 'Did Mrs Pascoe have any men friends? Regular ones?'

The housekeeper shook her head. 'No regular ones, and certainly no regular *close* ones.' Timberlake understood.

'Women friends?'

'A few. Mrs Greene, with an "e",' she added, unconsciously imitating Mrs Greene's poshed-up accent. 'She called to see Mrs Pascoe yesterday afternoon.'

'What time?'

'About five. I don't know what time she left. It was after I finished at six.'

'Harry!'

Timberlake turned. The police surgeon, Dr Lawrence Pratt, was entering the room.

'Good morning, Doctor.'

'I've finished up there for the moment, but I'll want to see her again when the SOCOs have done. Dr Pratt glanced at Mrs Coker. 'Any chance of a cup of tea?' he asked, giving what he thought was a charming smile.

'Of course, Doctor.' She picked up the tea tray and took it out.

Lawrence Pratt was just under six feet tall, and a stone overweight. His long hair, such of it as remained, was dyed a highly improbable black and combed carefully into a complex whorl from the back and over his scalp, then carefully plastered down with some sort of unguent that smelled like a tart's boudoir. It made him look as if someone had painted his head with black gloss paint. Anyone talking to him needed a great deal of will power to avoid staring at his hair. He wore a fawn-coloured three-piece suit; no one had ever seen him in anything else. If someone had told Timberlake the doctor went to bed in that suit he would have believed them.

'So what's the situation?'

Pratt trotted out one of the earliest of all medical clichés. 'They're as well as can be expected.' Webb, who didn't know Pratt all that well, regarded him curiously. The doctor was tortuously preparing a funny remark.

'What does that mean?' Timberlake asked wearily.

'They're dead,' he said with the sensitivity of a rhinoceros. 'I mean, considering what's been done to them, they're as well as could be expected.' If Dr Pratt was expecting applause, he was disappointed.

'Cause of death?'

'The younger one's been strangled, manually strangled. The fingermarks are quite clear. I'm not too sure about the older one. Might just be a natural death. It was dark: the curtains were closed and the SOCOs told me not to touch them, so I couldn't see too well. There was a bottle of pills beside the bed, and I couldn't get a good look at that either.' He paused. 'Still, there was one odd thing. The body temperature of the older woman was nearly thirty-

13

seven point five degrees Centigrade, nearly a hundred Fahrenheit. Of course, it was a warm night, and I couldn't tell how long she'd been dead. Which means—'

'It's probably asphyxia.' Timberlake interrupted. He knew that in cases of asphyxia, whether by strangulation or other means, body temperature of the victim actually *increases* for a while after death.

'Right.' Dr Pratt lapsed into a sulky silence.

Timberlake realized that he had made a mistake: the doctor had been going to say something more. He decided not to press it for the moment.

Sergeant Burton Johnson, the chief SOCO, appeared in the doorway like a daytime ghost. He was dressed in his working clothes: spotless white over-alls, plastic gloves and white cloth boots. Behind him other ghosts glided silently to other tasks. 'We've finished upstairs if you want to go up,' he announced. 'And in case you're going to ask, we've printed the bottle of pills next to the bed.' Timberlake wasn't going to ask, and Johnson didn't expect him to.

'Any signs of forcible entry?'

'Not into the house,' Burt replied enigmatically. 'Everything locked, bolted and unmarked.'

'Have you found anything?'

'Don't know, yet, until we've had the stuff in the lab. We'll give you a shout as soon as we can.'

'Thanks, Burt.' Timberlake turned to the other three men. 'Let's have a look at the bodies, shall we?'

They went up the heavily carpeted stairs, and the doctor led them into Mrs Pascoe's room. The curtains had been pulled back now and the room was light. There were off-white patches of fine aluminium powder left by the fingerprint officer on furniture and the toilet articles on the dressing table; otherwise the room was impeccably clean and tidy. Even the corpse lay neatly on the bed.

Mrs Pascoe's head, all of her that was visible, was slightly dark against the white pillows and the single sheet that had been pulled over her. Her eyes were closed and she seemed to be sleeping. Dr Pratt reached out to pull down the sheet but stopped in mid-movement when another voice spoke. 'I think I'd better do that.'

The three men spun round.

Professor Peter Mortimer had entered the room. Dressed in a

14

dark grey suit and a white shirt with an old-fashioned stiff white collar, he was carrying a black leather bag that could have seen service on HMS *Victory* at Trafalgar. He was accompanied by his assistant, Miss Gertrude Hacker, whose surname most people thought better suited to her principal. She was about fifty-five, dressed in a shapeless tweed suit and hat and a woollen jumper. She and Mortimer were apparently unaffected by heat. Timberlake had seen them dressed in exactly the same way in heatwaves, and had developed a private theory that the pair of them had different central nervous systems from the rest of mankind.

Once again Professor Mortimer had performed his uncanny trick of timing his arrival for five minutes after the scientific men had packed up their gear, leaving the scene of the crime clear for the pathologist. Mortimer, almost invariably referred to in popular newspapers as 'the eminent forensic pathologist, Professor Mortimer', would have been about six foot three inches if he'd ever stood up straight, but a lifetime of bending over dead bodies on beds, floors and mortuary slabs had made him stoop-shouldered.

'Good morning, Professor,' Timberlake said. Webb and Dr Pratt made vague noises; Mortimer was silent. He never wasted words on social pleasantries. 'Have you examined the bodies?' he asked Dr Pratt.

'Only to establish death and to take an anal temperature. Both of them were above normal: thirty-seven point five degrees.'

Mortimer put on a pair of rubber gloves then pulled the sheet off the dead form of Mrs Pascoe, pushed her peach-coloured nightdress up to her neck and carefully surveyed the surprisingly white body from feet to head. As he did so, he dictated to Gertrude Hacker the usual preliminary notes of the victim's sex, apparent age, colour and obvious symptoms. He bent over the head and lifted an eyelid and stared at it hard. When he took his hand away the one eye remained open. The effect was grotesque, as if Mrs Pascoe had died in mid-wink. Next Professor Mortimer closely examined the forehead, pulling the woman's hair back.

'Asphyxiated,' he pronounced.

'Yes, well, the body temperature—' Dr Pratt began, trying to establish his own expertise, but he could have saved his breath. Mortimer ignored him and continued, 'Obvious from the petechial haemorrhages in the white of the eye, on the face there . . . and there. As you can see, the skin of the head and neck is quite

15

dusky, and there is marked lividity in the lips and ears.' Miss Hacker continued to take notes.

'It takes twenty to thirty seconds of asphyxiation to produce these signs,' Mortimer went on. 'I'm confident that the autopsy will confirm that asphyxia by suffocation was the cause of death.' He pointed to a small pill bottle on the bedside table. 'Has that been fingerprinted?' Harry nodded.

Mortimer picked it up and looked at the label. 'Mild sleeping pill.' He peered into the bottle. 'Not many gone, although a whole bottleful wouldn't kill her.' He slipped the bottle into his ancient bag.

'Right, where's the other one?'

Dr Pratt led the others out of the room, his lips compressed into a thin line.

When they entered the second bedroom Darren Webb let out an involuntary 'Christ!' He shot a glance at Miss Hacker, but she was unmoved. Now Timberlake knew what Dr Pratt was going to warn him earlier, before he interrupted the doctor.

Veronica Newman was lying naked and uncovered across her bed. Her nightdress was neatly folded over the back of a chair.

A small corner at the back of Timberlake's mind briefly registered that she had a good figure, but this thought was driven out of his mind almost instantaneously as he took in the full scene. Veronica Newman's eyes were open and staring, her face spotted as if it were freckled. Her tongue lolled out of her open mouth; there were dark bruise marks of hands round her neck. But it wasn't her face that made Webb exclaim.

Veronica Newman was lying on her back, her knees up and spread wide; a pillow was under her buttocks. There was something indescribably obscene about the tableau. It was all too clear that Veronica Newman had been strangled during sexual intercourse. Or even worse, if that were possible, *before* sexual intercourse.

Professor Mortimer advanced to the corpse and again studied it intently from feet to head, dictating notes to Gertrude Hacker as he did. 'Large hands,' were the only words he said directly to the detectives, as he indicated the bruises on the neck.

Harry Timberlake was wishing he could get the hell out of it. He had seen dead bodies before, but a combination of the elements of the scene sickened him. The fact that the matronly looking Gertrude Hacker was there didn't help things. Professor Mortimer

16

bent down to peer closely at the dead woman's crotch. 'Interesting,' he said. 'She may have been raped. . . . yes . . . bruising and slight contusions . . . I'll know better when I've opened her up.'

Mortimer opened his bag and took out a glass tube containing a long-handled swab. He probed the corpse with it, moving it about to gather any traces of fluids or foreign bodies that might indicate sexual intercourse.

Gertrude Hacker caught Darren Webb's expression. 'She's dead,' she said. 'It's a body.'

'I didn't say anything,' he replied. He sounded like a man on a rolling North Sea ferry asking how long it was before they docked.

Mortimer was totally unaffected by these exchanges. He seemed to have as much emotion as an earthworm. He replaced the swab in the tube, closed it and affixed a small label on which he wrote in his small, crabbed handwriting before stowing it in his antique bag.

'Make sure the Scene of Crime Officers send the bedclothes to the laboratory, Inspector,' he said.

He took off his rubber gloves and put them into his bag as well. Rubber gloves cost money.

Chapter 3

There was a time when almost every detective story or film included the line of dialogue, 'Shall we call in the Yard?'

In real life these days local police in the Metropolitan Police area don't have the choice. Officers from Scotland Yard are going to turn up on the doorstep whether the local coppers like it or not. When a serious crime like murder is committed, Scotland Yard sends an Area Major Investigation Pool, or AMIP, commanded by a detective superintendent to take charge of the investigation.

London is divided into eight Areas and each has an AMIP, sometimes also called an Area Major Investigation Team or AMIT – it depends who you're talking to. A detective chief superintendent at the Yard has overall responsibility for the teams.

The AMIP's detective superintendent for the area that included Terrace Vale was Charles Harkness. He had been there before, accompanied by his usual driver and bag-carrier, Detective Sergeant Braddock, who could make a Trappist monk sound chatty. On that occasion Harry Timberlake had worked closely with Harkness on the Prendergast serial killing case, and knew the AMIP chief's methods.

So, at seven forty-five the next morning Timberlake, Webb and a couple of detective constables were ready and waiting in a spare CID office. Timberlake had ordered no smoking inside the room, which resulted in some muttered grumbles and a corridor thick with tobacco smoke where the two detectives had nipped out for a last few desperate drags on their cigarettes.

At the last moment Ted Greening slipped into the room. His 'act of presence' as the French put it, was a feeble attempt to show Harkness that he was in charge of the CID at Terrace Vale.

But his last encounter with the detective superintendent had been a painful and utterly humiliating experience.

If Harkness was surprised by the state of readiness of the CID team when he arrived at Terrace Vale at 8 a.m. he gave no sign. Sergeant Braddock wouldn't look surprised if someone stuck a ferret down his trousers.

Harkness was neatly dressed in a suit that looked as if it were made of something as creaseproof as armour plate. He wasn't very tall, probably just made the minimum height for the Met when they had that qualification; slender but wiry, clean-shaven, thin-lipped. His most notable feature was his eyes: dark for his medium colouring and deep set, they had stared down some pretty tough criminals and sharp solicitors.

Greening decided to brazen it out. 'Good morning, sir. I'm DCI Greening. If there's—'

'Good morning, Chief Inspector. Yes, we have met,' Harkness replied with apparent politeness. He wasn't going to embarrass Greening overtly in front of his own troops. But the message was clear. It was as if Wellington had greeted Napoleon with 'Yes, we have met . . .'

'Well, I've got a team together for you, sir,' Greening said with a ghastly grin. 'If you need anything . . .'

'Yes, thank you.' He gave a lips-only smile that could have frozen a bird in full flight. Ted Greening exited with all the dignity he could scrape up.

Harry Timberlake introduced the other officers to Harkness and then got down to business. First, he reported everything they already knew, including a check to see if Charles Henry Newman had a criminal record: there was nothing. Sergeant Webb would go through the two women's letters and papers, first to try to find the address of Veronica Newman's husband and then to compile a list of all their friends and acquaintances. He would interview Mrs Coker again, and from all these he would build up pictures of the women's lives. Harry himself would see the family solicitor and the bank manager. Detective Constables Wilkins and Slater would organize the house-to-house enquiries by uniformed officers.

'When are the post-mortems?' Harkness asked when Harry had finished.

'Tomorrow, four o'clock.'

*

19

As it happened Professor Mortimer had begun the post-mortem examinations well before four o'clock, but hadn't bothered to tell anyone. By the time Harkness, Timberlake and Webb turned up at the morgue he was sewing up the first body again. He didn't apologize for not waiting; he didn't even mention the fact. Nor did the formidable Gertrude Hacker, inevitably dressed in her tweed suit and woollen jumper, and armed with her fat notebook. A very large West Indian porter who obviously knew Mortimer's little ways stood in the background, out of Mortimer's line of sight.

The hospital morgue boasted three stainless-steel-topped tables. Ann Pascoe, sixty-seven years old at the time of her death, and her daughter Veronica Newman, forty-three, were laid out side by side. With unconscious deference to seniority Mortimer had started with the mother.

'First of all,' he said, like a teacher at a school for children with learning difficulties, 'the times of death. From the observations I made *in situ* of the degree of hypostasis, I made preliminary calculations as to the times of death, within a range of an hour on either side. Later I shall check those times on the basis of the stomach contents, if you know at what time they last had a meal.' Before anyone could ask a question he added, 'I shall provide you with the times as soon as I have made those checks, and not before.' There was an almost audible clang as Mortimer's iron shutter came down.

'The older woman is a straightforward enough case,' he said offhandedly. 'There were traces of diazepam in the blood and urine, but only enough to represent a normal dose for insomnia. I telephoned the doctor whose name was on the bottle, and he tells me that Mrs ... er ... Pascoe had no dependency on the drug. She used the diazepam only occasionally.

'When I first saw the body there were petechial haemorrhages in the white of the eye and on the face, but of course, as you are all aware, these signs are by no means peculiar to asphyxial deaths.' Webb nodded earnestly. 'However,' Mortimer continued, 'there were other outward signs: viz' – Timberlake had never heard anyone except Mortimer use 'viz' in the course of conversation – 'viz,' Mortimer continued with a glance at Timberlake as if he had read his mind, *'viz*, the skin of the head and neck was quite dusky, and there was marked lividity in the lips and ears. When I opened her up I found some frothy mucus in the larynx and trachea, the

20

lungs revealed a dark, frothy, blood-stained exudate. In the parietal, pulmonary and pericardial pleurae, the heart muscle and brain there were other petechial haemorrhages.'

Darren Webb made a small noise.

'Something wrong?' Mortimer asked. 'You look pale. Good God, man,' he said, realizing, 'don't say you're feeling queasy!'

'No, sir, I won't say that,' Webb replied with brave defiance. Mortimer looked at him as if he were a corpse that was trying to keep something secret, then turned to the others. In a tone of voice that suggested handing down stone tablets he concluded, 'Cause of death, asphyxia due to suffocation, as I said.'

Professor Mortimer then launched into one of his little lectures. Trying to stop him would have been like trying to push Niagara back up again. 'I say "asphyxia due to suffocation" because asphyxiation, of course, does not strictly mean suffocation in itself,' he began. 'It comes from the Greek, "a", meaning "not" and "sphixis", pulse.'

'Sph*u*xis,' Timberlake said involuntarily; he had read up the subject in a textbook some time ago.

Mortimer made no acknowledgement of his error and Timberlake's correction. 'So, asphyxia means "absence of pulse", which is caused by lack of aeration of the blood.'

'I'm sure we're most grateful for your explanation,' Harkness said. 'Do you have an opinion as to *how* she was suffocated?'

'I do not have opinions. I state facts. She was suffocated by a pillow over her face. I found minute traces of cotton fibres and what appeared to be duck down in the exudate of the larynx and trachea. There were down pillows on the bed, and one had traces of saliva and mucus.'

Harkness inclined his head. Fifteen all.

'Shall we get on with the other one?' Mortimer said ungraciously. He turned to the next table and signalled to the porter he had been observing with the eyes in the back of his head to remove the sheet from Veronica Newman's body.

She was lying on her stomach, her face turned towards Timberlake and the others. Both eyes were closed now, and she looked as if she were asleep. Her neck was in shadow from the overhead light and the dark, murderous bruises were hardly apparent to the detectives. For Timberlake dead bodies were usually that and nothing more, but for a reason he was barely conscious of and cer-

21

tainly couldn't explain, he felt a sudden surge of compassion, tenderness even, for the youngish woman lying helplessly naked in front of men she had never known.

Before Mortimer opened up the body and took out the organs he carefully examined the exterior of the body for any wounds or unusual marks. This was standard practice, and the reason why he began with the back, which he studied closely for some time. When he had done, he told the big, powerful porter to turn the body over. The man was strong enough to heave her over as easily as if she were a hollow dummy, but he did it gently and – there was no other word for it – respectfully. Once again Mortimer seemed preoccupied with Veronica Newman's genital area: he studied it with a magnifying glass, making faint sucking noises with his false teeth. He beckoned to Gertrude Hacker and drew her attention to something. 'See? There . . . there . . . and there,' he said. She nodded and made notes on her pad. Timberlake was about to ask what the hell it was all about, but Harkness, who knew Mortimer better than he did, signalled to him to keep quiet.

Mortimer finished examining the front of the body and made the standard big incision from under the chin to the base of the abdomen, and out came the organs for separate examination and analysis. Next, Mortimer sliced the scalp with a T-shaped incision, peeled back the skin, sawed open the top of the skull with an electric saw. There was a strong smell of burning bone, and Webb stifled a muffled exclamation. 'Useful device,' Mortimer said, brandishing the saw like a Swiss Army penknife. 'Saves a lot of effort compared with the old handsaw.' He removed the brain and dropped it into the pan of a spring balance. Webb studied the ceiling.

'Just over fourteen hundred grammes. A large brain for a woman,' Mortimer observed. Gertrude Hacker made no comment.

Mortimer finally finished the last stage of his examination and prepared to address his audience. 'There are a number of physical signs on and in this body which may well present difficulties for you in formulating your hypothesis.'

'You mean she *wasn't* strangled?' Webb asked.

A bishop eyeing a drunk who had started singing a bawdy ditty during his sermon could not have been more disapproving.

'Of course she was strangled! Any child of five could see that. Apart from the evident bruises on the throat, when I did the dissection you must have observed extensive bruising of the tissues

22

and fracture of the laryngeal structures.' Webb failed to mention that he had not been watching that closely. 'Although I suppose I shouldn't expect you to have seen the fractured hyoid bone,' Mortimer conceded. 'Now, if I may be allowed to continue without further interruption . . .' He paused for effect.

'The hypotheses are a matter for you, and in some regard you may consider the facts contradictory; I cannot say. As I have said, I do not give opinions; I state facts.'

This was Professor Mortimer's favourite dictum which he frequently launched like a guided missile from the witness box.

'The facts are these,' he went on. 'On the inner thighs, the vulva and the interior of the vagina there is considerable bruising. These signs are typical of those commonly found in cases of rape. However, there were no traces whatsoever of spermatozoa in the vagina, or, for that matter, in the vicinity. Ultra-violet light showed up no traces of seminal staining. Nevertheless, the interior of the vagina was still moist with natural secretions from the vaginal glands. It was present in such quantities as to indicate possible considerable sexual excitement. There were two separate dried patches of these secretions on the bed sheet, which are further indications of that considerable sexual excitement. Also present were minute traces of latex and traces of some vegetable oil or grease; which one I have not yet determined, although I shall do so later.'

The detectives were silent for a long moment as this sank in.

'Could you tell if the two patches of vaginal secretions were from two different episodes of sexual intercourse?' Harkness asked at last.

'No,' Mortimer replied with the finality which was often the despair or delight of counsel.

'No, they weren't, or no you couldn't tell?'

'No one could tell; not even me,' Mortimer said with breathtaking conceit.

Harkness rephrased the question. 'Are those two separate stains consistent with two separate episodes of sexual intercourse?'

'Yes.' Mortimer paused, and then with the air of a man who adds a third ace to pairs of kings and aces, he added, 'They are also consistent with a single episode.'

It seemed to Timberlake that Mortimer was speaking about sexual intercourse like a man discussing some fringe activity of which he had no personal experience, like morris dancing or mouse-fancying.

'Any foreign pubic hairs?' Timberlake asked.

'None. I was just about to mention that,' Mortimer said reprovingly. 'And although I cannot be absolutely certain before microscopic examination, it doesn't look to me as if the victim scratched her attacker. To the naked eye there does not appear to be any human skin, hair or blood under the fingernails.'

'How long would it take for the attacker to render Mrs Newman unconscious, would you say, Professor?' Harkness asked.

'Experience suggests that it would be a matter of seconds.'

Timberlake had learned that himself the hard way in the gymnasium, practising judo. Everything went black very quickly when an opponent got his arm across your throat from behind. There was just time to signal submission and have the hold released.

'Normally strangulation by hand is not the most efficient method. However, in this case the amount of bruising and the spacing of the separate bruises together indicate that the assailant was a man with large, powerful hands,' Mortimer continued. 'Of course, by far the most efficacious method of strangulation is by ligature.'

He sounded disapproving, as if criticizing manual stranglers for not choosing a better method. Killers who used ligatures were not spared censure either. 'Most stranglers keep on the pressure much longer than is necessary,' he said, patently blaming them for sloppy technique.

That, too, Timberlake knew. Three or four times he had known of cases of judokas' hearts actually stopping because the stranglehold had been left on too long. Always present during judo practice in the gym was a black belt judoka, expert in the technique of resuscitation by striking nerve points to jolt the heart back into action.

But in Veronica Newman's case it would have been instinctive for her to tear at her attacker's hands and wrists, even if it were only for a few seconds. Yet Professor Mortimer did not think she had scratched her killer.

'What the hell went on?' Timberlake asked himself.

Chapter 4

It was a question that they all asked themselves back at the Incident Room set up for the AMIP team at the Terrace Vale nick.

'In crude terms,' Harkness said, using an expression policemen rarely felt the need to utter, 'it might seem that Veronica Newman was raped, possibly twice, but enjoyed it; two things which are irreconcilable by definition.'

'And there was no semen anywhere,' Timberlake added. 'I've never heard of a rapist using a condom.'

'It has been known,' Harkness said. 'In 1980 a judge at York Crown Court gave a rapist a lighter sentence than he otherwise would have done because the rapist had used a condom when he raped an eighteen-year-old prostitute. He said, if my memory serves me, "You showed concern and consideration by wearing a contraceptive".'

The detectives looked at him open-mouthed. If it had been anyone other than Harkness they would have told him to piss off, at least.

'Well, our man didn't show much care and consideration,' Timberlake said. 'He killed them.'

After a moment Webb gave one of his apologetic coughs. 'Perhaps he – or she,' he added in a moment of inspiration, 'used a . . . some sort of instrument,' he said with some embarrassment. Harkness often made people feel embarrassed without even trying.

'That still leaves us with the physical evidence of her enjoyment on the one hand and the undoubted brutality on the other,' Harkness pointed out. 'Still, perhaps you'd better have a look through the house to see if there's anything that may have been used.'

'There are the other problems as well,' Timberlake said. 'How the murderer got into the house, which could be easy to answer, and how he got out and locked the door behind him, which definitely isn't.'

25

As if on cue from some detectives' patron saint, the phone rang. Webb answered, paused and then said, 'I think you'd better speak to Inspector Timberlake.' He held the phone out. 'It's Mrs Coker.' Timberlake took it, while Superintendent Harkness picked up an extension phone to listen in.

'Inspector, there's something I've remembered which I should have told you before, but with everything that happened, it went right out of my mind,' Mrs Coker said. 'I'm sorry.'

'That's perfectly understandable. What is it you've remembered?'

'When I arrived at the house yesterday, the Bramah lock wasn't locked. The other two were, but not that. I didn't take a lot of notice at the time; I just assumed that Mrs Pascoe or Mrs Newman forgot to do it. Could it be important?'

'Thank you very much,' Timberlake avoided answering the question. 'Sergeant Webb will be coming to have another word with you. Just routine.' He hung up, turning to Webb and the two detective constables. He repeated what Mrs Coker had just told him. 'The morning after the murders the Bramah deadlock wasn't locked although the other two were.'

'Which means that anyone could have just walked out of the house and pulled the door shut behind them,' Webb said.

'What about the keys to the house, apart from Mrs Coker's set?' Harkness asked.

'One set was in Mrs Newman's handbag, the other in a drawer in Mrs Pascoe's bedroom.'

'Did the husband have a set?' Harkness went on.

'I asked Mrs Coker, sir, but she didn't know.'

The detectives hardly had the time to consider the implications when the phone rang again. This time Detective Superintendent Harkness picked it up.

'Harkness.' He listened briefly, then asked, 'There can be no mistake?' The answer was indecipherable to the others, but the speaker was clearly indignant. 'Of course not. I beg your pardon,' Harkness said frigidly, and everyone knew he was talking to Professor Mortimer. He hung up.

The detectives waited impatiently while Harkness took two deep breaths. 'Professor Mortimer has come up with another of his post-post-mortem nuggets of information,' Harkness told them. 'His examination of the victims' stomach contents confirms his estimates – I beg his pardon, his *calculations* – that Mrs Pascoe died at approximately two a.m. and her daughter at six a.m. Give or take an hour. But the time difference between the deaths was definitely four hours.'

Eventually one irreverent detective recovered sufficiently from shock to murmur, 'Jesus Q. Christ!' The detective was, of course, a well-known Nonconformist.

Harry Timberlake stretched out in his favourite chair, rubbed the back of his neck and pinched his nose between his eyes.

Sarah Lewis handed him a medium-sized malt whisky and sat in the chair opposite. She was wearing a plain two-piece in a neutral colour that bordered on what the French call *caca d'oie*, or goose shit. At least, some of the French do. When she wore it on duty she was a perfect picture of a serious junior executive in a sober company. Now, lying deep in an armchair with her legs crossed, careless of how her skirt fell, she was a tired executive's dream of a stop-off on the way home: she looked practically illegal. Any wife would have detested her on sight.

'Rough day?' Timberlake asked.

She nodded. 'Another couple of burglaries last night, and a mugging. I've got a good idea who's doing the break-ins, but the clever little sod's got somewhere to hide the stuff. And he's all of fifteen years old. But I'll get him eventually. What about you?'

He got up to put on a tape recording from one of his own records while he answered. It was one of his occasional favourites: the powerful Bea Booth version of 'See See Rider' with Sammy Price on piano on a Sepia label. Sarah just managed not to hate it, but that was because she made an effort for Harry's sake. She preferred choral music, but then she was Welsh and could sing quite well in the bath, as Harry had discovered.

'I've had the council's leader of the opposition on to me again for the past couple of days about the stories of corrupt practices over council building contracts. I'm sure he's right, but all the people concerned are as crafty as Armenian carpet dealers and as slippery as a pound of jellied eels. I called on that man Soper again on my way home. You know, the council executive officer.'

'Is it a big fraud?'

'Not by Italian standards, or even compared with the Polson case. But it's serious enough.'

'What about the two murders?'

'Too many arrows pointing in different directions. But playing the percentages, I'll bet it's the husband, wherever he might be.'

He sighed. Not for the first time since he had begun the affair with Sarah – or she had begun it with him – he mused that he and Dr Jenny Long used to talk about work to each other without it becoming tiresome, but then they had different sorts of work to talk about. He wished he didn't think about her quite so often. 'Let's forget work for a while, eh?'

'I brought something back with me,' Sarah said. 'I'm going to do you sheep's brains with sauce Mornay and courgettes.'

As if it were an Alfred Hitchcock shock flashback Harry Timberlake had a sudden image of Veronica Newman's brain being tipped into a dish.

'You all right?' Sarah asked.

'Yeah.' He tried to sound light. 'Is there any part of a sheep you Taffs don't eat?'

'Only the baaa. But we're working on it.'

'I gulped down a couple of hamburgers this afternoon and I've got a touch of bovine revenge,' Timberlake lied. 'I'll just have some fruit and another malt.'

'Nothing to follow?'

'Welsh rarebit?' he suggested.

'Better than that. How about some Welsh hotpot?' Sarah said with a wicked smile that would have cost a couple of Hail Marys in Ireland.

Not many people enjoy night shifts. There are exceptions, of course: burglars, moonlighting watchmen earning untaxed cash wages, astronomers. Years of shift work had made the crew of Panda patrol car Hotel Romeo indifferent to night duty. In any case, this hardly seemed like night duty. There was a full moon and although it was nearly two o'clock in the morning it was still warm enough for the crew to doff their jackets.

The real disadvantage of doing nights was that there were very few cafés, hamburger bars or greasy-spoon joints open after midnight where you could have a feet-up. You could always go back to the Terrace Vale nick's canteen for Break for Refreshments, but that always meant running the risk of a Sod's Law operation which meant that you were lumbered with some unexpected

28

unpleasant task just because you caught the duty sergeant's eye.

So, PC Dick 'Rambo' Wright and WPC Marie 'Rosie' Hall brought thermos flasks and packets of sandwiches with them when they were on night turn. As it is with most members of close-knit communities like the police, army and football teams, they had acquired nicknames. How these were born was as mysterious as who starts rumours. In the inverse logic of nicknames Dick Wright was called Rambo because he was small and slight, had fine, gingerish hair and a sharp face with curiously pale eyes. He seemed as menacing as Bambi. Nevertheless, he had a black belt in judo and karate, something he largely kept to himself. His physical self-confidence made him quiet and unaggressive.

WPC Marie Hall was originally nicknamed Rosemarie. The Rosemarie became shortened to Rosie, and most people now thought that was her real name. Although she had spent all her life in a poorer part of London she looked as if she had come up from the farm two days ago, and was probably the only officer at Terrace Vale who thought it was a fairly peaceful area. Her previous posting had been in a part of south-east London where even the cats didn't care to go out at night.

Rosie was doing the driving on this shift. She carefully replaced the stopper and cup of her thermos, closed her sandwich box and prepared to take up the protection of Her Majesty's subjects again. Rambo Wright tidied away his own flask and sandwich wrappers, got out of the Panda and carefully brushed the crumbs from his trousers before getting back into the car. He picked up the RT mike and said: 'Hotel Romeo to Terrace.'

'Terrace receiving,' came a tinny voice over the loudspeaker.

'Hotel Romeo back on watch after refreshments, oh-two-one-oh.'

'Received, Hotel Rambo,' replied PC Phil Clapton, who considered himself something of a card. Terrace Vale had more than its fair share of would-be comics, but their combined witticisms would have been about as hilarious as a book of nineteenth-century German humour. 'What is your location?'

'We're in the bloody car!' Rosemarie Hall called across towards the mike. She had a voice that didn't need a microphone when she turned up her own volume control.

'Corner of Upper Vale Road on the motorway feed road roundabout. Hotel Romeo out,' Wright reported without expression.

29

'Romeo Hotel, observe correct RT procedure,' Clapton said grumpily, but he knew he'd lost this one.

'Oh, bollocks,' Rosie said as she put the car into gear. In her previous area that was polite, practically to the point of being a term of endearment. Rambo stared ahead without expression, although his silent disapproval was almost deafening.

'Shall we have a dekko round The Gut, see what's happening?' Rosie suggested. Without waiting for an answer Rosie pointed the Panda car in that direction.

'The Gut' was the local name for Valletta Street, one of a group of Terrace Vale's more sordid streets named after towns which were once part of the Empire. The Gut, as anyone who has been in the Royal Navy or Merchant Marine knows, is the main drag of Valletta in Malta which once boasted more whores per flagstone than anywhere west of Bangkok. Terrace Vale's The Gut had fewer tarts and dubious clubs than the Maltese original, but it made up for what it lacked in quantity with lots of bad quality. That's why Rosie said 'see what's happening' and not 'if anything's happening'. There was always *something* happening in The Gut.

They were halfway through the roundabout when Rambo Wright said, 'Hang on, look over there, just going towards the motorway.'

'What?'

'Someone on a bike without lights.'

'Riding a bike without lights?' Rosie said with withering scorn. 'That sounds real diabolical. Reckon it's a bank robber making a getaway?'

'Bicycles aren't allowed on motorways, and—'

'I know that.'

'He looks a bit young, anyway, and he's got a better than evens chance of being hit by someone on a motorway, especially riding without lights. Let's stop him.' There was an unusual edge of authority in Rambo's tone. Rosie changed direction and headed after the cyclist, whingeing quietly to herself.

When the police car pulled alongside the rider on the bicycle and Rambo Wright signalled to him to stop, the youth turned a pale, frightened face towards him. Rambo, who watched a lot of late-night films on television, was irresistibly reminded of the teenage Freddie Bartholomew. Both officers got out of the car and approached him.

30

'Don't you know bicycles aren't allowed on motorways, sonnie?' Rosie asked, keeping her voice down to a conversational level. Her earlier belligerence drained away at the sight of the youth's frightened face.

'Where are you going at this time of the morning?' asked Rambo.

'Just for a ride. You know.'

'Bit late for that, isn't it?' Rambo carefully studied the cycle. It was a moderately expensive one: not a flash mountain bike, but not a bone-shaker, either. 'Is this your bike?' The boy nodded. 'What's in the bag?' Rambo indicated a large bag on the luggage carrier.

The youth licked his lips. 'My things. You know.'

'You sure you haven't nicked the bike?' said Rosie Hall. 'Or borrowed it?' she added, giving the boy a ready-made half-excuse. 'Borrowing' a bicycle you say you had every intention of returning technically does not constitute theft. She surprised herself with her unaccountable lack of professionalism and objectivity, but there was something poignant about the youth.

'If you don't mind, we'll have a look,' Rambo said. The youth said nothing, which was a mark in his favour. If he had reacted by squawking 'You ain't go no right! Bloody coppers!' it would have classified him instantly in Rambo's and Rosie's minds.

The bag contained clothes and underclothes tightly packed, toilet gear and a few paperbacks.

'What's your name, lad?' Rambo asked, as Rosie helped the youth repack his bag. There was no answer.

'Running away from home?' Rosie asked gently. The youth still remained silent. 'How old are you?'

He turned this question over in his mind carefully and decided that it was harmless. 'Sixteen.'

'Come on, son. Let's have your name,' Rambo said, but without effect. 'Then I'm afraid I'm going to have to search you for any means of identification.'

'I haven't got anything like that.'

A body search turned up £15 in notes and eighty-seven pence in 'silver and bronze', in the time-honoured police phrase, although 'silver' had been a brass and nickel alloy for decades. The boy had no identification on him; no credit cards.

'Last chance, son. Tell us your name or we'll take you to the

31

station. You don't want that, do you?' Rosie said, trying to sound motherly. Still no answer.

Sergeant Rumsden was doing a rare night duty because the regular night station sergeant was off sick. When Rambo Wright and Rosie Hall brought in the still anonymous youth Rumsden raised an eyebrow. 'Can you manage him on your own or shall I call up reinforcements?' he asked. 'What's he done? Blown up Buckingham Palace?'

'Riding a cycle without lights,' sounded worse than anti-climactic; it sounded stupid, until Rosie explained the boy refused to give his name. Rambo dumped the boy's bag on the counter.

'All right, hang around,' Rumsden told the pair. 'Don't go before seeing me.' He called out to a constable sitting at a desk inside the main office. 'Vic, watch the front desk for a minute.'

'Why, what's it going to do, Sarge?' replied Vic, one of the Phil Clapton school of juvenile humour. Rumsden had had enough feeble backchat for one night shift. He stabbed Vic with a glance. 'Sorry, Sarge,' Vic said, getting smartly to his feet.

'Come inside, son. Bring your bag,' Rumsden said. He lifted the counter flap and led the youth to an interview room. 'Rosie, get us both a cup of tea, will you?' 'Why *me*? Why not Rambo?' she grumbled just not quite loud enough for Rumsden to hear. 'Because I'm a sodding *Woman* sodding Police Constable. You be mother and pour. . . .'

Interview rooms, with their harsh lighting and twin-track tape recorders can be intimidating places and it was clear to the sergeant's eye that the boy was not used to them.

'All right, sit down. This isn't the army.' Rumsden paused. 'Absconded, have you?'

'What?'

'From a detention centre?'

'No!'

Rumsden took a quick look in the boy's bag. 'No, this isn't official issue gear.' Rumsden switched himself into his homely, friendly father mode, which wasn't all that far from his natural character. 'So you're running away from home. First time you've tried it?' The youth nodded. 'How they going to feel at home when they find out you've done a runner?'

'I left a note.'

'Oh, great. That'll stop them worrying, won't it? What's the

32

matter – someone knocking you about?' After a moment he asked very gently, 'They're not doing anything else to you?'

'No it's nothing like that.'

'What, then?' The youth just shook his head helplessly.

'Where were you headed?'

'Oxford, I think. Hadn't thought, really.'

'No, you hadn't, had you?'

Rosie Hall knocked and entered, carrying a small tray. 'Two teas, Sergeant,' she said as sarcastically as she dared, trying to sound like a waitress. She placed them on the table with exaggerated care, and went out leaving a slipstream of resentment behind her.

'D'you live at home?' The youth nodded. 'What's your name and address, son?' He waited for a moment before saying with quiet reasonableness, 'You've got more sense than that. You know this can't go on for ever, and the longer it takes only makes things worse. So why waste both our time?'

'Jason Horlock. Five Manor Lane. It's a greengrocer's.'

'Yes, I know it.' Sergeant Rumsden didn't say how he knew it. 'That's fine. Now, what's it all about?'

Jason stared at the wall ferociously, then exploded, 'It's my dad!'

'What's he done?'

'He wants me to be an accountant! He won't let me leave school, and wants me to go on to be an *accountant*!'

Although Sergeant Rumsden was no great fan of accountants, he couldn't imagine anyone fleeing from home to avoid becoming one. 'And what do you want?'

'I want to be a motor engineer.' Not, Rumsden noted, a motor mechanic, but an engineer. 'I want to start in a garage and train to work on Formula One cars.'

'Not drive them?'

Jason shook his head. 'That's not my thing. I love engines. I mean, being an *accountant*!' He made it sound like being a baby farmer, a brothel owner, or even a politician. 'Besides, I don't want to go on studying all the time. I want to get a job . . . have my own money . . . be like my mates.'

It was the adolescents' old, old *cri de coeur*. 'I want to be like my mates.'

'Well, scarpering isn't going to solve anything. Go home, and have another talk with your dad.'

Jason Horlock's shoulders slumped. He said resignedly, without rancour, 'Talk to a brick wall. It won't do any good.'

'You'll never know if you don't try, eh? Right, now we'll get you home.'

Rambo Wright and Rosie Hall were waiting by the counter.

'Take Jason here home and make sure he goes in.'

'Right, Sarge.'

'And nice and quiet. We don't want the neighbours to think he's responsible for World War Three breaking out.' He turned to the boy. 'Can you get in again all right?'

'I've got a key.'

Rumsden smiled quietly to himself. Whether the lad realized it or not, subconsciously at least he wasn't cutting off all ties with home.

'Somebody'll be round tomorrow to tell your dad,' Rumsden said. Jason Horlock looked worried. 'He's got to be told, hasn't he?' The youth bit his lip and nodded. 'Don't worry, we won't make it heavy, and we'll make sure it's someone in plain clothes.'

'Come on, son,' Rosie said. She turned to Rambo. 'Then we can go and have a dekko down The Gut.'

Sir Tarquin Sparrowcroft was 'a Character'. Perhaps his eccentricity sprang from a reaction to his being a solicitor, which is generally less thrilling than being a deep-sea fisherman, say, or a film stunt man or even an illegal financial fraudster (there is a fine distinction between legal and illegal fraudsters). The tedium of poring over documents in an arcane language pushed him into rebelling against the general colourlessness of the firm of which he was head.

Sir Tarquin was bald, and some people swore he actually polished his head; he wore great, bushy, mutton-chop whiskers which went out with Sergeant Buzfuz. The shiny dome and the mass of hair below it gave the impression of a giant dodo's egg in a nest.

While everyone else, including the pretty receptionist, all dressed as if they were going to read a will to a family of old-fashioned undertakers, Sir Tarquin's appearance bordered on the bizarre. His suit was of a conventional enough material and colour, but its cut was idiosyncratic. It had wide, curved lapels of the sort to be found on what used to be called smoking jackets, and slanting pockets. From the top breast pocket cascaded a small sail of a lime green silk handkerchief which Pavarotti would have struggled to manage. Sir Tarquin's shirt was white with candy-coloured stripes as wide as the lines on a football pitch. He wore a bow tie that threatened to take flight and whirr round the large room at any moment. A broad silk ribbon with a gold-rimmed monocle hung from his buttonhole. His shoes were as shiny as glass and had large gold-coloured buckles.

When Sir Tarquin opened his jacket and revealed his waistcoat Timberlake felt as if someone had just let off a Catherine wheel. The waistcoat was of iridiscent silk with screeching colours that could have been painted by Picasso on speed. It was clear that he was very proud of it, for he smoothed it down from time to time with loving hands.

'You'll have a glass of sherry,' he said in a tone that was a mixture of bonhomie and command. His voice was plummy and studied, like Donald Sinden going further over the top than usual. He went to a cabinet and poured two glasses of sherry from an antique decanter that might have served to provide Charles I with his last glass of sack before his execution. The sherry wasn't quite good enough to be worth going to the block for, but Timberlake hadn't tasted better and admitted as much. Sir Tarquin looked as pleased as if he'd made it himself.

'So you've come to see me about Mrs Pascoe and Mrs Newman,' he said. He took a file from the side of his desk, opened it, and put his monocle in his right eye. Timberlake noticed the lens was plain glass.

'According to the pathologist Mrs Pascoe died first,' Timberlake said, 'which I suppose will affect the question of who finally inherits what.'

'Normally it would, but not in this case. In the first place,' the lawyer continued, 'neither lady made a will, despite my frequently reiterated advice to them to do so. They didn't see the necessity.' Sir Tarquin shook his head sorrowfully, tut-tutted extravagantly, then looked at Timberlake accusingly. He waited, challenging Timberlake to admit he hadn't made a will either.

Harry had a rush of guilt and was almost constrained to explain that he had no close relatives and nothing much of value to leave anyway, except for his jazz records and well-loved Citroen. In his head he could hear himself talking too much. He pulled himself together and managed a polite, 'You said "In the *first* place ..."?'

35

'Quite,' Sir Tarquin said. 'Mrs Newman owned the house and ninety per cent of the money. So if Mrs Pascoe died first, she had little enough to leave her daughter. If, on the other hand, Mrs Newman were the first to die, her entire estate would go automatically to her husband, even though they are separated – *de facto*, not *de jure*. A thoroughgoing rogue,' he added.

'I take it you'll be getting in touch with him. Do you have his address in Marseille?'

'Oh, yes. I wrote to him to tell him that his wife intended to sue for a divorce and to ask him whether he would accept service of the papers or a solicitor would do it on his behalf. He hasn't replied yet,' Sir Tarquin said with heavy understatement. 'My secretary will let you have the address before you leave. I've no doubt you'll wish to interview him.'

Harry considered the implications of this for a moment.

'How is it that Mrs Newman had most of the family money?'

'Mervyn Pascoe, Ann's husband and Veronica's father, was a stockbroker and an entrepreneur during the good years. He did very well, very well indeed. He was also a prudent and far-sighted man. He made a gift of most of his property to his daughter some seven years before he died, and so avoided inheritance taxes. He gave a relatively small sum to his wife.' He hesitated before adding, 'He was safeguarding his own position while he was alive: he had more influence over his daughter than over his wife.'

'So Mrs Pascoe lived on her daughter's bounty.'

Sir Tarquin was surprised. 'Curiously old-fashioned phrase for a young man.'

'I read a lot. A bit risky, wasn't it?'

'On the surface; but not really. Ann and her mother were very close, almost – if you'll forgive the cliché – like sisters rather than mother and daughter. There was no reason to think that anything could go wrong with his arrangement.'

'You said "on the surface".'

Sir Tarquin smiled with satisfaction. 'Indeed.' His expression changed, and he hesitated a moment before continuing. 'Of course, I have a duty of confidentiality towards my clients, even though they are deceased.'

Timberlake remembered how the dead women had been treated on the morgue tables, and thought that confidentiality was a little late now.

36

'Nevertheless, I shall be quite frank with you, Inspector, because I want to help you as much as I can to apprehend the murderer, and because I feel certain I can rely on your discretion. Veronica Pascoe was born to be a mother's companion and help, and an old maid. Men didn't interest her, and one had the strong impression that sexual activity with a man – or a woman, for that matter – was not one of the greatest impulses in her life.'

Timberlake waited for the 'But . . .'. He was disappointed.

Sir Tarquin breathed on his plain-glass monocle and polished it carefully with his massive lime green handkerchief before continuing his narrative.

'Then Veronica Pascoe encountered Carl-Heinz Rohmer. A German,' he added superfluously.

'*Who?*'

'Her husband. He and Veronica changed their name to Newman after they married. How they met, I don't know. Perhaps it's irrelevant. The gravamen of the situation is that she fell totally in love with the man.' He gave the single word 'love' more shades of meaning than Lady Bracknell's 'A *handbag?*'

There were three questions that immediately suggested themselves to Timberlake. He decided to ask them in reverse order of importance.

'What sort of man is Rohmer?'

'Complex. Physically large, good-looking, I suppose, in a coarse sort of way. Intelligent . . . or sly, more like it.' Bending over backwards until his spine creaked to be fair, Sir Tarquin added grudgingly, 'I must say that he could be charming sometimes, when he wanted to be.'

'You said Mrs Newman fell totally in love with Rohmer. How exactly?'

Sir Tarquin did not pretend he didn't understand what Timberlake meant. 'I am quite sure it was a purely sexual attraction. He had an extremely strong animal magnetism about him.'

'Mrs Newman's falling in love with him doesn't exactly match up with what you said earlier about her attitude towards men.'

'On the surface,' Sir Tarquin repeated. 'But I knew the family for many years. When Veronica Pascoe met Rohmer she was relatively inexperienced, I should imagine. As far as I know she'd never had a steady boyfriend and I think Rohmer's sexuality simply overwhelmed her. All her years of near-celibacy, had made her very vulnerable to a man like Rohmer.' But Timberlake appeared unconvinced.

'Tell me, Inspector, have you ever heard of the case of Samuel Dougal, of Moat House Farm?'

'It rings a rather unpleasant-sounding bell.'

'And well it might. In eighteen ninety-eight Samuel Dougal, a thorough fortune-hunting rogue and libertine, met a Miss Camille Holland, a retiring, virgin spinster of some fifty-five years of age. The man's hyper-sexuality made her lose her head completely, and she married him.' The lawyer waited for Timberlake to say something.

'Am I right in believing that he murdered her?'

'You are indeed. And he was hanged for it.'

The silence hung heavily between them. Then Timberlake asked his third, and most important question.

'How exactly did Carl-Heinz and Veronica Rohmer change their name to Newman?'

Chapter 5

'They did it by simple declaration,' Timberlake told Harkness and the rest of the AMIP team back at the Terrace Vale office. 'That's what fooled us at first.' He went on to explain for the benefit of the other detectives.

'Veronica Pascoe married Carl-Heinz Rohmer and adopted his name. Soon afterwards, the couple took up residence at the house in The Sycamores Avenue. Rohmer applied for and was granted British citizenship because of his English wife. Almost immediately they then told everyone, including the local council, their solicitor, bank manager and the rest, that in future they would be known as Charles Henry and Veronica Ann Newman. Although most people don't realize it, that's all it takes to establish a change of name legally.

'I'm pretty sure Rohmer knew it, and persuaded Veronica to do it his way. If they'd changed their names by deed poll it would get into all sorts of records . . . including the Criminal Records Office's computer. I've got the feeling that our Mr Rohmer/ Newman is a pretty crafty operator.'

While the computer came up with 'Not Known' for Charles Henry Newman, it had quite a lot to say about Carl-Heinz Rohmer, beginning with the already known fact that he was a naturalized British subject, formerly German. The next entries were much more interesting. Timberlake produced a computer print-out which he offered to Superintendent Harkness.

'No, tell us what's in it so we all know,' said Harkness.

'There are a couple of charges of drunk and disorderly. Apparently he got into fights, once in a pub – fined fifty quid – and once in a nightclub. There's a note that this second occasion it was a dispute with another punter over a prostitute. This time he was fined £150, ordered to pay £200 compensation for damage to a car and £500 for dental and medical expenses.' There was a heavy silence.

'That's not all,' Timberlake went on. 'Three months after the second offence he was charged with causing grievous bodily harm, alternatively with causing actual bodily harm.

'According to the file he badly injured a Gordon William Pettifer, aged sixty, a private detective who was formerly a police constable, by hitting him with a piece of wood. There's a note that he pleaded provocation, alternatively self-defence. His counsel just stopped short of alleging that Pettifer's injuries were self-inflicted,' Timberlake commented acidly. 'Anyway, Newman was found Not Guilty. Apparently he was defended by an expensive QC. The local police were totally satisfied that he was as guilty as John Gotti, but . . .' He shrugged.

'Where was he tried?' Harkness asked.

'Woodbridge Crown Court.'

This was greeted by knowing nods and a grunted 'That figures.' Urban Essex jurors are notorious for their extraordinarily high proportion of acquittals and their lack of love for the police, except when their own houses are burgled.

'I understand you speak French, Harry.' This practically took Timberlake's breath away. Although Christian names and nicknames are bandied about freely in the Met, particularly by senior officers to their juniors, this was the first time that Harkness had called him Harry. It was as unexpected as being called 'Mate' by the Queen. 'How good is it?'

'Adequate,' Timberlake understated.

'Right. You'd better get into touch with the Marseille police and start making arrangements to see Rohmer/Newman. In the mean time, I think it might be worth following up this Gordon Pettifer, to see what the altercation with Newman was all about,' Harkness said. 'If you have time, see Mrs Greene, the woman who called on them the day of the murders. Otherwise Darren can speak to her.' Sergeant Webb looked as startled at the use of his Christian name as Harry Timberlake had felt. 'Have another word with Mrs Coker, too. See if there's anything she's remembered.' Webb nodded.

The detective with whom Timberlake made telephone contact in Marseille was an Inspector Stanghelli, whose accent and name unmistakably identified him as a Corsican. He said he'd be pleased to help Timberlake interview Rohmer, which was probably an exaggeration, but to Timberlake's considerable relief he certainly didn't sound hostile. It occurred to him later that maybe Stanghelli was hoping that he'd take Rohmer off his hands.

Timberlake next rang to ask about air fares to Marseille. He couldn't believe his ears. An Apex fare was about £180. But the more flexible journey that he needed, with an open return date, was £430. Timberlake exploded. 'I could get to New York and back for that!'

'Twice,' agreed the clerk wearily, who had obviously heard it all before. And would hear it all again.

Although he wouldn't be paying for the trip himself, Timberlake opted for the train. He didn't believe in spending other people's money for the hell of it. As the Channel Tunnel still wasn't open, he decided on the overnight journey from Victoria to Paris St Lazare with the long Channel crossing via Newhaven and Dieppe; then Paris Gare de Lyon to Marseille on the *TGV – Train de Grande Vitesse.*

Timberlake rang Stanghelli and told him when he would be arriving. 'How will I know you?'

'You'll know me,' Stanghelli said confidently. 'Besides, I'll have a couple of cops with me. And fax me your photograph so I'll recognize you.'

Before he set off Harry Timberlake had time to see Gordon Pettifer. He found his number in the Yellow Pages and arranged to meet him at his office in Pimlico. 'Office' was an extravagant noun for the minimally furnished half-shop Pettifer occupied. The other half was a shoe repairer's; very convenient, Timberlake thought, for a private detective who presumably used a lot of shoe leather in the course of his profession.

After an exchange of professional courtesies Pettifer got down to outlining his to-do with Rohmer in a curious mixture of police prose – 'I was keeping the premises under observation . . .' – and what he thought were American colloquialisms.

He explained that he had been hired to watch Rohmer to see if he was cheating on his wife with other women. 'Well, of course I took the job. There's not a lot of work about these days, particularly divorce. People don't get married as much as they used to, and when they do do, getting a divorce is dead easy now, anyway.'

'And was he having other women?'

'Huh! I wish I knew what he was on! If he boffed only half the women he went with he should be in *The Guinness Book of Records.*'

'Anyone in particular?' Timberlake asked hopefully. If Rohmer had a regular mistress, she could have had a strong motive for murdering his wife, particularly one who was seriously loaded, although he had to admit to himself that cases of women stranglers were as rare as modesty in a politician.

'Particular was the one thing he wasn't. Brasses, pickups in pubs ... Some quality stuff, too.'

'So how did the fight start?'

'I thought Rohmer was acting a bit wary one night, and I didn't realize till too late that he'd made me.' By which Timberlake assumed Pettifer meant Rohmer had realized he was a private detective. 'I was following him, and as I walked round a corner he whacked me on the head with a lump of wood. I fought back, but that first whack had put me at a disadvantage.'

They continued fighting, Pettifer in self-defence, Rohmer trying to do him very serious damage. Someone called the police, who arrived, just in time as far as Pettifer was concerned. He was carted off to hospital and Rohmer was charged with GBH.

'Then things got real weird,' Pettifer went on. 'Mrs Pascoe, that's Rohmer's mother-in-law, visited me in hospital and offered me a couple of centuries to keep it quiet that I was watching Rohmer. She didn't want her daughter to know she'd hired me.'

'*Mrs Pascoe* hired you?'

'Yeah. When she first came here I thought she was acting on behalf of her daughter. Some women are a bit embarrassed at admitting their husbands have got a bit on the side, you see.' Pettifer reflected for a moment. 'Those that aren't as mad as a wet hen, that is. But apparently the old girl had done it off her own bat.'

'Why should she want to keep it quiet if the information was for her daughter anyway?'

'I dunno. People are funny,' said Pettifer, his expression as unfunny as a Faroes weather forecast. 'Perhaps she just wanted to put pressure on Rohmer for some reason, or maybe she had second thoughts and realized her daughter wouldn't thank her for the information. I mean, as long as Mrs Newman, Mrs Rohmer as she then was, didn't actually walk in on her husband schtupping somebody, she could always kid herself he wasn't cheating on her.'

This seemed the most likely proposition to Timberlake. 'What did you do?' he asked.

'To tell you the truth, I wasn't all that keen on keeping quiet. I wanted to tell the whole story in court so that bloody Hun would take a fall . . . go down . . . for duffing me up.'

'But?'

'Well, she upped the ante to a monkey – five centuries. Like I said, there's not all that much work about,' he added apologetically. 'So, I said in court that I was following another man for a client, and Rohmer must have thought I was following him. That was no excuse for him spanking me, though. But he'd got an expensive silk to defend him – his wife paid, I found out later.'

As Timberlake made his way back to Terrace Vale he could see only a one-candle-power ray of light from his meeting with the unhappy Pettifer. Rohmer had some sort of a motive for killing Mrs Pascoe . . . if he'd found out about her hiring a private detective to spy on him. As for Veronica, well, husbands have always got all sorts of private motives for killing wives, he thought misanthropically – not to mention inheriting a small fortune, particularly when the wives were on the point of getting a divorce. It didn't occur to him until rather later that subconsciously he'd already decided who the murderer was. Sternly he told himself to keep an open mind before he had all the facts. For all the good it was to do him.

He was halfway back to the nick when he realized he was not far from Beechcroft Avenue, where Mrs Greene with an 'e' lived. Her road was posh enough, but its name was without the definite article, so not quite as posh as *The* Sycamores Avenue.

Mrs Greene lived at Number 17, but the number was on a dark bronze plate half-obscured by laurel leaves that had probably been dragged across to hide anything as vulgar as a number. Much more prominent was a nameplate: *Cap-Ferrat*. Beneath the doorbell was another bronze plate: 'Tradesmen's Entrance at Rear'. Timberlake decided that he wasn't a tradesman, and pressed the doorbell. It gave a three-note gong which should have heralded an announcement about an aircraft now loading at Gate 25.

The door was opened a few inches with the security chain still in place, a practice Timberlake approved of, by a blonde young woman dressed in a sober dress of dark grey which seemed to be the local uniform for servants. 'Yes?' she asked.

'Can I speak to Mrs Greene, please?' Timberlake replied. He produced his warrant card and gave his name and rank.

'I'll see if she is at home.' The door was closed on him. After a few moments it opened again and the young woman showed him into a reception room that looked as if it had been furnished by the same decorator as the late Mrs Newman's. Mrs Greene came hurrying in with the jerky movements of a badly operated marionette. She was as thin as the late Duchess of Windsor and wore a black dress whose simplicity screamed its expensiveness and cruelly emphasized her scragginess. The amount of jewellery she wore seemed almost too heavy for her slight frame, but it didn't stop her waving her arms almost non-stop, reacting to what Timberlake was saying like an over-excited Neapolitan. This made her bracelets, rings, bangles, necklaces and the rest clatter and click as noisily as a box of castanets falling downstairs. She was carrying a cigarette-holder that could have been a Noël Coward cast-off.

When she spoke, Timberlake was shocked. She had a beautifully modulated contralto voice and unobtrusively cultured accent: the combination quite transformed her. It was as if an old wind-up gramophone suddenly burst forth with hi-fi sound. Talking calmed her, too; her almost spastic movements quietened.

'You called on Mrs Pascoe and her daughter that last day before they were killed. What time did you leave?'

'About six o'clock, I think.'

'Did anyone else call while you were there? Or did either lady say she was expecting anyone?'

'No.'

Timberlake asked her the standard questions about whether either of the two women had been acting oddly recently, whether, as far as she knew, they had received any strange telephone calls or letters that had worried them. She shook her head to all the questions. When he asked if they had any enemies it was as if he had pressed a secret spring.

'That bloody husband of hers!' Mrs Greene said venomously. 'Why the hell she ever married him, I'll never know. Yes, I do,' she added immediately. 'He addled her brains with that big cock of his.' Timberlake was briefly speechless. 'She got a few years' decent sex out of it, I suppose. But in no time at all that awful bloody Boche was carrying on with other women, spending her money... Veronica kept her eyes shut to it for a while, but eventually even she couldn't pretend any more. There were some awful public rows as well as the private ones. Finally she cut off the money supply and the bastard left her. I think he believed stopping the money was her mother's idea.'

The more Harry Timberlake heard about Rohmer, the more plainly he could see him as the number one suspect ... maybe the only suspect.

He could never have imagined what trouble that theory was going to cause him.

Inspector Stanghelli hadn't exaggerated when he told Timberlake he'd recognize him. At the Gare Saint-Charles he was flanked by two uniformed *agents de police*, which is the correct term for uniformed town policemen, but this isn't what made him identifiable. With a policeman on either side most people would look as if they were under arrest. In Stanghelli's case it looked more as if the two uniformed cops were under Stanghelli's arrest. He was the sort of man who would be recognizable as a cop lying on a beach, wearing only a pair of bathing trunks.

He was a big man, very big, and as overweight as Ted Greening, but in a totally different way. He gave the impression of being as hard as a lorry tyre. He was built on the lines of a student Sumo wrestler, not one of the older bags of lard. He was wearing sand-coloured slacks with a large white shirt outside them; not to disguise his bulk, but to conceal the holstered automatic at his belt. Timberlake raised his arm in recognition.

'*Monsieur l'Inspecteur!*' Stanghelli said, holding out his hand as he approached. Timberlake shook it.

'Inspector Stanghelli, glad to meet you. I'm really grateful for your help,' he replied. Stanghelli gave an airy wave.

The uniformed policemen saluted politely and shook hands with him, murmuring, '*Monsieur l'Inspecteur.*'

When they walked out of the Saint-Charles station the heat was almost tangible. Stanghelli glanced at Timberlake. 'It's only thirty degrees,' he said, which was about eighty-six degrees Fahrenheit. 'It's just that the traffic' – which was noisy, inconsiderate and bad-tempered – 'and the people make it seem worse.' He added, 'They make *everything* seem worse.'

Stanghelli first took Timberlake to police headquarters to make a courtesy call on his chief, Commissaire Piquot. The HQ building is called *l'Évêché*, which really means the Bishop's Palace. 'That's what the building originally was,' Stanghelli explained. 'Now it hears a different form of confession.' It was typical of most police buildings everywhere in the world: stark, functional and vaguely intimidating.

Commissaire Piquot, a sharp-faced man who reminded him slightly of Superintendent Harkness, received Timberlake unenthusiastically. 'So you've come to interview Rohmer,' he said in French. 'If you want to take him away, you're welcome. Just make sure the paperwork's in order.' He held out his hand for a second token handshake to signify the meeting was over.

'Have you fixed up a hotel?' Stanghelli asked.

'No. I hoped you'd be able to recommend somewhere.'

Stanghelli drove him to a small hotel near the Bas Fort Saint-Nicolas, the Marseille depot and recruiting office of the *Légion Étrangère*. 'It's cheap, clean, and the *patronne* is honest. The only problem is she doesn't sell liquor, but there's a bar next door. I'll call for you about seven and take you somewhere to eat.' He waved away Timberlake's thanks, and added, 'We can see that *salaud* Rohmer tomorrow.' This time Timberlake was ready for the handshake.

The restaurant Stanghelli took him to was on the Quai de Rive Neuve, overlooking the Old Port on the opposite side from the town hall. From the welcome and attention he received it was clear that the detective was a good friend and customer of the proprietor, who was named Marius. He and Stanghelli '*tutoyer*'-ed each other.

Timberlake reached for the menu. 'You won't need that,' Stanghelli told him. 'You've come to the home of the best bouillabaisse in Marseille, which means the best in Europe.'

'Only Europe?' said Marius in an exaggeratedly injured voice, moving towards the kitchen.

His first mouthful of the bouillabaisse made Timberlake's taste buds vibrate. 'What's in this?' he demanded.

'In the classic bouillabaisse there are six fish: white mullet, red mullet, *merlin, rascasse* and *vive* – I don't know the English for them – and one I forget. You cook them with onions, tomatoes, garlic, parsley, fennel, *sariette*, salt, black pepper . . . and saffron.

Those *croûtons* are flavoured with garlic mayonnaise.

'Chefs who respect the tradition of bouillabaisse are granted a charter by the Bouillabaisse Institute. That's Marius's on the wall there.'

Timberlake turned to see a framed, gold-coloured certificate which looked like an ornate university diploma. 'With the agreement of the institute a good chef can vary the ingredients as long as the spirit and tradition of the bouillabaisse is respected. This is Marius's unique recipe. 'You see, my dear Timberlake, although there are a thousand recipes for bouillabaisse, the true art is not only what you put into it, but the proportions of the ingredients, the amount of each herb and spice you add. And Marius here' – he nodded towards the proprietor – 'is the greatest of the artists. I tell you, *mon cher Timberlake*, Marius has done more for human happiness and culture than ... Picasso, or Rodin, or Beethoven, or ...' He made an all-encompassing gesture. Harry Timberlake was too busy spooning up his bouillabaisse to argue.

After a moment Stanghelli drew closer to Timberlake, looked around and then asked in a confidential voice, 'Tell me, how is Kreese Vadell doing in England now?' Timberlake was puzzled. 'Vadell?'

'Kreese Vadell, the footballer. The best foreign player we ever had in Marseille – probably in France.'

'Oh, Chris Waddle! Fine, fine.' He took another spoonful.

'Good,' Stanghelli said with satisfaction. He turned to his bouillabaisse, then checked. 'Oh, by the way ... if you're seeking company this evening ...'

'Not really.'

'Because I was going to say, there are a few *putes* in the Opéra area, but they are to be avoided. I can give you a couple of telephone numbers of reliable women.'

'No thanks, really.'

'As you wish. Now, let's eat.'

It was as well that Timberlake didn't know what the next day would bring. It would have ruined his appetite.

Chapter 6

In civilian clothes WPC Rosie Hall looked very different from her persona as the uniformed Terror of The Gut. She was having an evening out with her current boyfriend, a Terrace Vale optician named Rodney Swallow. They had just been to an amateur revival of *The Sound of Music*, which had brought tears to the eyes of Rodney Swallow, but left Rosie wishing that they'd left the show lying unrevived to die an unlamented death. She could imagine nothing more dire than a poor imitation of Julie Andrews, unless it was a good imitation.

At Southington underground station, which was in the next area to Terrace Vale, Rodney put a £1 coin into a ticket machine, and then another. The machine spurned the second coin with a disdainful clatter. Rodney tried it again. The machine was intransigent: the coin rattled into the 'Rejected Coins' cup. If a machine could sneer, this one did.

'It's a dud,' he said as he examined the coin carefully. Some time ago there had been a spate of slugs which had been specially made for ticket machines, forcing London Transport to tweak their machines to be much more selective. Rodney's coin was not one of those, which were clearly counterfeit and not designed to fool people; his was a genuine-looking coin. 'Maybe one of the other machines'll take it,' he said hopefully, moving off.

'*Rodney,*' Rosie said, using her official voice. He stopped in his tracks. 'You can't do that. Give it to me.'

He held out the coin with a tiny *frisson* of excitement. He loved it when she was masterful with him.

'I'll hand it in at the nick tomorrow. Now, see if you've got another one. And don't hang about. I want us to get home.'

She smiled lasciviously. Little beads of perspiration appeared on Rodney's top lip.

Next morning Stanghelli called on Timberlake at his hotel at 7 a.m. In the south of France – and Marseille in particular – the day begins early before it gets too hot, then everything stops during the afternoon for a siesta out of the sun. The two detectives sat on the hotel terrace with coffee while Stanghelli gave Timberlake the details of Rohmer's record, while referring to his notebook.

'Your Rohmer is not a very good citizen,' Stanghelli began. 'He has convictions for criminal damage, causing disturbances by fighting, and he has been in Les Baumettes' – the local prison – 'twice. Once for what you would call GBH' – he pronounced it 'Shay Bay Aysh' – 'and once for being in possession of an automatic pistol, an arm of the Fourth Category, contrary to the Law of twelfth of March, nineteen seventy-three.'

'How long did he get for the gun charge?'

'He could have been given two to five years, but he got two years with twenty-one months of it suspended. His lawyer said Rohmer was an ex-Foreign Legionnaire, and they enjoy a good reputation in France.'

'But . . .?'

'Yes, there is a but, *mon ami*. Rohmer boasts that he is an ex-legionnaire, and has photographs to substantiate his claim, but he was kicked out before the end of his three-month probationary period.'

'His *what*?'

Stanghelli grinned. 'Ah, you believe all you read in *Beau Geste*, no? Listen, when a man signs on with the Legion he has to give his real name, although he can use whatever name he chooses as a legionnaire. During those three months his background is investigated, and if he is not of sufficiently good character, he is rejected.'

'What exactly is "good character"?'

'Armed robbers, men who kill their wives' lovers in a *crime passionel*, they are accepted. After the war many collaborators joined, as Swiss or Belgians, because Frenchmen are not allowed in the *Foreign* Legion.'

'Collaborators?'

Stanghelli shrugged. 'Collaboration was a political error, not a

49

sordid crime. Snatchers of handbags, *aggresseurs* – muggers – abusers of children, are not admitted into the Legion.'

Timberlake thought for a moment before saying, 'I think I see the logic.'

'Rohmer was thrown out of the Legion during his probationary period for indiscipline, for a false machismo ... He was unstable ... liable to overreact. And although legionnaires aren't choirboys, there was an excessive degree of sadism in his character, according to the Legion psychiatrist.'

'I thought the Legion was supposed to be secretive. How do you know all this?'

Stanghelli gave a slow smile. '*Mon cher Inspecteur*, we have our sources, too, you know.'

'My apologies. What about Germany: does Rohmer have a record there?'

'Ah, this one is much more interesting. Rohmer was a detective in Dortmund, with a reputation for being a first-class thief-taker. He had a high clear-up rate in his cases. Unfortunately ... he began to get into trouble because an unnaturally large number of his suspects fell down steps, or walked into doors, or resisted arrest and had to be restrained by force. A few ...' He shrugged. 'That is to be expected, but Rohmer exaggerated.'

Timberlake nodded.

'There is more. He was suspected – to the point of virtual certainty – of having close associations with pornography and prostitution rings.'

'Was he chucked out of the force?'

'He was allowed to resign – loudly protesting his innocence, of course.'

Rohmer lived in the Rue Danube, in what was left of Marseille's Old Town after the Germans blew it up during the war. It had been a rabbit warren of criminals, deserters from both sides, black marketeers and members of the Resistance. Even Teutonic efficiency and ruthlessness could not sweep it clean, so the Germans blew up as much of it as they could, including the famous transporter bridge across the Old Port. This last act of destruction was simple maliciousness: in no way was the bridge a potential threat to the Germans.

The rue Danube was much the same colour as most of the

famous river: not blue, but dirty grey. The sunshine, brilliant even this early, cruelly exposed the street's scabrous blemishes: cracked and falling plaster, sagging roofs, rotting window frames, and rubbish in the gutters even though the street had been swept and hosed down an hour earlier. It was a street of no hope.

Carl-Heinz Rohmer lived at Number 19, a house that vaguely reminded Timberlake of some of the houses in the worst part of Terrace Vale: divided up into tiny apartments and let to people who were in no position to complain about exorbitant rents for rat-holes. When Stanghelli opened the street door Timberlake was assailed by a wave of the worst of human and animal smells. Marseille's climate is a great smell stimulant.

Rohmer's flat was on the second floor, up a staircase that sloped away from the wall and vibrated under the weight of Timberlake's feet. The contrast between this place and the elegant house in The Sycamores Avenue where Rohmer had once lived was almost too much for Timberlake to take in. He wondered how Rohmer-Newman, as he thought of him, was managing to adjust.

Curiously enough the card on the door of the flat read 'Rohmer-Newman'. Stanghelli pushed the bell. A man inside shouted *'Fous le camp!'*, which freely translated meant, 'Fuck off!'

'Police!' roared Stanghelli in a voice that set off scuttling sounds from some of the other residents in the house. *'Ouvre la porte, Rohmer! On veut te parler.'* He was using the second person singular, the *tu* and *toi* form. This immediately established either Stanghelli's friendship and intimacy with Rohmer, or his authority and superiority. There was no doubt which it was, and this was instantly confirmed by Rohmer's more formal answer using the second person plural: *vous.*

'Oh, bon. Attendez. Ne vous en faîtes pas. J'arrive.' 'Oh, all right. Don't worry: I'm coming.' His German accent was strong when he spoke French.

Rohmer opened the door. He was wearing only a dressing gown which had been expensive when it was new, but was now slightly tattered and stained. His feet were bare. He eyed Timberlake curiously as he entered behind Stanghelli. For once Stanghelli didn't offer to shake hands.

Rohmer-Newman was apparently fifty to fifty-five hard years old: his face testified that he had seen a lot of living. The man's potential cruelty was not heavily marked in his eyes and mouth,

51

but it was unmistakable nevertheless. He was a big man, much the same size as Stanghelli. They faced each other like two bull elephants about to dispute a territory . . . No, Timberlake thought, like two buffaloes, which are much more belligerent and dangerous creatures. Rohmer was the first to back off.

The door to the bedroom opened and a dark-haired woman of about twenty-five years of age came out. She threw Timberlake off balance for a moment.

She was wearing a wrap which she had thrown on carelessly: it emphasized rather than concealed that she had a marvellous body. She was large-breasted with a slim waist and 'interminable' legs like Mistinguett's. Her face was as striking as the rest of her, with large, dark, sleepy eyes that always gave the impression she had just got out of bed, or was about to get into it. The total effect was magnified – literally – by the fact that she was only an inch or two shorter than Rohmer-Newman. She was an absolute cracker.

Timberlake had the reaction most men under eighty who didn't have pacemakers experienced when they saw her: he speculated how she was in bed. He saw Rohmer giving him a slight smile, and knew that he had read his mind. His second thought was to wonder what the hell she saw in Rohmer. Maybe Mrs Greene's guess was right.

Rohmer introduced the woman as Carole Pradet. '*Bonjour*,' she said politely but without interest, and shook hands minimally with Timberlake. She started to shake hands with Stanghelli, but decided against it.

'Carole's Belgian,' Rohmer explained in French. 'She only speaks French, and a little Flemish. '*Chérie, va me faire un peu de café, veux-tu?*' he said. 'Sure you won't have any?' he asked the detectives. They both shook their heads, and Carole went off to make the coffee.

Timberlake decided to interview Rohmer in English. 'Do I call you Newman or Rohmer?' he asked.

Rohmer-Newman shrugged. 'If we're talking in English, *Mr* Newman, I guess.' He took the edge off his reply with a wry smile that David Niven or Cary Grant could not have outdone for charm, although for Timberlake it was as phoney as a £3 note. Timberlake remembered Sir Tarquin Sparrowcroft grudgingly admitting that Rohmer-Newman could be charming if he wanted.

Timberlake got straight to the point. 'I'm sorry to tell you that your wife is dead, Mr Newman.'

Unemotionally Newman asked, 'Suicide or murder?'

'What makes you think it's either?'

'Oh, come on, Inspector. Don't take me for a dickhead. An inspector doesn't come a thousand miles to tell someone his wife's had a heart attack, or been knocked down by a car, when he could do it over the phone.'

'It was murder. And your mother-in-law has been murdered, too.'

'What was it – a mugging? Burglary? Have you got him?'

'We're still making enquiries.'

Newman laughed. 'You mean you haven't a clue.'

Timberlake ignored this. 'I'm told that you visited your wife on Tuesday of last week.' Rohmer nodded. 'That's right.'

'How long were you with her?'

'A few hours. I asked her to drop the divorce, take me back. Then I asked her if she'd make me a settlement, for old times' sake. I gave her a pretty good pitch, and I even managed to get her into bed. Not that it was all that difficult. She obviously hadn't had any for some time, and I thought that was going to do the trick. I should have realized it was a total waste of time. Well, not quite total . . .' He smiled smugly. 'So, I returned here overnight.'

'You asked her to take you back?' Timberlake said.

'You don't have to look so surprised, Inspector,' Newman said. 'You've seen the house in London. Look at this place. Of course I wanted her to take me back.'

As he said it Carole Pradet came in from the kitchen with Newman's coffee. Involuntarily Timberlake glanced towards her. Newman caught the look, and shrugged. It could have meant anything. Carole merely smiled pleasantly and handed him the coffee. He kissed her on the cheek.

'Do you have a set of keys to your late wife's home?'

'I think so. Unless she had the locks changed after she chucked me out.'

'You didn't use them when you called to see your wife earlier last week?'

'No. I just didn't think of taking them.'

'Can I have the keys? I'll see that they're returned.'

Newman shrugged. 'Why not?' He addressed Carole in French. 'Darling, see if you can find that black crocodile-leather key-case I had.'

Timberlake returned to the attack. 'Where were you on the

53

night of Friday-Saturday last week, the twenty-sixth and twenty-seventh, Mr Newman?'

'I suppose that was the night she was killed. I was here.'

'Do you have any witnesses?'

'Carole, of course.' She nodded. 'And there's Michel le Nez. He'll have seen me. Him, and some of his customers. He's the owner of the bar across the street.' He grinned. 'When you see him you'll realize why they call him Michael the Nose. He used to be a boxer, not a very good one. Anyway, I couldn't have been in London on Friday.'

'Why not?'

'I didn't have a passport.' He paused for effect. 'When I got home on Wednesday I put it on the table and Carole spilled some wine on it and made the ink run.' She nodded again. 'I took it to the consulate when I applied for a new one. They've still got it, of course.'

He gave a smile of open sincerity with a full blast of charm. Instinctively Timberlake felt that somehow the whole story would stand up to scrutiny, although he was equally certain it was a blatant fraud. He just knew Newman had killed his wife and her mother, he *knew* it. But to prove it . . . He felt his heart turn to stone and start to plunge towards his boots. To give himself time to recover he changed tack.

'You don't seem to be very upset at your wife's death, Mr Newman.'

'Why should I be? She was a cold fish. When I married her I thought I might put some life into her . . . But Veronica was the original Englishwoman who closed her eyes and thought of . . . I don't know what the hell she was thinking of, but it wasn't sex. I've just thought of something,' he added with monumentally false ingenuousness. 'I must be inheriting something. I mean, even if she left a will she couldn't cut me out completely. That's the law, isn't it? D'you know if there is a will, Inspector?'

Timberlake shook his head.

Carole returned from the bedroom and handed the key-case to Newman, who passed it on to Timberlake. The case contained the front door keys, but that was all.

'Don't you have one for the alarm?' Timberlake asked.

'No. Veronica wouldn't give me one. I think it was her way of making sure I didn't come home late. Didn't work, though. I just stayed out all night.' He turned to the girl. 'Hey, Carole, we're going to be rich!' Newman exulted. 'We're going to live in a big house in England!'

'How rich?' she asked in French.

'Fucking filthy rich!' he replied in English, but the woman seemed to understand well enough. He returned to French.

'*Mais quand nous habiterons l'Angleterre il faudra que tu apprennes à être une dame, et que tu te souviennes de te mettre une culotte quand tu sors.*' He chuckled, and Carole giggled, like dirty water going down a drain. 'See you in England, Inspector,' Newman said cheerfully. 'I owe you one for bringing the good news. You must come and have a drink.' Newman grinned, but his eyes were full of hate.

Although Michel le Nez's brain had not been totally scrambled by his inglorious boxing career, it was definitely past its 'best before' date. He *thought* he remembered seeing Newman and Carole Pradet on the crucial Friday night, and he couldn't remember definitely *not* seeing them. Stanghelli asked one or two of the bar's regulars, but they predictably didn't remember having heard, seen, touched or smelt anything at all that day. To hear their answers it seemed that most of them were in a deep coma all day Friday and Saturday. Maybe some of them were. The place smelt like a fire in a Colombian garden.

Not so Michel le Nez Gondort's wife Hortense. Timberlake didn't believe that *anyone* was actually named Hortense. She appeared to be built out of something much less yielding than flesh and blood and capable of giving her husband a hard three or four rounds.

'They were both there on Friday night,' she said with a finality that Joe Stalin wouldn't have dared to contradict. 'I went to put out the rubbish and I could see them up there . . .' She nodded in the general direction of Newman's window. It was against the law to put rubbish out overnight, but Stanghelli wasn't going to make a point of it. 'See them *and* hear them arguing again,' Hortense added, nodding her head vigorously several times, like someone drawing a number of lines under a phrase for emphasis.

Timberlake's heart sank. It was the sort of positive testimony that would impress the hell out of a jury and make them liable to bring in a Not Guilty verdict for someone found standing over a shot and stabbed corpse while holding a smoking gun in one hand and a dripping dagger in the other.

Stanghelli looked at him sympathetically. Timberlake had one last card to play.

'Madame Gondort, are you sure it was Friday night?'

She brandished the ace of trumps before slapping it down on Timberlake's last card. 'Certain. I was thinking what a difference there was between *that* couple up there and Philippe and Desirée in *Valentina*. I was in a hurry to get back in because I wanted to see the latest episode. I never miss it.'

Stanghelli's jaw dropped. As he explained later, *Valentina* was a TV soap opera of a crashing sentimental banality that made Peter Pan look like *Crime and Punishment*. Hortense Gondort's devotion to *Valentina* was like Tinkerbell rushing home to see all-in wrestling.

Timberlake went through the formality of interviewing other local residents and hangers-about: it was fruitless. It was much the same story as in the bar. Most of them *thought* Rohmer-Newman was at home on Friday, some weren't sure, but no one could or would positively say he wasn't. A few didn't even know what day it was right then.

Long after Stanghelli was convinced that Timberlake was wasting his time barking up Newman's wrong tree, he remained indulgent of his English colleague. It was, Timberlake thought afterwards, his way of showing Corsican hospitality by being generous with his time. All for nothing.

While the sun was shining remorselessly in Marseille, rain was bucketing down on Terrace Vale and most of south-east England. WDC Sarah Lewis, plodding her soggy way to Manor Lane, knew she would have to exercise all her self-control not to be snappy with Derek Horlock when she called on him at his shop.

Derek Horlock's greengrocery shop was in the middle of a small parade which included a butcher's which also sold fish and delicatessen, a baker's, a launderette and dry cleaner's, sub-post office in a newsagent's shop, inevitably run by a hard-working Asian family, a mini-supermarket which stayed open late, a chemist's, a Chinese takeaway, and a hardware store. They all did better than merely surviving because the nearest large supermarket was a fifteen-minute – at the best of times – bus journey away. After a bus had actually turned up, that is.

Fruit and vegetables were laid out neatly on stands outside the shop; the inside was clean and tidy with produce displayed on two levels of shelves with strip lighting. A middle-aged woman with a bulging carrier bag coming out of the shop crossed Sarah in the doorway. Horlock gave the woman a smile and a polite 'Good day, Mrs Ward.' When he turned to Sarah his expression became bleak. She looked at him in some surprise.

Horlock was a small man, both short and spare. His forearms below the rolled-up sleeves of his clean blue shirt were like bunches of cords and ropes. In repose his face had deeply etched lines which dragged down his mouth into an inverted V of disillusionment: to a shrewd observer his eyes betrayed a permanent, bone-aching fatigue.

Horlock greeted her with, 'You lot never let go, do you?'

Sarah announced herself, 'WDC Lewis, Terrace Vale.'

'You don't have to tell me. I'd recognize you as a copper a mile off.'

This ruffled Sarah, who hoped she looked like a junior executive, or something. She felt bubbles of bad temper beginning to effervesce under her placid surface. 'You were saying?'

'Once we're in your book, we're fair game for ever, right?'

'I'm sorry, I've no idea what you're talking about.'

'Don't say they didn't tell you I've got form. That's what counts, ennit? Not that I've been dead straight ever since I came out.'

'As a matter of fact, no. Nobody did mention it. I've just come round to see you about your lad, make sure he's all right.'

Horlock studied her intently for a moment, then decided she was telling the truth. His expression softened almost imperceptibly. 'Well . . .' he conceded, 'it was all a long time ago.' He paused, and Sarah waited patiently to see if he wanted to say more. Something about her made him lower his defences a little and be more confiding. He went on, 'It's been eight – no, nine – years since I came out. Three years, for burglary. I did two. Never again.'

'Jason, does he know?'

He shook his head vigorously. 'He was only a kid. His mother told him I was a steward on a ship.' He answered the unasked question. 'She died, three years ago.' The anguish on his face was painful to see.

'I take it he told you about last night? Why he did it?' Horlock nodded. Sarah went on. 'If your boy's so keen on cars, if he's dead set on being a race engineer . . .'

57

'So he begins by sweeping up in a garage, and ends up where he started, only fifty years older?'

'Not necessarily. Some do become race engineers. If not that, he might be a qualified fitter . . . even get his own garage.' Horlock gave her a beaten man's look of cynicism.

Sarah pressed on. 'You might be underestimating Jason's abilities.'

Horlock shook his head violently. 'Accountants. They're the ones who get to the top . . . in every business. They're the ones who run things.'

'Suppose he's no good at it?'

'He will be, if he works hard. Nothing's for nothing. I'll see he works, all right.' Despite the heat Sarah felt a chill. Horlock seemed to know what she was thinking. 'It's for his own good. Don't you think I could do with more money coming in? I'm on my own here . . .' He waved his arm round the shop. 'You reckon I *like* getting up in the morning, when it's still dark, to go to the market, working all the hours the devil sends, knocking myself out just so he can go to a commercial college? I'm taking care of his future.'

'Or yours? Nothing's for nothing,' Sarah blurted out, and then wished she had bitten her tongue. The hot weather had got to her after all. More conciliatorily she added, 'What d'you think's better, Mr Horlock – a happy mechanic or an unhappy accountant?'

'Work's work. Happiness and unhappiness don't come into it. What do you know about anything, at your age?'

'I know Jason was unhappy enough to run away from home,' Sarah snapped, her Celtic temper getting the better of her again.

Horlock winced before recovering quickly. 'He's still here. Anyway, kids don't really know what they want to be at his age.'

'At sixteen?'

'Yeah. What did you want to be when you were his age?'

'The hell out of it, away from my father.'

Horlock stood frozen. At last he reached for a cigarette, but couldn't find a lighter or matches in his pockets. Sarah couldn't help: she didn't smoke. He went into the back room. After a momentary hesitation she followed him.

It was a small living room, with a tiny workshop area cut off by two large screens. In the main part of the room were excellent models of three of four racing cars, from an ERA to a 1990

Ferrari. They all shone with a lustre that almost glowed in the shadows: the Ferrari looked like a giant ruby. Sarah looked at Horlock. 'Jason's,' he said, without elaborating. He picked up some matches and lit his cigarette with an unsteady hand.

Sarah turned to the workshop area, where there were a number of clocks. She guessed they were partly home-made, home-assembled or home-repaired. Horlock noticed her glance. This time he was a little more communicative.

'I was an instrument basher in the RAF for a while. I got interested, and started on clocks.' With a sort of mordant humour he added, 'Apart from the time I was into locks.'

'They look quite good.'

Horlock was dismissive. 'Oh, yeah. Ever heard of a rich clockmaker?'

'I haven't heard of all that many rich greengrocers, either,' Sarah said. She was finding it difficult to remain polite.

'It's all I can do. I've got form. I couldn't get insurance for a clock repairer's shop.' Now Sarah felt a shit.

There was a footstep in the yard at the back of the premises. Sarah glanced out of the window. Jason Horlock was coming from a shed on the other side of a 20 cwt. van. He was carrying another model car.

'Hello, I'm WDC Lewis,' she said lightly.

'I told Dad,' he said defensively.

'I know,' Sarah said, and gave him the sort of smile that could make Harry Timberlake's toes curl up with pleasure when he wasn't wearing shoes. 'I just wanted to make sure you didn't do another runner after you got home.' Before Jason or his father could speak she said, 'That's a handsome looking model. May I . . .?' She held out her hand. Jason Horlock hesitated, then handed the model to her. She treated it with the care it deserved.

'It's a Williams-Renault. You know, Nigel Mansell's car the year he won the championship. There's his name, by the cockpit. I cut the Canon and Labatts logos from a magazine, stuck them on and then covered them with plain varnish.'

She gently ran her fingers along the length of the car. 'I think you did wonders. It's so smooth! How do you get that finish?'

'Takes a long time, rubbing it down,' he admitted. 'Then I put on three coats of cellulose, rubbing it down again between each coat. Racing cars have to be smooth, cut down the wind resistance.'

'It must come pretty expensive, all this.'

'Not really. I have to buy the wheels from a model shop, but most of the other stuff's just scrap. I get it from Mundy's garage, in Queen's Road. Old Mr Mundy's quite decent. And I've got my paper round at Watson's.'

'Really? They deliver my papers.'

'Where d'you live?'

'Harcourt Terrace, twenty-seven.'

'One of mine.' He searched the card-index of his memory. 'You moved in about . . . six months ago. *Guardian*, *Observer* and *Independent on Sunday*.' Which was a fairly unusual selection for a police officer.

'Dead right. Well done.'

'Here, have a look at these other cars—'

'She's got work to do,' Horlock cut across brusquely.

'Another time,' Sarah said, to keep the peace.

'Sure.' Jason looked back and forwards between his father and Sarah. 'Did you—?'

Horlock broke in again. 'Yes, she spoke to me. I'm not going to see you in some dead-end, dirty job just because—'

'It wouldn't be a dead-end—!'

'because of some kid's half-baked ideas—'

'I'm sixteen!'

Horlock moved towards the shop at the front to try to put an end to the argument, but his son followed him, with Sarah trailing along behind.

'Other blokes, my age, do odd jobs: packing supermarket shelves, cleaning cars . . . they got money, go out enjoying themselves, got girlfriends . . .'

'Oh, yeah, we know all about that! You're sixteen and you think you know it all. You know nothing! You'll study, make something of yourself. You'll thank me for it later.'

'What about *now*? How d'you think I feel, going out with my mates, always being the one who can't pay his corner? What d'you think the girls—?'

'Shut up about you and your bloody girls!'

Sarah felt it was time to cool the situation. Gently, yet firmly, she said, 'Look, let's calm down, shall—'

'Keep your nose out of it!' Horlock said fiercely. He turned to his son. 'I don't suppose you ever think how I manage to pay for your school just so you can be *somebody* one day? Scrounging pennies, cutting corners...' He caught Sarah's suddenly alert expression.

They all fell silent as the shop's doorbell rang like a ringside gong. It signalled the end of a round, not the end of the fight.

Sarah would have given odds that the situation was going to cause trouble, and sooner rather than later.

Stanghelli personally escorted Harry Timberlake to the Saint-Charles station to start his journey home.

'Sorry it didn't work out,' he said as they walked down the eighteen-carriage-long platform. 'I'm afraid Rohmer isn't your man.' He gave Timberlake a sidelong glance and saw he wasn't convinced. 'Look, Rohmer has a solid enough alibi with some credible witnesses on his side – let alone Hortense Gondort. Plus the fact that he didn't have a passport at the time. You couldn't even get a conviction in a Russian court,' Stanghelli added slanderously.

'Passport...' Timberlake said as a thought struck him. 'Would you send a fax to the German authorities asking if Rohmer, or Newman, has a current German passport? They can reply to me in London.'

Stanghelli sighed, and said the one word universal in all languages, 'OK.'

Chapter 7

Harry Timberlake's flat was dark and uninviting when he finally arrived home. He'd called at the Terrace Vale nick and typed out his report, which he had worked on during his journey from France. Then he'd made a detour from the station to the former Pascoe-Newman home to try the keys that he had taken from Newman.

They fitted. He couldn't make up his mind if that was good or bad.

The little green light on his answerphone was blinking steadily when he entered. He switched it on. The message was from Sarah Lewis. Without announcing herself – you could never be sure who might be listening – she'd said, 'Doesn't matter how late you get in. Give me a ring.'

He dialled her number. 'You said it didn't matter how late.'

'Half past eleven isn't late. Your place, or mine?' When he hesitated, she said, 'I'm on my way.' Gratefully, he hung up, then took the chain off the front door. Less than half an hour later Sarah let herself in with the keys Harry had given her long before, when he was faced with the Judgement of Paris between her and Dr Jenny Long.

'How was it?' she asked.

'I've got a perfect case against Newman ... except for the fact that he's got an unbreakable alibi.'

Sarah thought about this. 'Unbreakable ... Well, everyone said the *Titanic* was unsinkable.'

'I'll tell you all about it tomorrow.'

'Are you hungry?' she asked.

'I ate on the ferry.'

'I've eaten, too.'

So they had a glass of wine, and then another, and she asked, 'How d'you feel?'

'Tired, a bit.'

'I'll give you a massage in the shower.'

First she soothed him, then she started to excite him and he forgot his tiredness. When they went to lie on the bed, still slightly damp, he said, 'God, you're bloody marvellous.' In the very last nick of time he prevented himself from saying 'You'd make somebody a great wife.' I nearly buggered up things there, he thought. He lay and stared at the ceiling for a short while, wondering and worrying about the implications of that second thought.

'What're you thinking about? Something wrong?' Sarah asked.

'Anything but,' he lied skilfully. 'I was thinking of what I'm going to do to you.'

'I know *what* you're going to do to me,' she said with a giggle like the bubbling of a witch's pot. 'I'm just interested in *how* you're going to do it.'

Next morning life at the Terrace Vale station was staggering along in its customary fashion of semi-ordered chaos. The major talking points in the CID Office were Harry Timberlake's return from Marseille and the collapse with a heart attack of one of their colleagues, the unfortunately named DC Just Fullshawe. The attack hadn't proved fatal, but it was going to put him out of action for a few months.

Fullshawe's illness was not the main topic of conversation. His absence meant the cases he was dealing with had to be shared out among the other detectives. Chief Inspector Ted Greening was discussing the problem with Inspector Farmer in his office.

Detective Inspector Robert Farmer had recently been posted to Terrace Vale from Kingsmere-on-Thames, an upmarket area outside the London postal districts, but still part of the Met's bailiwick. Kingsmere had more than its fair share of well-kept parks and commons, was controlled by an enlightened local council; it was reputed that its population had the highest number of university graduates per head outside the university towns. As a result Kingsmere enjoyed a generally better-than-average class of crime. Inevitably in a well-to-do area there were burglaries, car thefts and white-collar crimes; but little of Terrace Vale's pimping, drug dealing, street prostitution, mugging and general nastiness.

Farmer's appearance reflected his previous background. He was the most elegantly dressed copper at Terrace Vale, and was tall and slim with it. When he took off his jacket in the office he hung it on a clothes hanger; he *always* wore a tie. Sergeant Rumsden reckoned he wore one with his pyjamas.

In his early days he was the butt of ribald remarks, but they bounced off him like spit off a hot iron. Many of the sallies were aimed at his lack of hair. He was called Kojak at first, but this was a gross slander; Farmer's hair receded at the temples and was less than luxuriant on the crown, that was all. He was apparently totally unconcerned by it. No one at the station dreamed he had a small cupboard at home full of lotions, creams, ointments, pills and homemade recipes. All useless. And it was quite evident that even if he was on the way to becoming a chrome-dome, it didn't stop him enjoying a rich, satisfying social life with young women.

When the CID performed one of their nice-guy-nasty-guy inter-rogations, Robert Farmer was always the nice guy. At the moment he was a cerebral rather than a streetwise copper; he had a long mile to go before he had Harry Timberlake's instinct and street-wisdom. However, he was highly accomplished at internal politick-ing and subtly brown-nosing his superiors. He was obviously a man with a future.

They had got down to the last packet of cases, which included a burglary at an alcohol and tobacco wholesaler's.

'Who do you suggest we put on this?' Farmer asked. 'We're a bit thin on the ground for troops at the moment, with one thing and another.'

'Yeah,' Greening said grumpily. 'Bloody AMIP grabbing bodies, and Harry swanning off to Marseilles and having a good time . . .'

To give him his due, Farmer didn't think Timberlake *had* 'swan-ned off', or necessarily had a good time, but he wasn't going to contradict his superior.

Greening studied Farmer uncomfortably. 'You know the people here far better than I do,' Farmer prompted.

Greening reflected. 'Bloody Dickless Tracy Lewis,' he said even-tually, using the slang title for any female police officer. 'She's supposed to be shit-hot,' he said with his customary elegance. 'Make the tart get off her fat arse and do something.'

Farmer nodded, keeping his face noncommittal. Although he was no great pro-female libber, he would never have called Sarah Lewis a tart, and she certainly wasn't lazy. Most of all, she didn't have a fat arse.

'Good idea, guv,' he said with a degree of genuine enthusiasm. Having Sarah working for him could give rise to all sorts of possibilities.

Detective Superintendent Harkness and his AMIP murder squad were in their commandeered office, most of them drinking canteen tea or coffee – the two liquids were difficult to tell apart – with one or two furtively eating a bacon sandwich. Sergeant Braddock was reading Harry Timberlake's report of his Marseille trip and interview with Newman. Harkness had already read it, and Timberlake had briefed Darren Webb and some of the others earlier that morning.

'Mmmm,' Braddock said as unsurprised as usual, and put the report on the desk in front of Harkness.

'When did you write this?' Harkness asked.

'Last night.'

'After you'd been to the house and found that Newman's keys fitted?' It wasn't really a question. Harkness silently calculated just how late Harry Timberlake had worked the previous night. 'So what are your views about Newman?'

Timberlake took a deep breath and nailed his colours to the mast. 'He did it all right: killed both of them.' He was fully aware that he had set himself up to come a humiliating cropper, but he wasn't good at prevarication. He went on, 'I think the fundamental factor is that he used to be a detective, and a very good one, till he turned corrupt. So, he knows the system and how it works; he knows how to fight it. He became a part-time crook, which in this case is an extra talent for him,' Timberlake added with a hint of a wry smile.

'Go on.'

'He knows all about transference: that a criminal always leaves traces of himself behind at the scene of a crime, and he picks up and takes away traces from it. He deliberately visited his wife a couple of days before the murder so that if the SOCOs found hairs, fingerprints . . . anything at all from him . . . he could say "Sure. That comes from when I was there on the Tuesday." The fact that Mrs Newman had just had sex with someone wearing a condom also fits with it being her husband.'

'Or a lover. And what about the keys?' Sergeant Braddock asked dubiously. 'If Newman's guilty he didn't have to admit he'd got a set. He could easily have said he left them behind when he left his wife.'

'We would have found out eventually there was a missing set: the manufacturers of the security keys keep careful records of how many they make.'

'Good point, Harry,' Harkness said eventually, which set a lot of heads nodding like toy dogs in car rear windows. 'But the evidence—'

'It's a gut feeling,' Timberlake interrupted boldly. 'I *know* he did it. And there were little things: for example, when he said he'd got his wife into bed on that Tuesday. He didn't have to tell me that, and I wouldn't mind betting that the Carole woman heard it even though she was in the kitchen.'

'You said she didn't speak English,' Braddock pointed out.

'*Newman* said she didn't speak it. That doesn't mean she doesn't understand it. He didn't have to tell me that,' he repeated doggedly. 'He was just laying the groundwork to explain any traces of him the lab people may have found in his wife's bed. In fact,' Timberlake said, realizing, 'that could have been his first mistake: we know now he could still talk his wife into having sex.'

'Perhaps he just wanted to show off, guv?' Webb said in his diffident manner. 'Maybe he wanted to prove he'd got the Belgian bit in the palm of his hand? Prove it to you *and* her?'

Slightly deflated, Harry stared at him. 'Yeah. Pretty shrewd, Darren,' he admitted honestly. He pulled himself together. 'But he did it all right: who else had a motive, particularly to kill both women?'

Harkness sounded almost apologetic. 'He had motive and means – his big hands – but no opportunity. And according to your report, he has a completely solid alibi.'

'There's a weak point somewhere: there has to be. I'll find it.'

'Right,' Harkness said without expression. 'In the mean time, we'll cover all eventualities and continue with following up all the two women's friends and acquaintances.' He nodded to indicate that the conference was over and the detectives moved towards the door. 'Harry,' he said quietly. Timberlake turned back. 'You seem to be convinced that Newman is our man. Is there any possibility that a personal dislike of him may be affecting your judgement?'

Timberlake had the common sense not to answer immediately.

'I have to admit that he got up my nose, but putting that aside, as I said, I'm absolutely certain he did it.'

'Despite the evidence against it.'

'Despite it. And I'll prove it.'

'Well, we'll see. Harry, I have a great deal of faith in your intuition and your ability.' He paused for emphasis. 'But make sure your conviction doesn't become an obsession.'

'Right, sir.' Timberlake never called Harkness 'guv'. The detective superintendent wasn't that sort of man. 'I'll be careful.' He turned and went out.

After Timberlake had gone Harkness stared at the closed door for a few moments, until a woman civilian clerk knocked and entered.

'Sir, we've just had a telex from Interpol, passing on a message from Germany.' She handed the piece of paper to Harkness. 'Carl-Heinz Rohmer's German passport expired two years ago and hasn't been renewed.'

'Thank you,' Harkness said slightly wearily. 'Put a copy in Inspector Timberlake's in-tray. In an envelope,' he added. There was no need for everyone to know of Harry's discomfiture.

Sarah Lewis looked dead scruffy. Her normally shiny, well-kept hair had dusty strings straggling out from under a Glasgow Celtic woolly hat; her only makeup was a dirty smear on her forehead. Despite the fact that it was a warm evening she had on a none-too-clean raincoat held in place by a twisted belt. Elephant-leg slacks and dirty trainers completed the bottom half of her toilette. She had with her a Marks and Spencer carrier bag that was new when Mr Marks and Mr Spencer served behind the counter. Although it was not the sort of outfit that would get you a welcome at the Savoy – unless it was known that your name was Getty, Rothschild or Berlusconi: nothing is too eccentric for that sort of serious money – it was not out of place in the public bar of the Peal of Bells, known locally as the Jingling Balls. It was a sort of last-resort pub, well away from Terrace Vale, and it suited her purpose perfectly.

She sat at a corner table with a half-drunk glass of Guinness in front of her, waiting for her 'boyfriend' to turn up. His name was Jocko McLeish and he was a small-time thief. He arrived a quarter of an hour late, which put Sarah in a bad mood: she hated to be exposed in public like this any longer than was strictly necessary. Jocko had a face that not even his mother had loved, and he was shaped like a half-deflated barrage balloon.

He looked round the bar when he arrived, noticed Sarah, and bought himself a pint of some strange Scottish beer which he took over to her table.

Sarah had inherited Jocko from a detective constable who had been posted to another station: Jocko was a snout or grass. On detectives' official reports he would be referred to as an informant.

The psychology of the informant has been a source of much speculation by criminologists, but his (or her) main motivations are fairly straightforward – for a twisted personality, that is. There is the sense of power over fellow criminals that excites many snouts, a close relation of the 'every man would secretly like to be a spy' syndrome. Almost equally important are the financial rewards: not just the odd fiver or tenner from the detective who is running the informer, but the percentage payments when the snout's information leads to the conviction of the criminals and the recovery of the stolen property. This is all black and white, but there is the dirty grey area which everybody knows exists, but no one admits. The informant's own little expeditions into burglary and thieving somehow never get cleared up ... as long as he doesn't overdo things and try walking into a bank wearing a balaclava while holding a gun. That would be considered to be taking a liberty.

'You took your time,' Sarah said sharply.

'I had to see a feller,' Jocko replied, his eyes sweeping the bar like a radar transmitter. 'You know, Sarah.'

'Miss Lewis to you, Jocko.'

'Sorry. Just trying to be friendly.'

'Well, don't.' She looked as cross as she felt, which added to their cover of boyfriend and girlfriend. She took a mouthful of her Guinness, which she hated, making her look even crosser. 'The fags and booze wholesaler's blag in Prince Regent's Road,' she said. 'Have you heard anything?'

'Och, be reasonable, Miss Lewis,' Jocko said reproachfully. 'There hasn't been time for word to get round.'

Mentally Sarah conceded that he was probably right. She tried another tack. 'Who's likely to take a load like that?'

Jocko shrugged. 'Any dodgy pub, or an off licence. This place, for a start. Maybe a drinking club.'

'Anything else moving on the manor?'

'Things are very quiet. You know I'll give you a bell if I hear anything,' he said reproachfully. Sarah nodded and started to get up. 'Miss Lewis, haven't you forgot something?' He put his hand on the table, palm up.

'You bring me nothing, I pay you nothing. Find out about the Prince Regent's Road job.'

'Bitch,' Jock said to her retreating back, taking good care that she didn't hear him.

'Good God, you pong like a zoo-keeper's heel. You need a bath,' was the gracious greeting Harry Timberlake gave Sarah as she came through the front door of his flat. 'And leave your things in the hall.'

'I was going to.' To anyone who didn't know Sarah, it would have been a perfectly neutral remark. To Timberlake, though, the unobtrusive harmonics that went to make up the whole sound came across as plainly as a police siren. He knew he would have to step as delicately as Agag brought before Samuel, if he wanted to avoid a row.

Sarah stamped into the living room as loudly as bare feet could manage, looking as grimly serious as a Spanish dancer in full fandango. It set parts of her barely clothed person jouncing and jiggling interestingly. Harry thought it best not to mention it.

'Bad day?' he said, trying not to sound patronizing.

'Bob bloody-Kojak Farmer has dumped cases on me, and my snout is being as much use as a hole in a bucket.'

Harry was wise enough not to offer help or advice. 'There're days like that,' he said briefly. 'You're too good at your job to let it get you down.' If this didn't exactly mollify Sarah, at least it didn't wind her up.

A cold gin and tonic and a hot bath with a massive overdose of Harry Timberlake's expensive 'special-occasions-only' bath essence smoothed off Sarah's jagged edges. Paradoxically, he felt himself becoming tense. Later, lying in bed with a soft and fragrant Sarah he tried to put everything out of his mind except what she was doing to him. In vain.

'What's wrong?' she asked.

'Nothing,' he said automatically.

This brought a derisive snort of amusement from her. 'Then why are we into Emission Impossible?' She paused. 'Did you

69

knacker yourself with some French tart while you were away?'
Saying that suddenly made her realize that although she had never
thought, let alone spoken about, either of them being faithful to
the other, she was actually jealous of what *might* have happened
while he was away.

'Come on. Can you imagine me going with some Marseille tom?'
Sarah pushed her jealousy away and began to laugh.

The tension between them was eased for a moment, but not
forgotten.

'Now, what *is* wrong?'

Briefly, he told her about Newman. Then, asking her as a friend
and not as a professional colleague, 'Do I sound obsessive about
him?'

As off-handedly as she could manage Sarah replied, 'Maybe,
a little.'

'Why the hell am I being so antipathetic towards him?' He
refused to accept he was being obsessive. Then he answered his
own question. 'Because of what he did to those two women.'

'Or somebody did.' Sarah felt Timberlake tense up beside her.
She could have bitten her tongue. Trying to make things better,
she only dug the hole deeper because she couldn't keep the doubt
from her tone. 'Even if you're right, despite his alibi, proving it's
going to be another matter. You mustn't let it get to you.'

He stared furiously at the blank ceiling.

'Harry,' she said tentatively.

There had been occasions when they had slept together without
making love, but for the first time he just turned his back on her
and said 'Goodnight,' with no kiss or tender gesture.

Just before Timberlake finally fell asleep it occurred to him that
it seemed that Newman was not only likely to ruin his professional
life but his personal life, too. He was depressingly aware of a nasty
crack that had appeared in the smooth façade of his relationship
with Sarah.

Chapter 8

After a cold, solitary breakfast Harry Timberlake set off for work at Terrace Vale nick in a very humpty mood. It wasn't simply the row – if he could call it that – with Sarah the night before, although that was the trigger action that set other thoughts firing off. They'd had no opportunity to make up in the morning, even if they'd wanted to, because Sarah woke early and left silently for work. She had changed into some of the clean clothes she kept in Timberlake's flat.

During the journey to Terrace Vale Timberlake began to analyse his relationship with her.

Sarah was a great-looking young woman, and very responsive sexually: he was dead lucky with her there. She was discreet and managed her side of keeping their relationship hidden from their colleagues at the station. Sarah was bright, and funny: she understood – only too well – the demands of police work and was uncomplaining about the disruptions it could cause to one's private life. She was supportive, and nearly always understanding of its stresses.

So what was the problem?

It was something he had already realized subconsciously. Sarah was a detective, and they talked shop most of the time: Jenny Long at least had other subjects of conversation. True, Sarah wasn't antagonistic towards Harry's favourite jazz like Jenny, but when he and Sarah went out together it was to musical comedies and falling-trousers-and-cuckolded-husbands farces or Inspector Clouzot films. Harry wasn't consciously an intellectual snob but he would have liked to see something a little more serious. His resistance to Jenny Long's dragging him to classics, he knew now, had been affected rather than real. And ... and ... Sarah was younger than Jenny. She was more streetwise, but she lacked the

71

wider background and experience of the slightly older woman.

Harry asked himself if he was capable of a permanent relationship. He recalled a visit he had made to the home of a retired detective superintendent named Lawrence Jordan to ask about a case he had handled some years previously. The visit scared the hell out of him. Jordan's home was as neat and tidy as a well-kept mausoleum, and had about as much life in it. Jordan had never married – which was not code for saying he was a homosexual: he wasn't – and his house made his solitude obvious. You could smell the aching loneliness which pervaded the place like dry rot. Timberlake was glad to get away, and was terrified for a while that he had seen a preview of his own old age. He decided to make the peace with Sarah that evening.

When Sarah got to work she found eight £1 coins neatly lined up on her desk. She regarded them fixedly, wondering if they were some sort of joke.

'Good morning, Sarah,' Inspector Bob Farmer said, coming up beside her. 'I take it you've seen the snide, there . . .' He used the old-fashioned slang for counterfeit coins. Sarah gave the coins a quick second glance.

'Yes. Good, aren't they?'

'Too good, if you ask me. Whoever made them went to a lot more trouble than he needed just to put them into slot machines.'

'Perhaps they were made to pass over a counter.'

Farmer nodded. 'Unnecessarily risky, though. Still, it might help you.'

'Me?'

'Uhuh. Find out where they've come from.' He said it as if it was quite straightforward instead of being like trying to catch a mouse in a pitch-dark room. 'Four of them have come from shopkeepers – I'll let you have the list – and another three were found picked up by banks. WPC Hall brought in the other one this morning. I think she's in the building – you can ask her where she got it.'

Farmer eyed Sarah calculatingly. His voice became softer. 'If you want any help or advice on this and the wholesaler's job, totally unofficially, out of duty hours' – he gave the merest suspicion of a friendly smile – 'to help you look good, just give me the nod.' He turned away in time to miss seeing Sarah's mouth go into a rat-trap line. She wondered how anyone who took so much care with outward appearances could be so heavy-handedly unsubtle. She said something quietly in Welsh which sounded much worse than the English translation.

Harry Timberlake's day was going from bad to worse, and his mood was matching it. He still had a sort of spiritual hangover from the previous night, and before he got to the nick he had another setback in his council corruption case.

He had arranged to meet a secretary in the town hall offices, Sharon Pettigrew, who was a possible source of vital information, to see if she had anything further for him. Now he found her shifty and evasive: either she had suddenly got cold feet, or she had been bought off. It seemed that the chief executive officer, Lawrence Soper, was going to get away with his graft.

This seriously annoyed Timberlake, and he made the unforgivable mistake of trying to bully the woman, something he normally would never have done.

Superintendent Harkness was studying typewritten lists of names and addresses taken from the late Veronica Newman's and Ann Pascoe's address books. The AMIP murder squad were about to undertake the mind-numbing routine of interviewing a murder victim's contacts, while the uniformed branch helped by going on the knocker – making house-to-house calls – to see if somebody had some small nugget of information that might prove to be valuable. The first one on Mrs Newman's list, which went to Timberlake, was Piers Aubusson at a Wallsend address, in the next Metropolitan Police area to Terrace Vale.

Wallsend was a Thameside area of expensive Edwardian houses and workmen's cottages that had been modernized into 'desirable town residences for executives' who thought that having a fashionable postal code for their address made it worth living like sardines.

The area was full of media people. Somebody said that if a bomb dropped on Wallsend, most of the BBC, ITV and the TV-commercials studios would go out of business the next day. A lot of people would have thought it no great disaster.

Timberlake called Aubusson at the number in Mrs Newman's book. He was answered by a recording. 'Hello! This is Piers Aubusson. Thanks for calling. Sorry I can't come to the phone right now, but I'm at the studio today. Leave a message after the bleep, and I'll get right back to you as soon as I'm home!'

Timberlake put down the phone, saying out loud, 'Why not put an ad in the papers telling burglars the bloody place is empty?' Which studio Aubusson was at was anyone's guess. Wallsend wasn't far, so Timberlake decided to go round to the Aubusson residence and see if any of the neighbours knew where he worked.

The house was one of the small ones with a cobbled space between the front window and the pavement large enough for a couple of tubs of geraniums and petunias, and a six-brick-high wall. Through the front window Timberlake could see a single through room with a small garden beyond. Plainly in view were an expensive stereo system, a large TV and a VTR recorder. The sash windows were secured – if that was the word – with a simple catch that a one-armed midget could open with a Boy Scout knife. Timberlake wondered which company had been rash enough to insure the place.

In front of the next house a middle-aged man was working on a car. About a third of its working parts were neatly laid out on a plastic sheet on the pavement. In some mysterious fashion the man had managed to keep his jeans and T-shirt clean and oil-free. Aubusson, Timberlake guessed, would probably consider that the middle-aged man was letting down the neighbourhood with his alfresco mechanics, even though the car he was operating on was a twenty-five-year-old Bristol with bodywork in immaculate condition.

'Nice car,' Timberlake said. 'Will it go?'

'Like a bomb. Eventually. Although I'll be gentle with her.' He grinned.

'What are you doing to it – her?'

'Putting in new valves and couple of little ends.'

'Not all that convenient, working here, I suppose.'

'Especially when it rains. I don't have a garage, and lock-ups round here are as rare as virgins in a brothel.'

Now he had established some sort of rapport with the man Timberlake got down to business. 'I'm trying to get into touch with Piers Aubusson, but his answering machine just says he's at the studio. Would you happen to know which one?'

'Oh, the old ocker. He's—'

'Who?'

'The ocker . . . digger . . . Australian. He's an Aussie. Peter Drugget. Born and bred in Pike's Gulch, Northern Territory. He'll be at the BBC.'

Timberlake chuckled. 'Peter Drugget?' The man nodded. 'Well, full marks for inventiveness. What does he do, exactly?'

'He's a director on *Riverside*. Can't have a name like Peter Drugget if you're a BBC director,' the man said with a slightly sarcastic smile. Timberlake looked blank. 'Don't tell me you don't know *Riverside*.'

'I don't know *Riverside*.'

'It's a twice-weekly soap, a sort of *Eastenders* with class and high comedy. I think it was originally based on this area.'

'What time is it on?'

'Seven.'

Which explained why Timberlake never saw it. He thanked the man and set off for White City, home of BBC Television Centre.

At the Centre Timberlake out-hectored a security guard on the front gate who tried to treat him as if he were at the front door of Buckingham Palace asking if he could use the bog. He even managed to bulldoze his way into the VIP car park, known to BBC-ites as the Golden Horseshoe.

The entrance hall of Television Centre had a long counter manned – if that is the word – by three business-like young women. Beyond the rows of benches at right angles to the counter a glass wall gave a view of the circular centre courtyard of the original building. It was designed in the form of a capital letter Q but it was already too small for its purpose before it was completed; subsequent additions and annexes had given the complex the shape of the Chinese ideogram for 'chaos'. In the centre of the courtyard was a tall fountain surmounted by a figure of a man seemingly ready to aim a kick at – it was popularly believed – the director general's office. The fountain was usually dry, because an expensive firm of management consultants considered that as soon as it was turned on half the people in the surrounding offices got up and went to pee. This, the consultants averred gravely, was counter-productive, although it would take a Sherlock Holmes with his magnifying glass to perceive any effect on output. In fact much of the organization's creative thinking and exchange of information happened in the loos. And a fair number of social encounters.

The benches were occupied by young women with immaculate

makeup and their most fetching clothes, young men in their interview suits and hopeful expressions, and a few self-conscious
bohemians of all four sexes holding briefcases, plastic shopping
bags or even large, bulging, battered and tattered envelopes containing scripts.

Harry Timberlake picked the middle of the three women behind
the counter. She was the plainest, and probably the oldest: she
appeared not unlike Elsa Lanchester. He figured that she was
always a visitor's last choice and anyone who went to her first
was likely to be favoured. He introduced himself and explained
he had come to see Piers Aubusson, although he knew he was in
the studio. 'Yes, but he's not nailed to the floor there,' the receptionist said unexpectedly. She consulted a list, made a phone call
in which she spoke sharply to the person at the other end, hung
up, then announced with satisfaction that Aubusson's PA would
come to collect him. 'Personal assistant,' she added.

Timberlake congratulated her on her persuasiveness and
thanked her just the right side of effusively with a smile. The
receptionist glowed and shot sidelong glances of triumph at her
colleagues.

A mouse in a drab cardigan and skirt approached Timberlake.
She had a clipboard under her arm, and on a cord round her
neck she wore a massive stopwatch that could have served as a
chronometer on a sailing ship. It was a standard BBC-issue instrument which served not only for measuring time but also as a PA's
unofficial shield of office.

She scuttled ahead of Timberlake through corridors and up a
flight of stairs to a door leading to the studio control gallery.

It contained a long horizontal control console with half a dozen
seats for the technicians in charge of lighting, sound, and recording, the director and his PA. The panel bristled with various knobs
and switches; microphones on long stalks reared in front of each
place like cobras ready to strike. On the top of the glass wall
facing the seats were ten television screens in a four-four-two
formation. Below them only small sections of the studio floor were
visible through the observation window.

There was only one person in the gallery, but even if it had
been crowded there would be no mistaking who was The Director.

Piers Aubusson was about forty, more handsome than nearly
all the men he directed and most of the women, too. His profile

76

was good enough to go on a gold coin; his hair was of such a shining gold with geometrically precise waves that it had to be natural. No hairdresser would try to get away with a false coiffure that flamboyant. He was wearing a silk shirt with a cravat, and when he stood up his hi-tech trousers had remained uncreased by six hours of sitting down.

'Piers,' the Mouse breathed like an incantation, 'this is Detective Inspector Timberlake.'

Aubusson gave Harry Timberlake a firm, dry handshake with his right hand, and held Timberlake's elbow with his left in a Hollywood greeting. His smile revealed what seemed like forty-four perfect white teeth. He was wearing a trace of after-shave that had the unmistakable whiff of money.

Despite himself, Timberlake, sensitive to ambience and character, *liked* Aubusson. For all his theatricality, inherent and adopted, there was nevertheless a sense of no-bullshit honesty about him, and anyone named Peter Drugget who called himself Piers Aubusson had a sense of humour and couldn't be all bad.

'We've got a thirty-minute break. Could we talk in the canteen, unless you're going to drag me off to the pokey right now?' Aubusson asked. 'I'm dying for a cup of tea out of a real cup and not one of these plastic horrors.'

'You should have told me,' the Mouse said hurriedly. 'I'd have gone to the canteen and got you one.' Timberlake guessed she would have walked to Edinburgh over hot coals for one if Aubusson had done as much as nod.

'I needed you here with me, sweetie,' Aubusson said. 'Couldn't have coped without you.' The Mouse gave him a regard of such incandescent devotion it risked scorching the wallpaper.

The main BBC canteen was much like most superior works or business house canteens, with two exceptions. There were people in costume, and voices were raised rather more vigorously than in most catering establishments. People in Piers Aubusson's line of work like to be noticed.

The Mouse ruthlessly elbowed her slight frame into the counter queue and brought Timberlake and Aubusson cups of tea, with a Danish pastry for Aubusson that was big enough to have made the North Sea crossing on its own. Then she went to a nearby table to watch.

'How can I help you?' asked Aubusson.

'I'm enquiring into the deaths of Veronica Newman and her mother, Ann Pascoe.'

'Never heard of them. What have they done?'

'Done?' Timberlake asked, baffled. 'They've been murdered.'

'I meant, what have they *done* . . . been in?'

'Oh, they weren't actresses.'

'In that case, I'm sorry they've been killed. But I don't know them.'

Timberlake mulled over the implications of this last answer, and made a mental note to pursue it later. 'Odd. You're in Mrs Newman's telephone book.'

Aubusson stared at him. 'Where does she – did she – live?'

Timberlake told him.

'Wait a minute . . . wait a minute . . . Veronica Newman . . . I remember now. We played bridge a couple of times at my – our – club. She asked for my phone number in case she needed a partner for one of our tournament nights. She left a couple of messages on my machine, but I never called her back. I wasn't all that keen on being involved with her.'

'Why not?'

'She had a reputation . . . you know, for being a bit of a goer.' He gave Timberlake an expressive look. 'Men.'

Timberlake thought of what Sir Tarquin Sparrowcroft had told him, which seemed to be at odds with Aubusson's remark. Sir Tarquin could be wrong: Mrs Newman wouldn't be the first woman suddenly to lose her head in middle age. If Veronica Newman had been having secret affairs with other men it could open up all sorts of lines of enquiry.

'Are you sure?'

'Well, I didn't actually bonk her myself, but three or four of the members of the club reckoned they did. And I'm inclined to believe them. I don't know why, but I had the feeling she could be trouble.'

'Who were these three or four members?' Aubusson was a little uneasy. 'I shan't say where I got the information. And we'll try not to talk to them in front of their wives.' Rather reluctantly Aubusson gave him four names and addresses.

'And you, Mr Aubusson, you only saw her the once at the bridge club?'

'God's honour. Hang on, maybe twice. But never outside the

club. And we definitely didn't play together: cards, nooky, bonking or Donald Duck.'

Timberlake believed him. 'Do you mind telling me where you were on the night of the twenty-sixth to twenty-seventh?'

Aubusson thought for a moment, then laughed. 'On Wimbledon Common. We were doing location filming till midnight. After that, overtime – *if* the crew are willing to do it – is horrendously expensive. Then I went home with Jackie Leeson – she's the one playing the licencee of the pub . . .' He gave Timberlake a look of the most deliberately phoney innocence '. . . and we rehearsed her lines till quite late.'

'We'll check of course. Discreetly,' Timberlake promised, but he knew the alibi would stand up.

'Excuse me, darling,' came a woman's voice just behind Timberlake. He turned to see a young Elizabeth Taylor bad look-alike wearing a floppy shirt outside straining jeans standing behind him. She was looking directly at Aubusson. 'I had to *fly* to the loo and I wasn't there for notes after the run-through.'

'I noticed your absence,' Aubusson said coldly, but the woman seemed to take it as a compliment.

'Did you have anything for me?'

'Just a couple of teeny-weeny, minor things, darling,' Aubusson said. 'I'll have a word with you on the set five minutes before we start again.'

The young woman flashed Aubusson a brilliant smile, turned to Timberlake and asked, 'Were you watching the run-through?'

'I'm afraid I wasn't.' Her smile disappeared as if a windscreen wiper had crossed her face. She turned and moved off.

'Silly bitch—' began Aubusson, but the woman had turned again and was approaching the table.

'Darling, it was all *right*, wasn't it? Not *too* underplayed?'

'It was super, lovey. Really.'

Satisfied, she went towards the exit, her eyes taking in all the tables en route, giving little nods, waves and smiles.

'Stupid bitch,' Aubusson said again, more in anger than in sorrow. 'You wouldn't believe—' He broke off, shaking his head, then resumed. 'There's a scene where her man friend asks her why she seems to prefer a man named Edward instead of him. She's been answering, "Oh, you appeal to my better *nature*, while Edward . . ." instead of, "Oh, you appeal to my *better* nature,

79

while Edward . . ." Actors,' he said with a sigh like a tyre being punctured. They're all the bloody same. Even Clark Gable couldn't get it right.'

'So why are you in the business?'

Aubusson gave a long, slow smile. 'I love kids. And they're just big kids who like to play Dollies Pretend. Actually, I used to be one myself, but then I grew up. Finish your tea. If you'd like to watch the recording, come up to the observation room, just behind the gallery, in about a quarter of an hour.' He moved to the exit, ignoring a silent barrage of classic attention-grabbing little gestures and movements from out-of-work actors. The Mouse shot away from her table and followed him like the tail of a comet. Timberlake shook his head. It was a new world to him.

'Do you mind if I sit here?'

Timberlake raised his head. A young woman wearing an old grey dressing gown and holding a cup of tea was standing beside his table. She was medium height and slender, with an air of fragility about her. Her face was pale and fine-boned, which made her eyes appear large. Her hair was an undistinguished mid-brown, but it was cut short in a deceptively simple-looking style which emphasized the delicate structure of her face.

'Of course not: on the contrary.' He smiled and rose from his seat, a gesture which slightly surprised her and Timberlake himself, for that matter.

Soon after she sat down she said to him, 'My name is Lucinda Fordham.' This was a significant phraseology. Most middle- and lower- rank actors and minor politicians who thought themselves well known said, *'I'm* Bill Bloggs . . .' or 'I'm Mary Plinge . . .' as if it were obvious you knew who Bill Bloggs or Mary Plinge were.

'Harry Timberlake.' They exchanged smiles instead of shaking hands. 'I bet you hate it when they call you Lucy.'

She nodded wryly. 'Especially since Pavarotti. You know: "Fat Lucy".'

'I don't think people will mix you two up. For a start, you haven't got a beard.'

She laughed. 'Are you working at the moment?' The 'at the moment' was a polite implication that he might well have been working recently, or was about to in the near future even if he wasn't right now, although Harry didn't get the nuance yet.

'Oh, yes.' As it often says in scripts, she looked a question mark. 'I'm a detective,' he added.

'Mmm, you're a bit too neat and good-looking for a detective,' Lucinda Fordham said matter-of-factly. 'Most of the detectives I've met were a bit more ... earthy.' She flashed him a brief, brilliant smile.

'Oh? What detectives were they?'

'A couple of technical advisers on cops-and-robbers series, and one when a friend's flat was burgled. And my ex-flatmate had a detective boyfriend for a while.' She paused briefly, looking puzzled. 'I didn't know they were doing a police show. Are you working here? What exactly are you in?'

'I'm not in a show. I'm a real detective.' Timberlake thought this might sound boastful, and added quickly, 'I mean, I'm a detective in real life.' He produced his warrant card.

'Oh, my God. That squelching sound is me pulling my foot out of my mouth.'

'Not in the least. You were quite flattering, even if you were a little unfair to some of my colleagues.' A mental picture of Ted Greening came into his mind. 'Earthy' definitely flattered him. 'Shitty' and 'drunken bum' were nearer the mark.

Lucinda looked at the big clock on the canteen wall. 'I'm due on the set in five minutes. I'd better go.'

'Are you in *Riverside*?' She nodded. 'Then I'll be watching you in the observation gallery.'

She smiled again. 'Perhaps we can have a drink in the club after the show.'

He hesitated; he had the four names and addresses of Veronica Newman's presumed lovers to follow up. But the hesitation was brief. 'I'd like that.'

Chapter 9

The collator at Terrace Vale was PC Brian Pegg, who managed to look like a dubious double-glazing salesman even in uniform shirt and trousers, and he had the ready chat of a junk-bond trader to go with it; yet he was basically quite a decent chap. As a beat constable, however, he was about as useful as a rubber crowbar. He looked the part, but could give more trouble than help. Pegg's handicap was that he knew *Moriarty's Police Law* from cover to cover, and he often browsed through ponderous law books for pleasure. As a result he knew a great deal about the law, but little about justice, and as it happened, less about common sense.

Somebody once said of Brian Pegg that if he arrested anyone fleeing from an armed robbery first he'd charge them with having an out-of-date Road Fund licence, and then ask to see their fire-arms certificate.

All this knowledge meant that he couldn't walk half a mile along a peaceful street without seeing half a dozen offences being committed. An early-morning paper boy ringing doorbells as he delivered the papers was 'wilfully and wantonly disturbing any inhabitant by pulling or ringing any doorbell, or knocking on any door', contrary to the Town Police Clauses Act 1847, as amended by several subsequent Acts, all of which Pegg could quote.

Not far from that scene of a crime two lads were leaning against a pillar box and kicking it with their heels as they talked, which is expressly forbidden by the Post Office Act 1953, as amended by the Criminal Justice Act 1967, the Criminal Law Act 1977 and the British Telecommunications Act 1981 (although what Telecom-munications had to do with pillar boxes was unclear; still, that was what the book said). The Post Office Act states that: '. . . no one

82

shall do or attempt to do anything likely to injure a post office box . . .'

Pegg's *pièce de résistance*, which made him celebrated in Terrace Vale and five surrounding Areas was when he saw old Mrs Joseph creating a scene as she tried to stop Mr Potter, the local green-grocer, from serving another customer with potatoes because she, Mrs Joseph, was there before her. Most coppers would have given the old lady a friendly talking to, but PC Pegg saw Mrs Joseph's action against Mr Potter as 'an intent to deter him from buying, selling . . . grain, flour, meal, malt, or *potatoes* . . .', contrary to the Offences Against the Person Act 1861.

His prodigious memory for detail, however, made him an ideal collator, concerned with every form of intelligence about criminals and shady characters.

When Sarah Lewis walked into his office Pegg was working on transferring the information on his filing cards on to his computer. Nevertheless, he had decided to keep the card system as a backup in case the computer had one of the dizzy spells computers are prone to. He looked up and gave Sarah a brilliant smile.

'Hel-*lo*, Sarah,' he said, sounding, if he'd realized it, like Liberace. 'What can I do for you?' He didn't get the answer he would have given his card index for.

'Hello, Peggy. Do we have any active or retired counterfeiters on the patch?'

Pegg had long since given up trying to get people not to call him Peggy and did not even wince. 'Cobblers,' he said. Sarah was on the point of replying 'And bollocks to you, chum,' when Pegg added, 'That's what they used to call villains who made funny money. Most of them went out of business about the same time as street gaslamps.' Sarah waited patiently. Pegg turned to his computer, hesitated and then went to his card index. As he riffled through it he asked, 'Why, has some turned up round here?'

'Pound coins.'

'How many?'

Slightly embarrassed, Sarah told him, 'Eight.'

'Eight! Enough to ruin the country's economy, if the sodding government hadn't done it already.'

'There could be more.'

'If the counterfeiter hasn't already retired to the Costa del Crime.' He took out a card. 'There's no one active in the area, as

83

far as I know, but we've got an ex-counterfeiter living on the Limetree Estate.' He took a pad and started writing the name and address. 'His name's Albert Spendlove. Age . . . sixty-eight.'

'What's his form?'

'Three convictions: six months, two years and three years. He was dead lucky that third time. He could have got seven.'

'When was the last one?'

'Oh, nine years ago. It seems he's kept his nose clean since then. Or at least, he hasn't been caught.' Pegg handed over the slip with Spendlove's name and address. 'He's been there ever since he came out.'

'Has he got a job?'

'Self-employed. He's a dental technician. Makes false choppers for dentists' patients.'

Detective Superintendent Harkness looked across the AMIP office at Detective Sergeant Braddock, who was working at a report on a word processor. Braddock sensed that he was being observed, and looked up. Harkness had the sort of stare that could be felt through a leather jacket.

'How are things going, Jim?' Harkness asked in his unofficial, off-parade voice.

'It's early days, sir,' he replied, trying to sound optimistic, although it was anything but early days.

'What do the team think about the way things are going? Any favourites for the murderer?'

'Haven't really got any runners yet, let alone any favourites.'

Harkness remained silent, but Braddock didn't return to his report. He had been with Harkness for some years, and the signal, 'Stand by for coded message', came through loud and clear.

'Uhuh. Where's Inspector Timberlake, do you know?'

Braddock decoded the message without difficulty. 'He's following up that first contact in Mrs Newman's phone book.' He paused to frame the rest of his reply as diplomatically as possible. He liked Harry Timberlake, but his loyalties were with his own chief. 'Inspector Timberlake's very keen and generally respected . . .'

'But?'

'Well, sir, it's not really my place . . .' Braddock wanted to be coaxed.

'Oh, come on, Jim. We're all on the same side.'

'Well, he's got one name in the frame. He's been banging on quite a bit about being certain Newman's our man, despite his solid alibi. Some of the lads reckon he's got a bee in his bonnet about him.'

Harkness wouldn't have put his own opinion in exactly those words, although he agreed with the assessment. Still, he had to admit to himself that Timberlake was conscientiously following up all the other lines of enquiry. But was his heart as well as his mind in his work?

On her way to see Spendlove Sarah passed the newspaper stand of Old Unusual, one of Terrace Vale's characters who had appeared on television and in a number of newspaper articles. Old Unusual's real name was Tom Jones, although he was no more Welsh than Sitting Bull, and probably couldn't sing any better. The nickname came, rather perversely, from the singer Tom Jones's early success 'It Ain't Unusual'. He was tall, white-haired and rather more distinguished-looking than the average person would expect a newspaper-seller to appear. In more ways than one, Old Unusual was like his name, out of the ordinary.

His stand was in an arcade near one of Terrace Vale's underground stations. It was a lock-up cabin arrangement, rather like a low-level coffee stall with the newspapers laid out on the long counter. Magazines were displayed on the inside of the lockable doors which opened out like wings.

His celebrity status was not due to the fact that he was a purveyor of newspapers to such gentry that Terrace Vale could claim, but to two talents. Old Unusual was blind, yet even under pressure at rush hours he could unerringly whip out the correct newspapers at a dizzy speed from the large display, his hands racing across the papers like a concert pianist's playing arpeggios. The secret, he explained, was in always having the papers laid out in the same order; and in any case each publication had its own size and feel. Even the ink on different papers had its own distinctive smell. He could identify his regular customers by their voice, of course, and many of them by the sound of their footsteps.

'Hello, Miss Lewis,' he said while Sarah was still ten yards away.

'How do you *do* that, Unusual?' she asked.

'You recognize people by shapes. Everybody's footsteps are different, so I do it by sounds. And maybe a little ESP. Besides, I recognized your perfume.' He smiled, and turned his head. If Sarah hadn't known he was blind, she would have sworn that Old Unusual was staring at a collection box for a blind charity at the end of the counter. A lot of customers put their change into the box when Unusual did the trick. Sarah fished a £1 coin from her handbag and was about to drop it into the box when a thought struck her.

'Here, have you heard about the dud pound coins that are circulating?'

He shook his head. 'No?'

'There's quite a few of them. One was on a tramp a PC picked up. It's a bit of a puzzler where he got it.'

'Oh, I don't know,' Old Unusual replied. 'Somebody gets stuck with one, he makes a business of looking generous in front of his girlfriend by tipping a tramp a pound. How many dud coins get into collection boxes in churches and on flag days, d'you reckon?'

Sarah considered this for a moment. 'I hadn't thought of that.'

'You haven't experienced it, Miss Lewis. I can tell when people put a two-pence piece in the box, or a foreign coin.'

'Really?' Old Unusual nodded. 'Well, this one's all right,' she said and dropped it into the collection tin.

'A pound? Oh, thank you, Sarah,' Unusual said in a surprised tone that fooled neither of them. He smiled again. Instead of being sorry for him because of his blindness, Sarah was unaccountably uplifted by his spirit. As she began to move on she gave him a wave without thinking, and said 'See you.' Since Old Unusual was the man he was, she felt no embarrassment at what could have been a verbal gaffe with someone else.

The floor manager of *Riverside*, who had seen Harry Timberlake with Piers Aubusson, took him through the studio to get to the observation gallery. Timberlake was astonished to see how threadbare, cramped and tatty the set was, giving lie to the cliché that the camera always tells the truth.

In the observation gallery behind the control room, Timberlake was absorbed by the technique and mechanics of television production. The first quarter of an hour was spent in recording two minutes of action which was stopped and restarted for a number of different reasons: an actor forgot a line, or moved from his mark on the floor, or a camera shot 'off', beyond the edge of the scenery. A couple of times there was a cry from Aubusson of 'Boom!' – not in congratulation but in anguish – when the microphone on the end of its boom came into shot at the top of the screen.

As soon as Lucinda Fordham appeared on the screens Timberlake found his attention riveted on her. She had presence; instinctively the viewer looked at her first. He realized why she had been in a dressing gown in the canteen: she was wearing only a slip as she prepared to dress to go out to meet someone. Her seminakedness was to emphasize her own natural air of personal vulnerability, her defencelessness.

She was playing the part of Penny, a young woman who lived with her elder sister, Ann. As the scene progressed it would become clear to Timberlake that the sister had virtually brought up Penny as a mother after their parents died, and Penny adored her for it.

The script called for Penny accidentally to come across a letter to her sister, written by Penny's fiancé Philip. As she read it Philip's voice could be heard, reading out the letter. It revealed that he had been Ann's lover for some time, while carrying on his affair with Penny. Ann had told him she was pregnant by him. Philip had a sense of relief, because at last he could find the courage to break it off with Penny, and he and Ann could get married.

When Lucinda, as Penny, read the letter she had to register curiosity, surprise, shock, nausea and finally personal catastrophe. At the end she had to look up to see her sister standing silent and white faced in front of her. Ann was dressed and made up to go out: the contrast between her and Penny was striking. The viewers would be deprived of knowing what the sisters said to each other, largely because the writer wasn't sure enough of himself to write that much of the scene.

During the recording Timberlake swiftly became unaware of the instructions coming from the control gallery. 'On two, coming to three ... one next ... coming to two ...' as the Mouse, now authoritative, called the shots for the vision mixer and the cameramen; and Piers Aubusson made interjections like 'Get in closer, Fred ...' '... Charlie, go left a fraction – that's enough! ...' Harry Timberlake's attention was totally on Lucinda.

There was only one break in the three-minute scene – long for modern television, particularly soap operas – when a boom crept into shot. Aubusson stopped the recording, then called to his technicians, 'We'll go from shot sixty-four, on two.' Next, to the floor manager to pass on to Lucinda, 'Pick up again from Philip's line "At last I can be honest with Penny, with both of you ...".'

Lucinda looked directly at camera and nodded to let Aubusson know she had got the instruction. She looked calm and unruffled, then thought herself back into her part again. As Philip, off camera, began, 'At last I can be honest ...' tears began to roll down her cheeks.

Timberlake was used to people acting parts and lying with total plausibility across an interview table. He reckoned he could smell a faker quicker than a bloodhound could sniff out a dirty sock. But now he was believing that he was watching a real *Penny*, not Lucinda playing a part. She was so totally convincing that he was overwhelmed.

Spendlove's address turned out to be a small shop with a window painted dark green to about a foot above head height. Sarah looked for a door leading to the flat above, but there didn't seem to be one. She rang the shop bell and Albert Spendlove opened it. He looked like a minor civil servant who was bullied by his boss and his wife, and very probably by his children as well, if his wife had permitted him the familiarity of impregnating her. His face was round and smooth as a peeled hardboiled egg; he had neither eyebrows nor eyelashes. However, he wore an incredible wig of a Dayglo marmalade colour. Sarah kept her eyes firmly on the space between Spendlove's eyes.

She politely introduced herself. Spendlove looked at her without expression, and said, 'You'll want to come in.' He unselfconsciously adjusted his wig, which had slipped to a rakish angle like Maurice Chevalier's straw hat. He held the door open for her and stepped aside.

The shop had a workbench with three or four lamps, a large sink, what was obviously a small kiln, some unusual-looking tools and various jars, bottles and pots and various other odds and ends that Sarah couldn't quite identify. There were many plaster casts of mouths with great gaps of missing teeth, and some of mouths with gums that could not boast a single molar among them.

Two things struck her immediately. There was a small, modern-looking safe . . . and teeth. Lots of teeth. Lots and lots of teeth in dental plates lined up along shelves. It was all rather grisly. Faced by the unnerving grins of the disembodied, brilliant teeth, Sarah found it difficult not to give them back an ingratiating smirk.

She dragged her eyes away from the teeth, kept her gaze from the outrageous wig and smiled at Albert Spendlove, a gesture that seemed to disconcert him. His mouth dropped open a little, to reveal that he had a perfect set of gums, totally toothless. Well, the saying is that the shoemaker's children go barefoot. 'I've come to ask for your help,' Sarah told him.

'Oh, yes,' Spendlove said guardedly. 'You want me to help you with your enquiries. Well, I gave up snide a long time ago.' He met Sarah's gaze with the irritatingly expressionless gaze of a civil servant dealing with an importuning member of the public on the other side of a glass screen. You felt that if you threw a tennis ball at his face it would drop straight down without bouncing back. Sarah was uncertain how to deal with him, so she decided to cut out the pussyfooting and stride straight in. She produced the counterfeit pound coins from her bag and put them on the workbench in front of Spendlove.

He looked at them for a moment. 'Not mine,' he said. 'I told you: I haven't done anything like that since I came out the last time.'

'I just want your professional opinion, any help you can give me.'

Spendlove picked one up, rubbing it between his fingers, and then dropping it on to a metal plate on the bench. He repeated the process with the others.

'Very good work,' he judged at last. 'Too good.'

'What do you mean?'

'There's a lot of private-enterprise coins floating around, but not like this. They're mass-produced – washers of the right size and thickness, with lead in the middle to make up the weight, just enough to bamboozle slot machines. You don't need workmanship of this quality for machines. These are meant for passing over counters.'

'So?'

'The profit margin's not big enough. I mean, a quid! By the time you've got your change, how much profit you got? It's taken time and effort to make these ones. And craftsmanship. They're as good as anything I ever did. Well, nearly.'

'As a matter of interest, what did you make?'

Spendlove gave a toothless grin. 'I started with half toshes. Half a crowns. Twelve and a half pence these days. But you could buy something with half a dollar then. Inflation's ruined the market for counterfeiters. Then I got ambitious. I made sovereigns. Flogged 'em to foreigners. I should've got the Queen's Award for Industry.' He picked up one of the pound coins again. 'Feels good, not too soapy . . . right weight. I wonder what the metal is?'

'Any idea who might be making them?'

'An amateur. Has to be. These simply aren't a commercial proposition.' He paused, thinking. 'Or could be someone doing it just for the hell of it, and the satisfaction of fooling people.'

'Oh, come on,' Sarah said, dismissing the idea as too fanciful.

Spendlove saw her scepticism and asked her, 'You ever been inside the Black Museum at Scotland Yard?' She shook her head. 'One of the exhibits is a postal order for five shillings. It was originally a sixpenny postal order, but some master penman spent, oh, it must have been *days*, of work with bleaches, and close meticulous work with a fine-pointed pen. It wasn't for the four and a tanner, it was for the pride in his craft. Van Gogh couldn't have done better.'

Sarah thought Vincent Van G. couldn't have done as well, come to that, but she stayed silent.

'There aren't any craftsmen like that any more,' Albert Spendlove said regretfully. 'People don't have pride in their work.'

'And you can't get a plumber to come out on a Sunday,' Sarah said. 'But as far as these pound coins are concerned . . .'

'Can't help you,' Spendlove said regretfully. 'Though if you do catch him, I'd like to meet him and congratulate him.'

A thought struck Sarah. 'How did you get into the Black Museum?'

'Wrong question. How did I get *out* of the Black Museum?' But he didn't enlighten her.

Sarah nodded, picked up her dud coins and prepared to leave. At the door she asked him, 'Oh, what's in the safe?'

'Gold.' She looked startled. 'For bridges.' Spendlove bared his gums again for his version of a smile, lifted his wig an inch and scratched his scalp. 'I make more money making teeth than I ever did making money, if you get my drift.'

*

The customary post-recording drink in the BBC club was boring for Timberlake: he knew no one and he found the 'You were marvellous, darling,' exchanges farcical. There was one bright moment when the actor who played Philip asked, 'Lucinda, would you like a lift home?' She gave an almost imperceptible glance at Timberlake, and said without hesitation, 'No thank you, darling. I've already got one.' Timberlake didn't have to be hit with a brick.

Lucinda Fordham lived in Rancliffe Square, an area of large houses divided up into habitable apartments, not like some of the rats' nests in Terrace Vale's poorer backwaters. The square and its adjacent streets were a sort of staging post for actors and actresses where sheep were sorted from the goats. The successful ones usually moved on to larger flats in Wallsend, while the less talented, or less lucky, sank to West Southington or even Terrace Vale.

Her first-floor flat in an Edwardian house consisted of one enormous sitting/dining room which overlooked the dusty communal garden, a small bathroom, an equally small kitchen and a bedroom. The place had ceilings so high that there was a danger of cloud formation in winter. Timberlake thought it must cost a fortune to heat. The main room was economically furnished almost to Japanese standards of sparseness, but it was roomy, and pleasant with bright curtains, flowers, some good prints and a few posters for theatres with names like 'The Backyard', 'The Firehouse', 'The Green Barn' and 'The Second Best Bed'. Timberlake guessed that at the last place they put on forty-five-minute Shakespeare plays with the cast dressed as soldiers, sewage workers or spacemen, with mumbling compulsory.

Although they had only just met and knew almost nothing about each other, Lucinda Fordham and Harry Timberlake were completely at ease. It was as if they were old friends who had been separated for years and were catching up on what had happened to them in the mean time.

She offered him a drink, which he refused, explaining that he never had even one when he was driving. He hoped he didn't sound smug or sanctimonious.

Lucinda told him that she had always wanted to be an actress from the moment she had helped as a dogsbody and gopher for her local dramatic society. 'I got a job with a repertory company in the north—'

'Doing what?'

'Everything but acting. I helped paint the scenery, swept up, changed light bulbs, gave the wardrobe mistress a hand, did babysitting, prompted ... Actually, that was how I made the breakthrough into acting. The whole thing was a shoestring operation, and Julie Short, one of the actresses, had a bad fall one night and couldn't walk. The so-called understudy didn't turn up for some reason. Well, I'd been there for all the rehearsals and then I'd been prompting, so ...' She gave a deprecating gesture. 'Oh, God, this is so corny. Real Hollywood nineteen thirties. Anyway, I went on, and ...' She flung her arms wide and hammed outrageously to say, 'I became a star.' Lucinda smiled impishly. 'Well, not quite. But it was a way into the theatre.'

Timberlake was fascinated by her anecdotes of show-biz, a world that was as alien to him as early Egyptian hieroglyphics. He was brought back to the real world when at last Lucinda looked at her watch and said, 'I'm sorry, but I'm going to have to throw you out. I've got another rehearse-record day tomorrow and I'm going to look an old hag if I don't get my beauty sleep.'

Timberlake was horrified: it was a quarter past one. He bounded up, spilling over with apologies. 'I really am sorry. I was enjoying myself so much I didn't realize how the time had gone.'

'Nor did I,' Lucinda said brightly.

'I must make it up to you. Dinner sometime?'

'While I'm in the show my day off's on Thursday,' Lucinda said without hesitation.

'A Thursday evening, then?'

'No. Make it a Wednesday. That way I won't have to worry about getting up early the next morning.' She gave him a meaningless social kiss on the cheek at the door.

Timberlake was still mulling over the implications of that last remark – or the lack of them – when he walked into his flat.

'You're late,' came a voice from the bedroom. He walked over and opened the door. Sarah Lewis was sitting up in bed reading a magazine. The bedclothes were tucked round her neck. A half-empty wine glass was on her bedside table.

'Oh, hello.' He went across and kissed her, then gently pulled the bedclothes away from her chest. He raised his eyebrows. 'Hmmm. Aren't you afraid of catching cold?'

'No. I've got a glass and a half of wine inside me.' She paused for half a heartbeat and added in a voice of virgin innocence, 'For a start.' The bland tone was contradicted by a stare straight into his eyes with her Welsh witch look.

It was a highly satisfying session of love-making. The two and a half glasses of wine that Sarah had drunk – she had another one – made her even more enthusiastic than usual. When they were relaxed and recovering, wondering whether or not they should start again, Sarah asked casually, 'Where'd you been all evening?'

'Oh, following up Veronica Newman's contacts. At the BBC.' All at once he had a mental image of Lucinda Fordham, lounging with unstudied grace on her settee, looking young and vulnerable . . . and attractive.

'Uhuh. See anyone famous?'

'No.'

Sarah made a movement towards him. He shook his head. 'It's been a long day – for both of us, I expect – and it's going to be another one tomorrow.'

'Perhaps you're right.' She sighed. 'Anyway, I've got to go to a funeral tomorrow, somewhere in Hertfordshire.'

'Somebody dead? Oh, what a stupid question. Sorry. Who was it?'

'Some distant relation I've never heard of, left Wales donkey's years ago. It's too far for my parents to come up, so they want me to represent them.'

'I hope it's not too dreary for you.' He leant over towards her and kissed her. 'Goodnight, darling.' She responded to his kiss, sexlessly at first, but then with increasing desire as her tongue probed his mouth.

Gently and without haste Timberlake drew away from her. 'You may not be, but I'm satiable,' he said, trying to make it sound light.

'You're getting old, Harry.'

'No, just tired.' But he did not fall asleep for some time, and when he did he was haunted by brief, shadowy dreams of that vulnerable pale face.

Next morning Timberlake reported on his meeting with Piers Aubusson, and Detective Superintendent Harkness agreed that he could be eliminated from the enquiries. The four names he had given Timberlake were added to the list of contacts to be interviewed.

93

Only a matter of seconds after he returned to his desk his phone rang.

'This is Tarquin Sparrowcroft. Is that Detective Inspector Timberlake?' Timberlake admitted he was. 'I thought you might like to know that Rohmer-Newman and his . . . er, companion . . . took up residence in The Avenue house two days ago.'

Timberlake was instantly alert. 'Is he entitled to do that?'

'Any action to prevent him will be extremely ill founded and there is no other claimant to the property. He was still married to Veronica Newman at the time of her death; he has a set of keys which he came by legitimately and it's certain since neither lady made a will that he will inherit all her estate.'

'What about money?'

'When Mrs Newman's bank manager contacted me I was reluctantly compelled to inform him that *legally* Newman was not yet entitled to touch her funds. Newman has not asked me to advance him any, although I was prepared for the eventuality.'

It didn't take a mind reader to know Sir Tarquin was prepared to give Newman a firm refusal, quoting fifty-seven varieties of legal justification.

'Thank you for the information, Sir Tarquin. I think I'll call in on Mr Newman.'

'I thought you might.' When Sir Tarquin spoke again he had dropped his Donald Sinden delivery. 'Good luck,' he said.

Timberlake picked up his jacket from the back of his chair and went to Detective Superintendent Harkness's desk. 'Newman is back in London,' he announced. 'I think I'll go and see him, clear up one or two things.'

'I thought we'd decided he has a solid alibi?'

'On paper,' Timberlake said doggedly. 'But there are holes in it somewhere. There must be: he murdered them all right. I'll stake my reputation on it.' As soon as he said it he realized how much of an awful cliché it sounded.

Harkness avoided the temptation to counter with one of his own: 'You may be doing just that,' and contented himself with saying, 'Well, just don't waste too much time on him.' Timberlake appreciated his reticence. 'There are still a lot of people in the two women's address books to be interviewed,' Harkness added.

'Yes, sir.' He left quickly before Harkness changed his mind. The senior detective wondered why it was he hadn't stopped Harry Timberlake going, and decided that next time he would.

When Newman opened the door he was wearing the same expensive but tattered dressing gown he had on at the rue Danube flat in Marseille. Harry Timberlake briefly felt an odd sense of time-slip.

'Ah! Inspector Timberlake!' he said, slightly thickly, although it was not yet eleven o'clock. 'I suppose that poofy solicitor told you we were here. Have you come to welcome us back to England? Don't stand there, man! Come in!' He led the way into the sitting room at the back of the house. The french windows were open, and the morning light poured through them mercilessly. Newman looked terrible: unshaven, his eyes baggy and bloodshot, his mouth slack. Carole Pradet, dressed in a négligé that was too small for her, which Timberlake guessed had belonged to Veronica Newman, was sprawled on a sofa.

'Give the inspector a drink,' Newman told her, gesturing to her so she understood. Before Timberlake could refuse, Carole struggled to a sitting position to reach for a bottle of champagne and a glass. The movement made her négligé fall open, revealing her nakedness from her navel down. Newman roared with laughter. Totally unembarrassed, Carole took her time covering herself, and winked at Timberlake. To his own surprise he found himself almost liking her.

'How's your enquiry going?' Newman asked slyly. 'Found the villain yet?'

'Oh, I know who did it all right. The problem is that I can't prove it . . . for the moment.'

'I don't fancy your chances, then,' Newman said. 'You know as well as I do that every day that goes by the trail gets colder, the proof harder to find.'

'True enough, but I've got something on my side.'

'What's that?'

'Every criminal makes at least one mistake.'

'Every *stupid* criminal, every *ignorant* criminal,' Newman replied with a nasty grin.

His smile faded when Timberlake replied, 'All criminals are stupid. Otherwise they wouldn't be criminals. The odds are against

95

them. I'll get the bastard who killed your mother-in-law and wife if it takes me the rest of my life.'

Newman looked at him venomously for a moment, then relaxed. 'We'll see. Hey, d'you happen to know whether that miserable bitch Mrs Coker was still cleaning for my wife?'

Timberlake glanced round the room. It was more of a mess than might be expected from a couple of days' occupation. There were a number of glasses with the dregs of different drinks in them, half a dozen used coffee cups and dirty plates. The expensive carpet was littered with crumbs.

'Yes, although I don't think she'll be too keen to deal with this lot, particularly if the rest of the house is in the same state.'

'She will, if I pay her well.'

'Incidentally, how are you doing for money?'

Newman turned on his charming smile. 'Have a look at this.' He went over to a writing desk. 'Genuine Louis Seize.'

'I believe you. I'm sure Mrs Newman wouldn't have another fake in the house.'

At first Newman looked ready to attack Timberlake, but he quickly controlled himself, and let out a great bellow of laughter. But it was too late: he had given a revealing glimpse of the dark, violent side of his character. He took out one of the upper drawers of the desk, and did something inside the empty space. Two wide, flat, secret drawers sprang out of the side of the desk. There were bank-wrapped bundles of £50 notes in both the drawers. There was a space in one of them where a bundle had been removed.

'Veronica always liked to have lots of readies in the house,' Newman said. 'It's a good thing the killer didn't know about this, or he'd have been off with the lot.' He gave Timberlake a smug, pointed smile.

It was blindingly clear what both men were thinking. Newman himself knew of the secret store of money, but when he murdered Veronica Newman and Ann Pascoe, he hadn't touched it. Now he had a witness to the fact that if *he* had killed the two women he could have made off with the cash and no one would have been the wiser. But the money was untouched. If it ever came to a trial it was a powerful point in his favour that any defence counsel would make the most of. And the witness was Timberlake himself.

96

'Call again, Inspector, any time,' Newman said, his smug smile growing wider.

It was Timberlake's morning for clichés. 'Count on it.'

But he felt a sudden wave of depression. Newman had outsmarted him once again.

Chapter 10

Although the AMIP's Pascoe-Newman murder case was obviously
the major preoccupation in the Terrace Vale nick, the local officers
there had the usual long catalogue of outstanding cases to deal
with, including several burglaries, robberies, aggressions, possession of drugs of various potencies for dealing and for personal
use, car thefts, criminal damage, hooliganism, racial incitement to
violence, indecent exposure, soliciting, fraud, Sunday trading,
illegal parking, lost bicycles, unmuzzled dangerous dogs within the
meaning of the Act, and all the rest. In other words, things were
pretty normal. Also in the catalogue were the counterfeiting of
£1 coins and the burglary at the wholesaler's that Sarah Lewis
was investigating.

Sarah was slowly getting nowhere with her burglary enquiry,
and just as far with the counterfeit coins case, which was making
her feel rather ragged.

Bob Farmer thought it was time for him to have another go at
her. He repeated his suggestion, with embroidery, that if her workload was proving too heavy for her, he'd be pleased to give her
an unofficial hand. And I know where you'd like to give it to me,
she thought furiously.

'I won't mention it to any of the others,' he said, 'but if you like
I'll meet you for a drink after work, somewhere away from the
patch, and we can talk it over.' He gave her a smile that would
have worked well with many women, but once again he had played
his hand badly with Sarah.

The self-satisfied prat hasn't even got a new line, she thought
with furious contempt. She forced something like a smile in reply.
Farmer didn't know how lucky he was there was nothing heavy
or sharp within Sarah's reach. 'That's very good of you, guv. Just
the same, I'd prefer to battle on by myself for the time being.' She

took a chance and added, 'Unless you want to take me off one of the cases.'

Farmer considered this option for a moment, then quickly dismissed it. No; keeping the pressure on her was the best tactic. 'Of course not,' he said heartily. 'I admire your spirit. Good luck. And remember, the offer's open any time.'

'I appreciate that, guv. Definitely.'

Farmer moved away, hiding his chagrin. He straightened his tie, and making sure he wasn't being observed, redeployed his hair with little pats to cover the maximum possible area. Typical of his puncture-proof ego, he could think of only two reasons for Sarah's turning him down. 'I wonder if she's gay?' he asked himself. 'Nah . . . It's just because she's pretty new to CID. I expect she's a bit intimidated by the difference in rank. Yeh, that's probably it.' Which showed how little he understood Sarah Lewis. She couldn't be intimidated by a Prince of the Blood. Particularly these days.

The AMIP team were doing no better than Sarah, and doing it much more expensively. Their door-to-door enquiries, interviews with the people in Ann Pascoe's and Veronica Newman's address books and studies of their private papers had produced nothing of substance. This was no surprise to Harry Timberlake, who was quite convinced that the whole thing was a waste of time. His attitude was, Sod the evidence: Charles Henry Newman was the murderer, and they should all be concentrating on breaking his alibi. Sergeant Rumsden privately commented that Harry could represent Britain with the certainty of an Olympic gold medal for Being Boring.

As a matter of routine Harry Timberlake had got PC Brian Pegg to run a check on the four men Piers Aubusson had said were particular friends of Veronica Newman. They all came up as clean as Shirley Temple. Except one. Pegg's remarkable memory had done it again.

'Those names you gave me, guv,' Pegg said. 'One of them seemed to ring a bell . . .'

'Theodore Heptonstall?'

Pegg was taken aback. 'Yes. How did you know?'

'All the other names were pretty ordinary. They wouldn't set off chimes.'

'Right, guv. I remembered reading about him in the *Daily Telegraph*. So, I got on to the CRO. He's in the files all right.' He put a sheet of paper on Timberlake's desk. 'It's all there. He was nicked twice for indecent assault, found not guilty, once for attempted rape: three years.'

'Gay, or straight?'

'All straight, and no juveniles. They were all in Lancaster, before he moved down here.'

'When did he get out?'

'Six years ago. They were the only recorded incidents, and God knows how often victims don't report them.'

Timberlake nodded. He looked at the CRO photograph clipped to the sheet. Theodore Heptonstall looked like a vegetarian butterfly collector. The thought that he was a nasty rapist seemed as unlikely as Rambo doing petit-point. 'You wouldn't have an address, by any chance?'

Pegg was sufficiently pleased with himself to both nod and wink as he passed over another piece of paper.

'This is the second AMIP enquiry where you've been helpful. I'll tell the superintendent,' Timberlake promised.

'Thanks, guv. Any time.'

'Where we going, guv? asked Detective Sergeant Darren Webb.

'Out towards Kingsmere. I'll explain on the way. You can drive.'

'Your car?' asked Webb incredulously. Everyone knew that Timberlake never let anyone drive his Citroen, not even to move it in the car park. Timberlake looked at him. 'OK, my car.'

The last known address of Theodore Heptonstall was about eight miles south of Terrace Vale, in a modern block of flats which was one of a moderately elegant development. The back of the flats overlooked a commuter railway line, but double glazing kept the noise down below tolerable limits. Beyond the railway was one of Greater London's attractive commons. The blocks were all named after rural English counties, and Heptonstall's address was in Shropshire Court.

There were sounds of movement from within the flat when Timberlake first rang, but he had to persist with the ringing and knocking before anyone came to the door. When it opened Timberlake was taken aback. For a brief moment he thought the man in the doorway was standing with his back to him. Then he could make out that what he took to be the back of the man's head was an untidy mass of black hair above a great tangled clump of facial hair: beard, moustache and Denis Healey eyebrows. He was wearing a rather scruffy Arab *djellabah*. His only other visible features were two baggy dark eyes. The whole effect was curiously like a St Bernard dog peering through a bush. If Heptonstall had decided to let Nature run rampant to prevent himself being recognized, Nature had done a magnificent job.

'Mr Heptonstall?' Timberlake asked politely.

'No. He doesn't live here any more,' came a Scottish voice from somewhere within the thicket.

'Ah. Do you have any idea where he is now?'

'Mortfield Road.'

'What number, can you tell me?'

The two dark eyes regarded him for a moment. 'Ah, you're not from round here. Mortfield Road's the cemetery. They say victims of the Great Plague were brought out here in 1665. That's how it got its name: *Mort*field.'

'When did he die, do you know?'

'Ye've got a lot of questions, young man. You're the polis, aren't you?' Timberlake nodded. 'A couple of months ago.'

A female voice with a strong Scottish accent bawled out from somewhere inside the flat. 'Come back in here and finish off what you were doing, you selfish sod!' The hairy man began to shut the door. Just before it closed completely he opened it again and added, 'Good riddance to bad rubbish,' then slammed it shut.

Harry Timberlake wasn't sure whether the furry Celt was referring to Heptonstall or himself.

'I've only just realized,' Timberlake said, as they drove away. 'It's taken me all this time. I've been involved with quite a few murders, and fatal accidents when I was a beat copper. There's always been someone to cry for the victims, or at least be badly shaken. Someone who's needed to be comforted. In this case, there's been no one, there hasn't been a single tear, a single sense of loss for Veronica Newman and her mother. Sad, really. Says a lot about their lives.' He thought for a moment.

'We're going right near The Sycamores Avenue on the way. We'll drop in on Newman and that woman,' Timberlake said suddenly. He needed to see the man, to reinforce his own certainty of his guilt. Webb decided not to point out that The Sycamores

Avenue almost being on the way to the nick was like Bristol being on the way from London to Birmingham.

A light at the rear of the Newman house was visible through the glass panel of the front door, and Timberlake could hear music, although it was too faint for him to make out what it was. Newman didn't come to the door until Timberlake's third, long ring. When he opened it, the music poured out as if a floodgate had been opened.

Although Timberlake was a jazz devotee, he could at least tolerate most music. Wagner, however, he simply could not stand, and it was Siegfried's Funeral March from *Götterdämmerung* that was blasting out from an expensive four-speaker hi-fi system. That particular passage either makes the listener feel exalted or that he has his head in a bucket that is being walloped.

Newman was in an expensive new silk dressing gown and pyjamas and was holding a balloon glass of brandy.

'Inspector!' he roared. 'Welcome! Come in, you and your friend, whoever he is.' It was a perfect feed line for 'He's no friend, he's my sergeant,' but Timberlake wasn't tempted. Newman led the two detectives into a rear room. 'Veronica used to call this the music room,' he said.

'Sounds more like the rumpus room,' Timberlake said.

Newman laughed extravagantly. 'It's my favourite music to screw by,' he said, looking across at Carole Pradet who was lounging on a dark red settee, negligently holding a glass of brandy like Newman's. She was wearing a rumpled Chinese cheong-sam, slit up one side to the hip-bone. Darren Webb looked at her wide-eyed as if she were a cheque for the jackpot on the football pools. He wondered if he changed his position what he would manage to see.

'Detective Sergeant Webb,' Timberlake said, introducing him. It made Webb drag his eyes away from Pradet.

All at once Timberlake was aware of a sense of strain about the couple. His first reaction was that they had been having a row; they were both slightly flushed. No, he thought, it's not that. For a moment he thought they were embarrassed at having been interrupted in the middle of a bonk, then he quickly dismissed that. Both Newman and Pradet were brazen enough to get up on a stage and sell tickets. There were no outward physical signs, but the tension was there all right. Timberlake could *feel* it.

'Drink?' Newman said to the two men.

'No thanks,' Timberlake replied, pre-empting any acceptance from Webb. With an acidly wry smile he added, 'We're on duty.' Newman laughed. The fictional convention that detectives don't drink on duty has even less relation to reality than an estate agent's brochure. They all knew that drinking with villains is one of the major ways of getting involuntary admissions from them as they become boastful and careless.

The feeling of stress was still there; there was something *wrong* in that room. Timberlake knew that if he could find the right question, the right, penetrating question, it might well force a crack in Newman's self-assurance.

Timberlake spoke in French directly to Carole Pradet. 'Has he asked you to marry him yet? Because *he* knows, even if you don't, a wife can't testify against her husband.'

Before he had finished the sentence Timberlake knew it was the wrong question. The tension collapsed like a broken spring. Newman laughed again.

'So you still don't know who did it?' he asked.

'I told you: I know all right. I just can't prove it. Yet.'

'You've had experience in these cases. It's too late, Timberlake. There won't be any evidence now. That's if there ever was.'

Newman's self-satisfied arrogance made Timberlake want to strangle him. He took a long breath to make sure his voice was steady before he spoke again. When he did he surprised himself with the authority of his own tone. 'You were a detective, Newman. They say you were a good one . . . once.' Newman gave an exaggerated mock bow, spilling some of his drink. 'I'll say it again: you know as well as I do that a criminal always makes at least one mistake. It's inevitable.' He paused for effect. 'And there's the Sod's Law effect.'

'What the hell's that?' Newman asked.

' "If anything can go wrong, it will." Or, to put it another way, there's always the random factor, the unpredictable element that even the cleverest criminal can't foresee.'

At last Timberlake was pleased to see the tension return in Newman's expression. It was the moment to go, leaving Newman to stew.

*

103

Back in the car Timberlake was silent for a long time, until at last Darren Webb asked him tentatively, 'You all right, guv?'

'I blew it.'

'What?'

'There's always a crucial question, one that catches them unawares, sends them off balance. I asked the wrong one, about them getting married. If I'd asked the right one, he might have given something away.'

'What was the right question?'

'If I'd known that I'd have asked it, you prat! Still, it wasn't a dead loss; we learned a couple of things.' Webb stayed silent. 'Newman's not worried about the Pradet woman dropping him in it, which can mean only one thing.'

'Yeah?' Webb ventured.

'She's the only person who could shop him over that phoney alibi. Newman's vain and a heartless, murdering bastard, but he's not stupid. He knows eventually he'll elbow her for another woman. The only way he can keep her quiet, short of killing her – and that's too risky here in London – is to have something on her. So she must be involved in the murders somehow. She can't shop him without implicating herself.'

Darren Webb felt slightly light-headed. It seemed to him that it was a dubious proposition, based on guesswork and wishful thinking to say the least. Timberlake was like one of those archaeologists who find a toe-bone and conceive an entire new dinosaur from it. That was apart from his begging the question by assuming that Newman's alibi *was* phoney. Webb essayed a noncommittal noise in reply.

'But it wasn't a dead loss,' Timberlake went on. 'It's the first time I've seen him worried. There was something wrong between them. Tension. Couldn't you feel it?'

Webb made another noise, this one a little more positive than the last.

'And when I said there was always the unpredictable element, something the cleverest crook couldn't foresee, it got to him. There's a weak link somewhere, and I'll keep pulling until it breaks.' Timberlake lapsed into an introspective silence, nodding his head gently. Darren Webb began to wonder if his guv'nor had slipped a couple of cogs.

They were within a couple of minutes from the Terrace Vale

nick when Webb took his courage in both hands. He cleared his throat and said in a small voice, 'Guv, man to man?'

Timberlake looked at him in surprise. As far as he was concerned that was always their relationship. 'Of course.'

Webb cleared his throat again. He suddenly felt as if he'd swallowed a ball of knitting wool. 'Guv, have you ever considered you could be wrong, that it wasn't him; somebody else did it?'

Timberlake stared directly into his eyes in a way that made the inside of the back of his skull tingle.

'No,' he said, sounding like a portcullis coming down.

Timberlake doggedly forced himself to write a report on his aborted interview with Theodore Heptonstall before leaving the nick to go home. He started to rise from his desk, stopped in mid-movement, swore and sat down again. He wondered whether or not to add his call on Newman. If he failed to note it officially, it might look suspicious if Newman ever made a complaint about Timberlake harassing him. He decided to report it, then changed his mind. Newman would never complain, he was enjoying playing cat to Timberlake's mouse too much. On the other hand, Darren Webb could well report the interview with Newman and Carole Pradet. Timberlake didn't want to be the sort of officer who tells his subordinate to leave something out of his report as a favour to him. He groaned and started typing.

By the time he had finished, Timberlake was uncertain whether or not to call into the canteen and have a coffee before returning home. He felt a sudden wave of tiredness and knew that if he sat down at a table it would take a major effort of will or a firecracker to get him up again. He locked his desk drawers and made his way towards the station car park.

PC Nigel Larkin, manning the front desk, looked up in surprise as Timberlake clip-clopped his way down the worn wooden stairs from the upper floors. 'You're working late, sir,' he said. He couldn't bring himself to call Timberlake 'guv'.

Timberlake scratched around for a snappy answer. 'Yes,' he said.

'Well, you'll get your reward in heaven,' Larkin said boldly.

He was wrong. Timberlake was going to get his reward in the next few minutes, and it was the last one he would have expected.

He was driving home on autopilot, stifling an occasional yawn, when a warning light started flashing in his subconscious. He had that instinct for something slightly odd shared by people of a natural or acquired suspicious character, like income tax inspectors, detectives and jealous wives. It was akin to that seventh sense that makes a dog, its hackles rising, stare fixedly into an empty corner of a room, and growl.

Ahead of him was a Jaguar XJ6 driven by a man with a woman beside him. She was resting her head on his shoulder, and from time to time the couple contorted their necks to kiss each other. They didn't look comfortable and couldn't have been enjoying it much. Well, there was nothing in that to set his antennae quivering. Even from behind them Timberlake could see that the man was considerably older than the woman, but there's a lot of that about, too. Yet there was *something* ... Timberlake had the feeling that he knew them from somewhere.

The Jaguar slowly turned into a small side road. Timberlake stopped his own car opposite the side road, switched off his lights and ducked down so that he could just see over the top of the door. All of a sudden he felt foolish and told himself he was being paranoid. Maybe his tiredness was playing tricks on his judgement. He was on the point of setting off again but curiosity got the better of him when the driver of the Jaguar parked his expensive car in the shadows under some trees, instead of under a street lamp where it would be less vulnerable to car thieves. Both the man and the woman opened their doors and looked cautiously up and down the side road before getting out. Timberlake knew then his instincts had not let him down: the couple were providing a perfect performance of Behaving in a Suspicious Manner. Since the Police and Criminal Evidence Act 1984 that alone is not sufficient ground for nicking a suspect, but the Act does not say a policeman can't keep an eye on someone Behaving in a Suspicious Manner.

The couple hurried back out of the side road and, some fifty yards along the road where Timberlake's car was waiting, passed under the light of a street lamp. Timberlake saw the man plainly: it was Lawrence Soper, the council chief executive involved in the alleged corruption case. Accompanying him was Sharon Pettigrew, a senior secretary in the council administration department ... the woman who had inexplicably changed her mind about giving Timberlake information on the case.

They went into a large house divided into flats, looking as furtive

106

as amateur spies. A few moments later Timberlake went up to the front door to study the names next to the bellpushes. 'S. Pettigrew' was Flat 3, on the second floor. He returned to his car just as lights went on at the second floor. A quarter of an hour later the main light went out, leaving only a shaded lamp burning. Timberlake's tiredness had quite gone, and he hummed cheerfully to himself. He waited a full hour longer but Soper didn't come out, and the last of the lamps was turned off. It was a fair bet that the couple weren't discussing council business.

Before Timberlake drove away he made a careful account of his observations in his official pocketbook. He always took time to do his notes before returning to the station. This personal rule occasionally led to a ritual exchange in court. When Timberlake asked permission 'to refer to my pocketbook to refresh my memory', the defending counsel would sometimes ask in a sceptical tone, 'And when exactly did you make this note?' in the reasonable expectation that the answer would give him an opening. However, this was the point when the time-honoured dialogue took a sharp turn. Harry would pause before saying clearly, 'Ten minutes after the interview' – or 'observation', as the case might be. It impressed the hell out of the jury and had the supercilious counsel shuffling his papers as if he expected to find a £50 note among them.

As he drove on home Timberlake began to whistle. Normally a sordid little affair between a boss and a secretary wouldn't be worth a moment's attention, but in this case it could be important if charges of conspiracy arose. Now, however, for the first time he could see a crack in the carefully constructed wall of secrecy around Soper's corrupt practices. All he had to do now, Timberlake told himself, was to apply pressure at that point. Soper didn't even have the excuse of Barabas in Marlow's *The Jew of Malta*, who admitted committing fornication, 'but that was in another country'. Soper should have remembered what St Paul told the Corinthians: fornicators would not inherit the Kingdom of God. Not to mention the old adage: don't crap on your own doorstep.

In the excitement of the moment, Timberlake totally forgot two important facts. First, that when it came to fornication, he was in no position to throw stones; and second, that he was not an inch nearer to proving Newman guilty of two murders.

Chapter 11

Before leaving for work next morning Harry Timberlake telephoned Lawrence Soper's home. A servant answered the phone.
She told him that Mr Soper was away on business.

'And Mrs Soper?' Timberlake asked, almost certain of what the
answer would be. He was not disappointed.

'She's been visiting her mother for a couple of days.' She was
expected back that afternoon, the woman added. She also volun-
teered the information that Mr Soper said that he would be home
about five o'clock . 'Can I take a message?' she concluded.

'No, thanks. I'll call later.'

He hung up, and smiled like a tiger who has just seen a sleeping
goat. The situation was almost too banal for words: the wife was
away and the husband took the opportunity to spend the night
with his bit on the side. Timberlake decided on his plan of action,
a move that came well within the definition of a Right Dirty Trick.
He was aware that it was unscrupulous, but that didn't bother
him for a second. Although Timberlake would never manufacture
evidence to catch his man, abstract concepts like scruples and
morality were never allowed to affect his dealings with criminals.
Malefactors forfeited those considerations.

Harry Timberlake didn't like asking favours, particularly not
from Detective Superintendent Harkness. Harry admired the man
and wanted to impress him, but he needed the favour to achieve
his plan.

'Sir, could you do without me and Sergeant Webb for a while?
There's been a development in a major case I was working on
before the murders. The council corruption case. I think I mentioned it.'

'Yes. Isn't there anyone else who could deal with it?'

Harry Timberlake hesitated. 'Perhaps. But I'd really like to take care of it myself. I should manage to clear it up in a couple of days.'

Harkness studied him for a moment. For all his own toughness of spirit, Timberlake found the stare uncomfortable.

'Of course, Harry, if you think that'll be enough.' After a moment: 'Have you seen Newman again?'

'Yes, sir. Yesterday. It's in my report.'

'I haven't read it yet. And?'

'Nothing new, I'm afraid.'

Harkness walked over to the window and looked out towards the slow-moving traffic in the nearby main road. 'The other day you quoted *Crime and Punishment*. The book isn't a real-life case history, even if the psychology of it is accurate. There's a vital difference between Inspector Petrovich's relationship with Raskalnikoff and yours with Newman.' Harry didn't try to deny that he was hoping that constant, almost daily pressure on Newman would eventually squeeze some sort of admission from him, or at least push him into an unguarded remark that would reveal how he had fabricated his alibi.

Harkness turned round. 'Raskalnikoff was racked with terrible remorse and guilt. Even if Newman *had* murdered the two women – and all the evidence is against it – *do you think he would feel any sense of guilt?*'

Timberlake could have kicked himself long and hard. At last he realized that for the first time in his career he had approached a case with tunnel vision and total belief in his own ability to break down a suspect's resistance. And yet, what alternative did he have? Once again he had to suppress the nagging thought, Suppose I'm wrong and he's innocent?

Harkness went on, 'Intuition, a gut feeling: they can be invaluable in a good detective, but it takes painstaking, routine police work to build a case we can take to court.' His tone changed. Cheerfully – or what passed for cheerfully with him – he said, 'So take the time off with Sergeant Webb if you need to.'

'Thank you, sir.'

'It's for your other enquiry. Not to interview Newman. Understood?'

'Yes, sir.'

Harry Timberlake turned away to leave the AMIP office. His doubts had already disappeared again. 'But the bastard did do it,' he said to himself furiously. The thought was so positive he wondered if Harkness could actually hear him thinking it.

On his way to the main CID office he met Sarah alone in the corridor. He said quickly, 'I might be home for a couple of hours this afternoon. If you can get away, give me a ring to see if I'm in.' The words were hardly out of his mouth when he wondered what the hell had made him say that.

She winked and licked her lips lasciviously. 'Thanks, guv,' she said surprisingly. Behind Timberlake's back she had seen Inspector Bob Farmer appearing at the top of the stairs on his way to DCI Greening's office. He called out to Timberlake, who turned and returned the greeting with all the enthusiasm he could muster, which wasn't a great deal. Recently Farmer's brown-nosing Greening had become a little too obvious, Timberlake thought. He wasn't going to bother to tell Farmer, relatively new to the Terrace Vale nick, that hitching his star to Greening's wagon was like trying to get a high-speed tow from a brewery dray with a wheel missing.

'How're things?' Farmer asked Sarah.

'Struggling on, guv,' she said evenly. 'I've had a report from forensic. The metal in those dud pound coins is mainly old threepenny bits – you know, the ten-sided ones, or whatever they were. I'm starting on rounds of the coin dealers today, see if anyone's been buying them.' She moved past him, just out of touching distance as a matter of principle. Her heart beat a little faster at the possibility of some summer afternoon nooky.

'Where are we going, guv?' Darren Webb asked Timberlake as they went to the car park.

'Town hall. The corruption case. I think we've got a breakthrough.' He explained while they drove there.

The town hall of the local council was a would-be grandiose building. At reception Timberlake asked if Mr Soper was in, and was gratified to hear that he wouldn't be back that day. They would be able to interview Sharon Pettigrew without interference from her boss. While they waited for her to come to the reception area Timberlake briefed Webb on how she had promised to give him information about Soper and his accomplice, Norman Dawlish, the entrepreneur and builder, but then had, unaccountably, backed out.

Webb was curious to get a good look at Pettigrew. At first sight she appeared to be an attractive, efficient woman executive with good taste. After a moment, though, small false elements became evident. None was important in itself, but the cumulative effect was ruinous. Her skirt was just a fraction too short, her *décolleté* a few inches too deep, her blouse half a size too tight, her heels too high and spindly, her makeup a shade too blatant, her evening perfume a little too obtrusive, her eyeshadow too heavy ... She could have got away with one or two of these errors of judgement, not the whole bag. Nevertheless, she had an attractive figure and an undisguised latent sexuality. It was easy to understand how a man thirty years older than her had become infatuated to the point of reckless imprudence. After all, there were recorded precedents – going back two thousand years or more.

'Is there somewhere we can talk privately?' Timberlake suggested.

Without speaking Sharon Pettigrew led them to a door marked 'Interview Room'. It was strictly functional, not unlike the interview rooms at the Terrace Vale nick. It lacked only a twin-track tape recorder and the tenacious stink of a mixture of stale tobacco and fear-generated perspiration to make the two detectives feel thoroughly at home.

Sharon sat down, crossing her legs in an automatic conditioned reflex which revealed an expanse of thigh. When she spoke her voice was another mistake: it was just a little too 'refained'. She would have been better off with an early Michael Caine accent. It would have given her integrity. 'I hope this isn't going to take too long,' she said sharply. 'I'm very busy.'

The tone of this simple statement told Timberlake a great deal. She was self-possessed and unworried, which was a dead giveaway as to why she had changed her mind about giving him evidence to implicate Soper and Dawlish. It wasn't because she had been threatened and was afraid; it was because she felt secure and protected ... and, in a manner of speaking, rather cocky. It confirmed what he had seen the previous night.

He remained standing, giving her The Look. The first tiny crack appeared in Sharon Pettigrew's self-composure. She licked her too-red lips.

Timberlake changed tack and spoke gently, almost genially.

'As you know, Miss Pettigrew, I'm investigating possible corrupt practices in the awarding of council contracts and other offences.'

'I don't know noth—, anything about that.'

111

'On a previous occasion you said you could provide me with evidence that Lawrence Soper and Norman Dawlish were involved...'

'No, I didn't, and you can't prove I did,' she said with returning confidence.

'It's true that I can't prove it. Nevertheless, I have to warn you that if you are involved in the matter and are knowingly withholding evidence for any reason whatsoever, you could lay yourself open to charges yourself...' He paused. 'Including the very serious charge of conspiracy.'

Darren Webb added weight to Timberlake's words by nodding gravely. Sharon Pettigrew licked her lips, which were looking dry despite their liberal coat of lip-gloss. Still, she continued to put on a good defensive show. 'Why should I hold any evidence back?'

Timberlake moved forward and sat facing her from a couple of yards away. It is a scientific fact that the amount of light falling on an object varies inversely with the square of the distance from the light source. By halving his distance from her Timberlake quadrupled the power of his Look at Sharon. She shifted uncomfortably in her chair, and tried to pull her skirt down over her knees like an embarrassed television presenter on a too-low settee.

'Why should you hold any evidence back?' Timberlake echoed before adding in an Orson Welles timbre, 'Because you are Mr Soper's mistress.'

'Oooh, that's disgusting! Let him...? Me have sex with *him*?' she said with ladylike restrain. 'That's a diabolical lie! It's slander! I'll complain to your superiors!' Webb observed her admiringly, and reckoned she deserved an A for Effort.

'Surely you can't have forgotten?' Timberlake said with silky sarcasm. 'Only last night he drove you home at half-past eleven and stayed the night with you.' Webb permitted himself a 'Tsk, tsk.'

Timberlake was taking a chance with parts of the accusation, but it was a heavily odds-on bet that it hadn't been the first time Sharon and Soper had shacked up together. The shock of the accusation so stunned Sharon Pettigrew that her footwork deserted her.

She began to crumble like Mrs Lot in a thunderstorm. A few minutes later she agreed to accompany the detectives to Terrace Vale to make an official statement.

'I'll just go along to my office to pick up my things,' she said.

'Detective Sergeant Webb will go with you,' Timberlake said with a smile like an icicle. He wasn't going to take any chances of her trying to phone Soper to warn him. Or get near a shredder. He need not have worried. Sharon had already decided to co-operate fully in a bid to save herself. When she returned with Webb he was carrying a bulky file marked 'Private and Confidential' in red. Webb winked at Timberlake.

In all his career as a detective Harry Timberlake had never sneaked off in the middle of the day to go to bed with someone. Never. As he lay on his bed staring at the ceiling he wondered why the hell he'd done it this time. Beside him Sarah stirred, stretching one leg straight out, leaving the other with the knee still up, and with her head turned to one side. It was one of the positions that Harry liked most. It reminded him of a painting he had seen somewhere, although he couldn't remember which one.

Sarah was attractive, amusing, lively, had a marvellous body and had an all-over sexy look which could make wood smoulder. Even if the earth hadn't moved enough to rock the furniture they'd made love satisfactorily, and occasionally noisily. So why the hell was he thinking so much instead of just luxuriating in the after-glow? He should be feeling triumphant and sprightly after his success in getting Sharon Pettigrew to make a statement.

And then it hit him.

He had wanted to prove to himself that he still found Sarah irresistible, that the relationship was still strong and had a future. And if he had to prove it to himself, it wasn't, Harry thought. The memory of the night when he had turned his back on her with a flat 'Goodnight', with no kiss or tender gesture, came flooding back. He again felt a very real fear that he would progress through a series of semi-long affairs to a final arid loneliness.

His introspection was jolted when Sarah turned towards him and said, 'I don't know how long it is since I had an afternoon session of blanket bagpipes.'

The post-coital mood of *tristus* was broken. 'Good God! Where did you get that expression?'

She shrugged. 'I read it somewhere.'

If Fate had left things just there, Harry Timberlake's day might have been saved, but as is well known, Fate has as much sense of humour as a Tokyo undertaker.

The phone rang.

113

'Harry Timberlake? This is Lucinda Fordham. I hope you won't think me *too* shameless if I remind you that tomorrow's Wednesday.'

His mind stalled as abruptly as if someone had turned off the ignition. It spluttered into life again and he recalled she had told him that her day off was Thursday, so she preferred to go out on Wednesday evenings after her day in the studio.

Harry turned to catch the full power of Sarah's stare. 'Ah, thanks very much,' he said, trying to sound nonchalant. 'I'll come back to you on that, if I may.'

'It was a moment before Lucinda spoke again. 'It's a bad moment, isn't it?'

'No, not altogether.'

'You've got someone with you.'

'That's right,' he replied, trying to make it sound harmless.

'Perhaps you'd better call me later, if you want to.'

'Oh, I do,' he said, and wondered what the hell was making his mouth run ahead of him for the second time in one day.

'Goodbye.' He hung up.

'Who was that?' Sarah said, making a decent fist of sounding incurious.

'Oh, one of the people I met at the BBC. They wanted to know if I'd like to see a recording of the show.'

'*They*?'

'She.'

Sarah was far too shrewd to ask whether 'she' was attractive. 'Uhuh,' she said.

The bedroom temperature was going into free fall. I'd better be getting back to work,' Sarah said.

'Me, too,' was the best Timberlake could find to say.

Mrs Avril Soper, née April Clinch, opened the door to Harry Timberlake and Darren Webb. She looked very much like a former public house manageress who had married above her and was now the status-conscious wife of a newly appointed governor of a minor colony, ready to receive guests for a candlelight supper. As soon as she realized who the two detectives were, her expression slipped down three notches. She admitted that Mr Soper was at home, and said she would find out if he was available to see them. 'You can wait in the parl—, in the sitting room,' she said.

Avril Soper's generous figure put her expensive dress under strain, but 'I bet when she was younger she was a fair bit of crumpet, guv,' said Darren Webb. Timberlake agreed. In fact she must have looked very much like Sharon Pettigrew, which explained a lot. There was one significant difference between the two women, nevertheless. Avril Soper had the sharp, ferret-like nose of a born-curious busybody. Timberlake's spirits soared.

The Soper house looked ordinary enough on the outside: one of a series of four-bedroom, two-garage, large-garden homes in a tree-lined road that could have served for filming *The Good Life*. On the other hand, the interior was well out of the ordinary. It managed to combine no-expense-spared with a taste that was, well, common kitsch. On a silk flock wallpaper was the portrait of a green-faced oriental lady, which had a costly frame better suited to a water-colour. Near it was the Annigoni portrait of the Queen. The fitted carpet had a tartan pattern which would have been fatal to any chameleon that tried to cross a foot of it. Timberlake guessed that the only reason there were no flying ducks on the wall was that Mr or Mrs Soper could not find any that were gold-plated or had pink lights concealed in them.

'Good evening, Inspector, Sergeant,' Lawrence Soper said breezily as he entered the room. He favoured his wife with a nod. 'What can I do for you? I hope this won't take too long,' he added, using the same phrase as Sharon Pettigrew earlier. 'We're going out for dinner soon.'

Timberlake repressed a desire to say, 'You'll be lucky, chum,' and contented himself with, 'I'll be as quick as I can, sir. I've come to ask you for your comments on a statement that's been made to us.' Soper's eyes narrowed, but he didn't look alarmed. Yet. Timberlake gave him a 'We're all men of the world' look and added, 'Perhaps you'd prefer to continue this interview in private, sir, without Mrs Soper?'

Soper had the anguished appearance of a man who has suddenly felt someone take a firm grip on his balls. If Timberlake had suggested this with anyone other than Mrs Soper present he almost certainly would have accepted the offer, but there was no way out of it now. 'No, that's perfectly all right,' Soper said with a totally unconvincing smile. 'My wife and I have no secrets from each other.' He had a flash of inspiration. 'Unless, of course this is something to do with confidential council matters?'

Timberlake yanked on the line, making the hook dig in deeper. 'No, it's not that sort of confidential . . .'

Now Soper couldn't have got his wife out of the room with a pack of wolves.

'Before I go any further I have to tell you that I suspect you of offences contrary to the Public Bodies Corrupt Practices Act of 1889. You are not obliged to say anything, but anything you do say will be taken down in writing and may be given in evidence. Do you understand, sir?' Soper nodded. 'Will you please say yes or no?'

'Yes, I understand.'

Webb ostentatiously took out his pocket book and clicked his ball-point pen. It sounded as loud as an executioner testing the trapdoor.

'Do you wish to have a solicitor present?' Timberlake asked quietly.

'Am I being charged now?'

'No, sir. Not now.'

'Very well. I am a solicitor, as you know. I am totally innocent of any wrongdoing and I have nothing to conceal. Please make a note of that, Sergeant,' he said with bravado.

'Miss Sharon Pettigrew, who I understand is your private secretary, has made a long statement in which she alleges that you accepted gifts, money and a holiday from Mr Norman Dawlish, in exchange for your assisting him to obtain council building contracts for his company. Furthermore, she states that on your orders she opened sealed tenders from other companies, and you then passed their prices on to Mr Dawlish so that he could tender a lower price.'

'The lying little rotten bitch!' Avril Soper exploded, but there was a false note in her voice.

Soper shot her a warning glance before turning to Timberlake. 'There's not a scintilla of truth in that,' he replied, forcing a laugh. 'Any advice I may have given the council supporting Mr Dawlish's company was disinterested and based on my honest judgement of the merits of the tenders. *If* Mr Dawlish had prior knowledge of the tenders offered by other contractors, it must have been a private arrangement between him and Miss Pettigrew. *I* most definitely didn't receive any gifts or money from Mr Dawlish whatsoever.'

116

'Can you think of any reason why she might have made these accusations, Mr Soper?'

Soper's brain was whirring almost audibly. Timberlake guessed what he was thinking. If he admitted having an affair with Sharon, and she was doing this out of revenge because he broke it off, his loving wife wouldn't let him forget it. However, if he didn't admit to a busted affair there would be no way of diminishing Sharon's evidence. He opted for staying in the frying pan and not risking a leap into the fire.

'Spite. She's doing it out of spite.' He addressed his wife, who was going red and then white by turns. Her lips were compressed into a thin red line. 'I'm sorry, darling; I didn't want you to know this, but I had a brief, a very brief, affair with Sharon some time ago. You see, Inspector, I broke it off, and she took it very badly. She's been pestering me ever since. She's made it all up out of spite.'

Soper's suit suddenly seemed a couple of sizes too big for him. He made another attempt to moderate his wife's rage. 'It was some time ago – when you were away at your mother's place for a week,' he added inspirationally. 'I was lonely, overworked, and tired. It was a moment of weakness, I admit it. I'll make it up to you,' he said pleadingly.

Every single day for the rest of your life, Timberlake thought.

'Miss Pettigrew claims that she has been your mistress for some time,' Timberlake continued mildly.

'Not true. It was a weekend affair, little more.'

'When did you break it off, Mr Soper?'

'Oh, it would be a month or more.'

'Yet you stayed overnight at her flat only last night.' In the ensuing silence Webb thought he could hear Mrs Soper bubbling internally like a kettle on the boil.

'That's a lie! She's just saying that to bolster up her story,' Soper said smoothly.

'Mr Soper, you were observed entering her flat at eleven-thirty last night, and you stayed all night.'

'Who said they saw me? One of her friends, I suppose.'

'No. *I* saw you enter and you had not come out again by three-thirty a.m.'

Soper gulped several times, his mouth opening and closing like an Indian Ocean grouper fish. But he was a battler, and managed to scrape together some self-composure. 'Yes, it's true. I was there, but I didn't admit it because I didn't want to cause Avril any more pain. I've been trying to break it off with Sharon for weeks. I went there last night to make one more effort, but...' He shook his head sadly. 'And when I... refused her, it must have been the last straw to make her make up all these lies about me.'

Mrs Soper was no great aid and support to her husband. She gave him a blowtorch stare, turned on her heel and stormed out of the room, slamming the door behind her so forcefully that it made the green oriental lady and HM the Queen rattle against the wall. A row of real-ivory little elephants lined up in diminishing size fell like a set of dominoes, making a noise like teeth being knocked out.

When Soper had recovered, he began to explain how Norman Dawlish had suggested the scam to him but he had indignantly refused to be involved. Because they had been friends, he promised to forget Dawlish had ever said it, but he must never mention the idea again. 'Dawlish must have turned to Sharon Pettigrew for information about his rivals' bids,' Soper concluded.

'Will you come to the Terrace Vale police station tomorrow afternoon to make a formal statement, sir?' Timberlake asked.

'Of course. I'm as anxious to clear up this matter as you are.'

As Timberlake and Webb walked away from the house they thought they heard crockery hitting a wall.

Driving back to Terrace Vale Timberlake whistled cheerfully to himself. Webb was puzzled. 'Doesn't look like you've got much of a case against him, guv. At the moment it's all on the Pettigrew woman. Why did you see Soper at home instead of at the nick? Putting him in an interview room with the tape recorder going might have made him less cocky.'

'I rather think you'll see the answer to that one tomorrow morning.'

But there was to be a lot of unwanted excitement before then.

Chapter 12

When she had just half an hour left to live, Mrs Brenda Hardie had a noisy, bitter argument with a member of the local Conservative Party committee, of which she was chairwoman. In the local Labour Party Brenda Hardie would probably have been called the chairperson, or even the chair, but the Conservative Party is a little more conservative in these matters – except for sections of the Young Conservatives, of course. The member with whom Brenda Hardie had words was a Harold Golightly, who was as spiky in temperament as his chairwoman. He was to regret for some time that his last words to her were, 'Oh, drop dead, you bossy bitch!'

Brenda Hardie used up twenty-four minutes of her remaining thirty minutes of life with a few cronies, drinking sherry and slanderously dissecting the characters of absent fellow members. In other words, having a convivial political evening.

Her customary walk home from the local party headquarters, a converted shop, usually took her eight minutes, but she didn't have that long left. Two minutes and 180 yards from home and safety she was murdered. She was dead before she hit the ground under a handsome chestnut tree. The local milkman, Charlie Trinder, found the body the next morning.

The subsequent official record noted that the body was that of Mrs Brenda Hardie, apparent age fifty-five years (which was a spot-on guess), medium build, bleached blonde hair (in a Lady Thatcher cast-iron bouffant style, a detail that the report omitted), blue eyes, two four-tooth bridges in the upper mouth, two molars on the right side and one on the left side of the lower jaw missing. She was dressed in a dark blue suit with a white blouse, bra and knickers, black tights and black court shoes.

There was no handbag to be seen, and there were no rings or other jewellery on the body. The pockets of her suit were turned

119

inside out. At first sight there were no signs of any sexual attack, and this was confirmed by the later post-mortem. There were two puncture marks on her blouse, but there was hardly any blood.

The corpse lay on its back in a leafy pathway unimaginatively called The Pathway, which ran from the main road, through the car park of a supermarket and into Milton Avenue. Access for the cars of The Pathway's residents was only from the main road end. Because of the pedestrian right of way from the main road to Milton Avenue, the supermarket's car park was never closed, which meant that God knows how many people could use The Pathway.

Charlie Trinder was an intelligent and resourceful man. At home in the West Indies he had been a technician in a pathological laboratory, but in England he was glad to get any job, and one as a milkman was a bonus, because it meant he could go to early evening classes to study to become a solicitor. He calculated that life being what it was in England there would always be work for a solicitor.

Two early risers, an elderly man and his wife, who seemed to be acting as foreman, were working in their front garden. Charlie told the woman to phone the police, and the man to stop anyone entering The Pathway from the car park end. They carried out his instructions without demur for Charlie exuded a natural authority which would have enraged the Ku Klux Klan, particularly if they'd known he was also a Catholic. Charlie himself blocked off the Milton Avenue end of The Pathway by the simple expedient of parking his milk float across the entrance.

Within minutes the first police presence was on the scene and the rituals of the long, laborious murder investigation procedure were under way. Screens were erected round the body and broad white tapes were tied to trees and fences to keep gawpers away. For a time some residents of The Pathway were prevented from approaching their own houses, others were politely prevented from leaving them. Dr Pratt pronounced the corpse dead, and stated that it was a stone-bonker, racing certainty that the victim had been stabbed right where she was found.

The murder had taken place on a gravelled stretch of The Pathway, and there were no discernible footprints. A meticulous search of the immediate area was carried out. It turned up, among other rubbish, empty cigarette and crisps packets, a torn pair of woman's tights, one woollen glove on which cress was beginning to grow, a used London Underground ticket six days old, and a sticky used condom containing more than enough material for genetic fingerprinting of the two people who had been involved in its use. The corpse's underwear was firmly in place and showed no signs of interference, which meant that the condom was only of sordid academic interest. It was not a promising start, and none of the items found in the vicinity of the murder was to prove of any value to the investigation.

Harry Timberlake missed most of the excitement in the Terrace Vale CID offices. He worked very late on the Soper case paperwork and was up early the next morning to call on builder Norman Dawlish while he was having breakfast. He 'invited' Dawlish to call at Terrace Vale police station to help him with his enquiries – after he'd finished his cornflakes of course. But somehow Dawlish had suddenly lost his appetite.

It was going to be Timberlake's day. As he walked in at the back door of the nick, Sergeant Rumsden called to him that someone was at the front desk, asking for him.

It was Avril Soper, who showed no signs of having calmed down from the previous evening. Timberlake reckoned that if he did manage to put Soper in jail, he might well be grateful for the peace and quiet. He led her to an interview room, sweeping Darren Webb along with him like a train picking up a mailbag.

Mrs Soper had come in to spill the beans – more accurately, to pour them all out, making sure none was left in the tin. Darren Webb listened to her wide-eyed.

'That time my husband and I were supposed to be on holiday in Bandol,' she said venomously, 'the second day we went on to Cannes, where Dawlish paid for us to stay at the Carlton. Last September my husband' – she made it sound like 'Hitler' or 'Dracula' – 'and I went to Marseilles where Dawlish picked us up in his yacht and we had a three-week cruise round the Greek islands . . .' She dumped a pile of photographs on the table. They were holiday pictures of the Sopers and the Dawlishes together obviously having a marvellous time in nightclubs, on beaches, and on Dawlish's yacht.

Then the real detonator that had set off her explosion of rage and bitterness was revealed. 'Dawlish and my husband went off

121

on what he said was a strictly business trip. *On their own.* I can guess what sort of business it was. They took their secretaries with them.' She slapped a piece of paper on top of the photographs. 'There are the details of his other bank accounts and the names they're in.' She hadn't stitched up her husband: she had riveted him.

'You know, of course, that you wouldn't be allowed to give evidence against your husband in court,' Timberlake began, but almost before he finished she snapped, 'I won't need to, now you've got all that.'

When it was all over Avril Soper went to the WPCs' loo to repair her makeup. The two detectives waited to escort her to the front of the building, where a police car ordered by Timberlake was ready to take her home.

'So this is what you were expecting, guv. How did you know?' said Darren Webb.

'It's a classic situation. So many cheated wives or mistresses grass in a fit of temper . . . to the income tax people, the police or the husband's employers. Hell hath no fury, and all that. People wouldn't believe how often it happens. Of course, tomorrow she'll regret it.'

'I shouldn't have thought so, guv. She struck me as being the type who'll stay steamed up for weeks.'

'Ah, but she hasn't realized yet that when Soper loses his job, has to forfeit all the money he got from Dawlish and pay a thundering great fine, it's not going to leave her a lot. Then she'll start hating herself – and us as well.'

Yes, it was definitely Harry Timberlake's day, for as Mrs Soper walked down the steps, Norman Dawlish and his solicitor were getting out of a taxi. As soon as Dawlish saw her accompanied by the satisfied-looking Timberlake and Webb he turned several shades of grey.

Dawlish started by denying that there was any truth in any of the allegations. However, if there were, it was nothing to do with him. But as soon as Timberlake marked his card about Sharon Pettigrew's statement, the documents she had handed over and Mrs Soper's contribution, Dawlish's paler shade of grey had faded into a dirty off-white. He began to wriggle and try to get out from under by blaming Sharon and Soper for everything.

By the time he had made a formal statement and agreed to

hand over all relevant documents, Timberlake had an almost bomb-proof case. Now it was simply a matter of paperwork to submit to the Crown Prosecution Service. Lots of paperwork.

Since this latest murder was on the Terrace Vale patch, and Detective Superintendent Harkness and his AMIP team were already installed there, Harkness took charge of this case as well. It meant recruiting more bodies from the Terrace Vale CID. Harkness approached DCI Ted Greening – reluctantly, because he liked the man as much as an ingrowing toenail – to ask for reinforcements. He was determined not to let his dislike show.

Greening pondered the question. 'You've got a tough one there, sir,' he said ingratiatingly. 'It's got all the earmarks of a simple mugging, probably by some spade trying to make some money for his next fix who got a bit too enthusiastic.' Harkness felt his irritation with Greening rising. It was true that violent crime in Terrace Vale was perpetrated by a disproportionate number of West Indians compared with the local White population, but then a disproportionate number were also unemployed, on or under the poverty line. Harkness took exception to the easy assumption, statistically supported or not. And anyway, there was apparently one detail that didn't fit with the simple mugging theory.

Some of Harkness's disapproval must have leaked through his expressionless mask. Greening looked slightly ill at ease, coughed and said he'd see who was involved with which cases and get back to Harkness right away. As soon as Harkness closed the door behind him, Greening took a swig from the whisky bottle in his bottom drawer, allowed himself a noisy burp, and sent for Bob Farmer. While he waited he lit his ninth cigarette of the morning.

Farmer's first choice of someone to join the AMIP team was Sarah Lewis. He hoped that adding to her workload might make her more amenable to his advances. For a detective inspector he was a poor judge of character.

His second suggestion was Detective Sergeant Lennart Gundersson, whose name would have betrayed his Viking origins if his six foot four inch height, almost white-blond hair and blue eyes hadn't already done so. He had a lot of success with women, but he had as much future as an undercover detective as he had of being cast as one of the Seven Vertically Challenged Persons, a.k.a. the Seven Dwarfs.

123

Ted Greening, adopting an air of brisk efficiency that fitted him like a Pavarotti suit, reported to Harkness that he had given the question of reinforcement for the AMIP team his best consideration and decided that, for a start, Detective Inspector Farmer, Detective Sergeant Gundersson and WDC Sarah Lewis were ideally suited. Harkness received the part about 'best consideration' with all the credulity of a Swiss banker being offered Tower Bridge for sale.

'All right, Chief Inspector. Tell them to report to me,' Harkness said.

'Inspector Farmer and Sergeant Gundersson are here, sir, but WDC Lewis is out on enquiries.' He tried to make it sound as if Sarah was out picking flowers.

Sarah was suffering from the mental equivalent of a small stone in her shoe. She had been worrying about her lack of progress with her caseload, when she became aware of something at the back of her mind. She had seen, heard or half-remembered something important that had a bearing on one of her cases, but what the hell was it? – It niggled and niggled at her, distracting her, infuriating her. Sometimes she tried telling herself it was empty imagination, but this didn't work. She knew that the solution to one of her problems was, infuriatingly, almost within reach. She tried to think of something else, but that didn't work. One of her uncles used to joke with her, saying, 'Whatever you do, love, for the next five minutes don't think of a white horse!'

'How the hell can you *not* think of a white horse when someone's said that to you?' she used to say.

Then there was the matter of her relationship with Harry Timberlake. Until now they had no secrets from each other, but now she had a Big Secret. It wasn't yet a Very Big Secret, although it had all the makings of one.

An angry hooting from another motorist jolted her out of her introspection and made her concentrate on the business of driving. In an attempt to take an orderly approach to her problem she had decided to visit all the people she had interviewed in the past week – even including her noxious snout Jock McLeish.

First on her list was Derek Horlock. He had form, he was short of money, he had transport, and he had the perfect excuse for being out early in the morning. On a scale of one to ten he scored seven as a prime suspect.

Sarah stopped her car round the corner from the shop's yard, and walked the rest of the way. As she entered the yard where the van was parked, Jason came out of the shed, a gleaming model car still shiny and wet with a new coat of white cellulose, smelling like peardrops.

'Hello,' she said genially. 'What's that one?'

'Auto Union,' Jason answered tersely. 'German. Pre-war.' His attitude softened. 'I've been working on it for weeks. Couldn't get proper drawings of it at first. D'you want to see Dad?'

'No,' she said, edging nearer to the van. 'Just happened to be passing, thought I'd look in.' She glanced through the half-open doors, but the van appeared empty. Jason watched her intently, suddenly suspicious. Sarah decided she'd have to come back another time when no one was in the yard. She smiled at Jason.

'Everything all right with you?'

Jason was suddenly suspicious. 'Yeah. Why shouldn't it be?'

'No reason. Like I said, I just happened to be passing.' When she got back to her car and switched on her radio, PC Phil Clapton was in the middle of trying to contact her. She was told to return to Terrace Vale nick. Clapton tried to make it sound as if she was in deep trouble, but in fact it was only to be told that she was now officially on The Pathway murder.

The initial problem with The Pathway murder was to identify the body, for there was nothing on it, and no handbag – it was never found – to help with the identification. It was not until Brenda Hardie was taken to the morgue that she was recognized, by one of the porters who worked there. He was able to tell the police who she was and of her Conservative Party connections. The local office furnished her address and the fact that she was a widow who lived alone.

Since there had been no handbag with the body, Sarah Lewis and Lennart the Viking, accompanied by two SOCOs, were sent hotfoot to her home to see if her murderer or murderers had found her address and house keys and gone there to steal. Harkness wasn't all that worried about a robbery as such, but there should be a better chance of finding clues in a house than in a well-used street or pathway.

The detached house in Milton Road had a couple of decent locks on the front door, but the back door put up as much resistance as a zip fastener.

It was evident within the first two minutes that the house hadn't been burgled: it was as neat and tidy as if a photographer from *Homes and Gardens* was going to call. As the team moved slowly from room to room they could see no obvious signs of an alien hand having been at work. There were valuable, easily resold items in full view: a carriage clock, silver candlesticks, a camcorder, television and video recorder among other pieces. In a sort of study there were photographs on the wall of Brenda Hardie, trying to look suitably modest, with various Conservative Party dignitaries, pride of place going to one showing her with the Iron Lady. In what appeared to be the earlier photographs Brenda Hardie had shortish hair; but in the later ones she had adopted the Thatcher starched coiffure.

On the desk was a silver-framed photograph of Mrs Hardie with a shorter, younger woman, which looked as if it had been taken on holiday somewhere. Mrs Hardie was wearing slacks, the other woman a frilly dress. She looked too old to be Mrs Hardie's daughter, and had no family resemblance.

There was another photograph of Brenda Hardie and the other woman on the dressing table in the large, double bedroom. Sarah studied the toilet articles beside the photograph with a knitted brow.

'Found something?' Gundersson asked.

'I don't know.' She moved to the bed and sniffed, then leaned over the pillows and sniffed harder. 'There's been another woman in this bed.'

'Don't tell me you can smell her,' Gundersson chuckled.

'I can smell her perfume. There's only Poison and Chanel Number Five on the dressing table.' Sarah sniffed again. 'This is something else. Something cheaper.' An idea struck her and she went to the wardrobe and opened the doors wide. She ran her hand along the dresses and suits, then nodded with satisfaction. Next Sarah looked through a chest of drawers. Triumphantly she pulled out two bras and two pairs of knickers and put them on the bed. Gundersson, who had seen many such items of women's underwear *in situ* and on beds and chairs and on floors and once on a chandelier, recognized instantly that they belonged to two different women. And as Sarah pointed out, not only two different women, but two different *kinds* of women. The larger items, which were clearly Mrs Hardie's, were expensive but no-nonsense,

126

practical devices with the minimum of feminine trimming. The others were the sort of lingerie described in advertisements as 'Seductive and sexy: send for our catalogue, price £2, reimbursed with first order'.

'It looks to me,' Sarah said heavily, 'that our Mrs Hardie probably had a little friend.'

'This could be a weird one,' Gundersson said with Scandinavian gloom.

He was right. And it was going to become a lot weirder.

'The first important element of this killing,' Professor Mortimer pontificated in the cold and echoing morgue, 'is what are generally called defensive wounds, sustained on the hands or forearms when a victim tries to ward off blows.'

His audience consisted of four detectives: Superintendent Harkness, Inspector Farmer, Sergeant Gundersson, and WDC Sarah Lewis. Also present were Mortimer's assistant Gertrude Hacker, dressed in her usual thick tweeds and holding her thick notebook – Mortimer scorned tape recorders – and the porter who was at the post-mortem of Mrs Pascoe and Mrs Newman. They were grouped around the mortal remains of Mrs Brenda Hardie.

'There are none,' Mortimer said. He was not trying to be what passes for humorous in forensic pathologists, nor had he ever heard of Sherlock Holmes's dog who was remarkable because he hadn't barked during the night. 'Make of that what you will.'

What the detectives made of it was fairly obvious.

Her corpse was lying on a dissection table, her body cut open from beneath the chin to her pubis. Some of her organs had already been removed ready for closer examination. Mortimer was drawing attention to Mrs Hardie's heart. Only Sarah and Inspector Farmer had not seen one separated from a body before. Sarah was surprised that it was so small: an inverted conical shape, five inches long and three and a half inches across its broadest part and about two and a half inches thick. Even more surprising was its golden sheen: Sarah thought it looked quite beautiful.

'Death was caused by two penetrating-lacerated wounds to the heart,' Mortimer droned on. 'The first is situated over the sterno-clavicular articulation of the left clavicle.' He indicated the position, but the detectives couldn't see any gaping wound. 'The second penetrated the aorta at the junction with the left auricle.'

127

As far as the detectives were concerned, there was still nothing much to see.

'After the blows were struck, how long did it take for Mrs Hardie to die?' Harkness asked. He avoided the mistake of asking Mortimer how long he *thought* it had taken or what his opinion was.

'She died almost immediately. Apart from the damage to the heart, there was the shock.'

'Well, it would be a bit of a surprise,' Farmer said to Sarah *sotto voce*, but it wasn't too *sotto* for Mortimer, who had surprisingly acute hearing for a geriatric.

'I was referring to *clinical* shock. I should have thought someone of your experience would realize that. Good heavens.'

Harkness intervened smoothly before Farmer could aggravate his offence by saying he was only joking. 'What can you tell us about the weapon, Professor?'

'It was not a conventional knife or dagger. The "blade" section, if I can call it that, was round, between eighteen and twenty-two centimetres long, and five to six millimetres in diameter. That is one of the reasons that there was so little blood present.' He paused for dramatic effect. 'Oh, yes. It had a chisel-shaped point.'

'A screwdriver,' Sarah said involuntarily.

Mortimer stared at her. He had just been about to make that announcement himself and he hated it when people anticipated him. He rapidly continued his exposition. 'To conclude . . . to conclude, the killer either had some knowledge of anatomy, or was lucky with the blows.'

A fat lot of help.

Chapter 13

The time of Brenda Hardie's murder was easily and accurately established. It was known that she left the party committee rooms at 10.37 p.m., and she was killed before she reached home, eight minutes' walk away. There was the faint possibility that she had stopped somewhere on the way home before she got to The Pathway and had been killed later than 10.45, but it was most unlikely. And there was a witness who thought he had seen her entering The Pathway at about ten to eleven. So the police went on the assumption that she had been stabbed at about 10.42 p.m.

The first witness to be questioned – it was too early to call him a suspect yet – about Brenda Hardie's murder was her fellow committee member, Harold Golightly. He had frequently been heard to say he could strangle/murder the domineering/arrogant/ high-handed/tyrannical/stupid bitch/cow ... and other unparliamentary expressions. They hated each other with the calculating hate that only politicians can manage. Maastricht mentioned in their presence resulted in their spontaneous combustion.

Golightly was in the clear five minutes after Lennart Gundersson interviewed him at the local party headquarters. On the night that Brenda Hardie was killed he had stayed on for an hour after she had left. There were half a dozen members who had been there with him, then another member gave him a lift home.

Tactfully Gundersson asked Brenda Hardie's former colleagues whether she had any enemies. This was greeted with an embarrassed silence. He changed tack and asked if they knew of any of her friends. The silence intensified, if that were possible. Timberlake would have been tempted to quote Oscar Wilde's description of G. B. Shaw: 'He hasn't an enemy in the world and none of his friends likes him.' Gundersson ploughed on. He asked whether Brenda Hardie lived alone? The silence became deafening. He

129

could get no hint of a relationship with a younger woman.

It was Sarah Lewis who got a lead to the young woman whose photograph and some of whose clothes were at the Hardie home. She had the job of sorting through the dead woman's papers in her study at home. Although they were as voluminous as in a French civil service office, fortunately they were in perfect order. Sarah found vouchers and confirmations of orders from a travel agency that went back four years. For three and a half years the bookings had always been for two persons; then they had been for Brenda Hardie alone.

The name of the companion for those three and a half years was a Ms Sandra Dawlish. A call to the travel agency, a local firm called Diana Huntress Ltd, produced her address.

Farmer decided that he would interview Sandra Dawlish, and Sarah Lewis would accompany him. Sarah was less than thrilled by the prospect, but Farmer had learned his lesson from the deep-freeze reaction to his first two approaches. Slow but sure was his motto now. When he drove them to Sandra Dawlish's small flat near Victoria Station his hand never slipped from the gear lever, and he kept his conversation as asexual as a railway time-table.

A neat-looking young woman, barefoot and wearing a man's long shirt over shorts, opened the door when they rang. She had a headband to keep her dark hair back, and a duster in her hand.

'Ms Sandra Dawlish?' Farmer asked, turning up his charm to about half-power.

'No. Well, yes, I was, but I'm not now. Mrs Sefton. I'm married.' When the two detectives identified themselves she said calmly, 'Oh, I suppose you've come about Brenda. I read about it in the papers. You'd better come in.'

After they had explained how they had traced her, it was a straightforward interview. She made no bones about her relationship with Brenda Hardie and said finally, 'She talked me into it, you know, when I was seventeen. I had no parents, few friends, and I was absolutely inexperienced. At the time it seemed – you may find this difficult to understand – rather, I don't know, *daring* and sophisticated. She was terribly impressive and dominating with everyone else, but she was sweet to me, honestly. She took

130

me abroad on holiday . . .' For the first time she spoke with some embarrassment. 'She was the only experience of sex I'd ever had; I thought that was *it*. I thought I was . . . like her.

'Then I met Derek. I became confused about my own sexuality, but when Derek . . . Well, I knew it had all been a mistake.' This secretly confirmed Farmer's theory that all any lesbian needed to make her heterosexual was a good screwing, but he kept this philosophical nugget to himself. 'I couldn't tell Brenda to her face, so I wrote to her, and phoned.'

'How did she take it?' Sarah asked.

'She didn't carry on. Stiff upper lip stuff, you know. She said she wouldn't send back the things I'd left at her place: she knew I'd come back. There wasn't any chance of that. I didn't want them anyway.'

'When exactly did you leave her?' Farmer asked. He had allowed his charm to slow down to tickover.

'About eight months ago.'

'Does your husband know about your former relationship with Mrs Hardie?' Sarah asked.

Sandra Dawlish Sefton looked Sarah straight in the eye and said, 'Yes.'

So that was that. One more name to cross off the list. If anyone of the triangle had a motive for murder, it was Brenda Hardie herself: Derek Sefton had taken her lover from her.

Maybe this is how married couples become, Harry Timberlake thought, glancing sideways at Sarah Lewis, who was looking at the television without actually seeing it. They'd eaten a takeaway meal, because both had worked late and neither had felt like preparing any food. Timberlake was being particularly morose these days for he was forced to go through the motions of conducting an enquiry into the murders of Veronica Newman and her mother, knowing all the time that it was all a total waste of time.

Although Sarah was tired and was wearing an old bathrobe that was about as fetching as a potato sack, Harry still found her physically attractive; he felt warm towards her and comforted by her presence . . . yet there was something lacking. Was it unpredictability, or mystery, or the ability to surprise him? He wondered if this was the beginning of a break-up. Perhaps it was the beginning of a descent into a sort of tolerant mediocrity, which would be much worse.

He decided he would have to do something about it. What, exactly, he wasn't sure.

In common with Gaul, the London Borough of Southington is divided into three parts. West Southington may sound rather more up-market than plain Southington, but in fact it is definitely a good few rungs below it on the social ladder. There are those who admit to having heard of East Southington, but no one confesses to actually *living* there unless forced to. Applications from East Southington addresses for credit and for mortgages to buy property there are considered with reluctance and subjected to severe scrutiny and scepticism.

Jacqueline Clayton lived in Southington. She was fifty-eight years old, and in a favourable light could have passed for fifty-seven.

Miss Clayton was popular and well liked by almost everyone and loved by many. She had *charm*, was good-hearted, kind, and funny. She had a good degree from Oxford. Before she was made redundant – with a reasonable golden handshake and a good pension – she had been an English teacher at a girls' private school that was hardly up to Cheltenham Ladies' College standard but was definitely better than Dotheboys Hall and Borstal. She augmented her income by writing occasional amusing articles for women's magazines and newspapers.

She had been a spinster all her life, a well-satisfied spinster, and lived in a small semi-detached, end-of-terrace house in a side road. Its garden gave on to a pathway which ran the length of the street of some thirty houses each side, and parallel to it. When the doorbell rang at five to nine one evening she was surprised, but not alarmed. Maybe one of her younger neighbours had been let down at the last minute by a baby-sitter and the mother was hoping Miss Clayton would help out at short notice. Jacqueline Clayton was that sort of woman. Nevertheless, she looked through the security viewer in the front door. What she saw reassured her and she opened the door.

The caller referred to a clipboard and asked politely, 'Miss Clayton?'

'Yes?'

132

The caller gave a disarming smile, then produced a long, thin screwdriver from under the cover of the clipboard. Before Jacqueline Clayton could move, the caller plunged the screwdriver accurately into her heart, withdrew it and gave a second blow. There was surprisingly little blood.

Jacqueline slowly sank to her knees, and was dead before she rolled over on to her side. Her killer stepped inside, quickly pushed the body to one side and shut the front door.

When the SOCOs and police arrived, as far as they could see nothing in the house had been stolen, or even touched.

Within two hours of Jacqueline Clayton's body being found and the method of her murder established, Terrace Vale nick was informed of the correlation between her killing and Brenda Hardie's. Twice. The first time was on the inter-station network direct from Southington, the second from Scotland Yard's Criminal Intelligence department. The three parts of Southington were all in the same AMIP area as Terrace Vale, so Detective Superintendent Harkness's group were lumbered with the investigation of the Clayton murder as well as their other enquiries.

The extra workload made Harkness quail internally, yet he preserved his appearance of total imperturbable calm. The fallout affected Ted Greening, for there were demands on him to provide more detectives for the murder squad. If he wasn't careful, he'd have to get out of the office and do some real detecting again.

Harkness managed to turn the situation to his advantage. He called his two teams into his office and announced changes in the disposition of his forces. Farmer and his group would take over the investigation of the Pascoe-Newman murders, and Timberlake's team would be responsible for the Hardie-Clayton enquiries. It was an unusual move, and Harkness departed from his normal practice of not giving reasons for his decisions.

'Inspector Timberlake and his team have worked very hard on their case and I think it may be time to bring a new outlook on the problem. Since he has had recent experience in 'serial' murders and there is a very strong possibility the last two killings were committed by the same hand, he will lead this new investigation.' He paused. 'Any questions?'

There was an uneasy near-silence, broken only by some foot shuffling and stifled coughs. Harry Timberlake was reminded of a report of a meeting of the then Soviet Republic when Gorbachev was President. Someone called out, 'If you knew all that about Stalin and Brezhnev, why didn't you say something at the time?' Gorbachev glared into the hall and said sharply *'Who said that?'* The place went deathly quiet. 'That's why,' said Gorbachev, smiling.

Harry didn't feel like smiling, though. He knew why he had been taken off the Pascoe-Newman case, and it was nothing to do with his recent experience. It was because no one believed his theories about Newman. And with another officer in charge of the enquiry, he couldn't even approach him.

From the beginning of the investigation into Jacqueline Clayton's murder Timberlake knew it was going to be a tough one. It could be summed up in a well-worn cliché of 1970s television: 'Who could have wanted to murder Walter? He didn't have an enemy in the world, Inspector.' *Nobody* had a bad word to say about her, not even some sour-looking married neighbours. The local shopkeepers liked her, her former colleagues liked her, and there was nothing in any of the magazine articles she wrote to provoke the most touchy subject.

She was not rich, and as far as the detectives could tell from their preliminary enquiries, she had no relatives who would want to kill her to inherit money or property. From all accounts, her affairs were only with unattached men, so there were no jealous spouses to wish her harm. She had not been sexually assaulted; her house showed no signs of being robbed.

Timberlake and Darren Webb decided to try to find something or someone Jacqueline Clayton and Brenda Hardie had in common, yet on the face of it the two women could not have been more different. His failure with the Newman-Pascoe murders, the Brenda Hardie killing and lack of a lead in this last murder thoroughly depressed Timberlake. He began seriously to wonder if he was losing his touch.

'Still fond of peppermints, Sergeant Rumsden?'

Rumsden, absorbed with making notes in the Incident Book, looked up to see Old Unusual standing in front of the counter. 'Oh, hello Old Unusual. What can I do for you?'

'I'd like a word with WDC Lewis, please.'

'I'll see if she's in.'

'She's in. I can hear her talking to someone in the back office.'

'You can't!' Rumsden said.

'*You* can't,' Old Unusual said. 'But I can. Ah, here she comes.' Rumsden turned to see Sarah coming through into the reception area.

'Hello, Sarah,' Old Unusual greeted her. 'I think I've got something for you.'

'Hello, Unusual,' she replied. 'D'you want to come upstairs?'

'No, it'll do here. It won't take long.' He took a coin from his pocket and dropped it on to the counter.'

'Dud?' asked Sarah.

'Couldn't you hear it? I can feel it as well.'

'Don't tell me someone's passed one on you,' Rumsden said, disgusted.

'No, they didn't try to buy anything. It was dropped in my collecting box. But it was an accident. People don't usually try it on with blind men. Beggars, drunks, yes . . .'

'What?' Sarah said sharply.

'Beggars. I told you. People often give them foreign coins, tokens, you name it. They think it's a bit of a joke. Or maybe it's to impress a woman, or get a cheap thankyou.'

'Uhuh,' Sarah said, unimpressed.

'Ask the vicar how many fifty-centime pieces and German pfennings get into the plate. End of the summer holidays it's all pesetas.' He paused, and turned his sightless eyes directly on Sarah. 'I reckon the person who gave me this might be the person you're looking for.'

'What makes you think that?' she asked.

'Well, when I heard it drop in the box I said, "That sounds a bit funny. It could be one of the duds floating around." They were sort of taken off balance. Surprised.' He gave a quick intake of breath. 'Like that. Then they ran off.'

'So?' said Sergeant Rumsden sympathetically. 'That doesn't necessarily mean—'

'No.' Old Unusual shook his head. 'If it had been a genuine mistake, they'd have just said, "Is it? Oh, sorry. Let's have a look. If it is a dud, I'll give you another one." But they were surprised. Shocked. I could tell.'

Sarah believed him. 'You could well be right. Even if you are,

135

it doesn't help much. You can't tell us much about him.'

Old Unusual smiled. 'Don't make assumptions, Sarah, if you'll forgive me for saying so. First of all, it wasn't a him. *She* was about so tall . . .' – he held a hand up to about his own chin level – 'in shoes. A non-smoker; I can always smell stale tobacco smoke on people. She was young, was wearing flat heels.'

'How could you tell *that*?' Rumsden this time.

'The sound of her footsteps. Quick, firm steps, and definitely not high heels.' He paused, and smiled.

'Come on, Unusual,' Sarah said. 'I know you're dying for us to ask you. How do you know it was a she, and not a he?'

'She'd only just done her nails. I could smell her nail varnish. It was faint, but I could smell it all right.' He smiled with satisfaction. 'Ten out of ten?'

If – *if* – Old Unusual was right, Sarah reasoned, it drastically limited the area in which the counterfeit £1 coins originated, *if* the young woman who put one in the collection box was the manufacturer. She wouldn't have had time to go very far before the odour of her fresh nail varnish disappeared. *If* she was only an accomplice who was passing them for the actual maker she still must have set out only a little time before. Sarah didn't know the statistics, but it seemed improbable to her that there had been many female counterfeiters. When it came to passing the coins, though, a young woman would be far less of a suspect, particularly if she were attractive.

That's a hell of a lot of ifs, Sarah thought. And anyway, there's not much I can do about it while I'm on the murder enquiry.

The first of the turns for the worse came the next morning, soon after Timberlake got into the office. There was an expected phone call for him.

'That you, Harry?' came a familiar voice.

'Inspector or mister to you.'

The phone squawked as the caller at the other end laughed.

'Sorry, *sir*. Hey, why haven't you been to see me? What's the idea of putting that tailor's dummy on my wife's case?' asked Carl-Heinz Rohmer, a.k.a. Charles Henry Newman.

'Not my idea.'

'Come round and see me.'

Timberlake pondered this for a long moment. *Why*? he asked

136

himself. What was Newman up to? He looked round the room to make sure he wasn't being overheard. 'I can't. I'm off the case.'

'Not business. Just for a drink. Show there're no hard feelings.'

It would take a whack on the head with a lead pipe for Timberlake not to have hard feelings for Newman. Nevertheless, his curiosity to find out what the man was up to was too strong. 'I'll be there in half an hour.'

Newman must have found someone to come in and clean the house, which was almost back to its state when Veronica and her mother were alive. Newman was shaved and neatly dressed; Carole Pradet was fully clothed, for all the good that did. She exuded sensuality like a steaming kettle. Timberlake thought she looked much more sexy fully dressed.

It was a weird meeting. When she brought Timberlake a coffee she leaned over him as if she was going to blow in his ear and smiled. Newman didn't seem to notice.

The whole conversation was oblique, hinting at much more than was actually said. It had the formal politeness of duellists before they turned back to back and took twelve paces.

Then Timberlake understood. Newman was showing Timberlake that he was safe now, established in his wife's home, assimilated into local society . . . untouchable. He was quietly gloating, with finesse. He had won, and was taunting Timberlake with his failure. *That* was the point of the invitation, Timberlake was certain.

He was wrong.

Chapter 14

There weren't many places in Terrace Vale where you could have wholehearted outdoor nooky, even in a car, without being seen and attracting either applause or derision. The best place was a long, horseshoe-shaped, earth-surfaced road which left the main road and returned to it half a mile further on. It enclosed a group of allotments, playing fields and sports clubs. In one of its inspired flights of imagination the local council named it Playing Fields Lane. They probably had a heated debate and a vote on whether it should be called Allotment Lane. There were few lights, lots of trees and aptly named lay-bys.

Police cars rarely patrolled the lane, and when they did, they had their headlights on and their blue light flashing. It cleared the place up without lots of paperwork. Their arrival provoked muttered oaths, the sounds of clothes being hurriedly adjusted and groans of disappointment. There was the occasional muttered cry of 'Sod the police! Don't stop now!' Cars started up and raced off like the starting-line at Silverstone circuit.

This time, all except one.

'There's one up ahead,' PC Paddy Paterson said. He was driving a panda car with PC Herbert Fanshaw beside him. There was no reply from Fanshaw, who was turning over in his mind a problem that occasionally exercised him. If the name Featherstonehaugh was pronounced 'Fanshaw' in England, why wasn't Fanshaw pronounced 'Featherstonehaugh'? Although he had to admit to himself that Featherstonehaugh would be a rather heavy handle for a West Indian police constable.

'I said there's one up ahead,' Paterson repeated. He switched on full beam headlights. 'Might as well give 'em a chance to get away. I expect he's having trouble getting his cock back in his trousers.'

'I hope he hasn't caught anything important in his zip,' said Fanshaw, who was well known at the nick for being soft-hearted. Paterson, who wasn't, chuckled.

The approaching panda's headlights at last caught the unmoving car. It was a Volvo Estate, parked beside a tree, with its near side hard up against the hedge. Paterson eased the panda up behind it, leaving room for Fanshaw to get out his side. They waited a moment. The whole atmosphere had changed; there was something wrong. They could see no one in the vehicle.

'Maybe they're having some nooky away on the grass somewhere,' Fanshaw suggested. Neither of them believed it. They were both wondering whether it was a motor belonging to a gang of villains up to something near by.

Fanshaw used the radio to call Terrace Vale with the car's number and ask for a vehicle check. It hadn't been reported stolen, they were told, but it could have been nicked before the owner noticed.

Paterson slowly got out of the panda, carrying a large torch. He approached the estate car, and shone his torch through the large back window.

'Oh, Christ,' he muttered.

A woman lay in the back, her head towards the rear of the vehicle. Her eyes were wide open and her mouth was open wide for a scream she did not live long enough to make.

Harry had been seeing Lucinda Fordham a few times, taking her out to dinner, and once to the theatre. He was amused and interested by her show-biz anecdotes and fascinatingly scandalous backstage gossip about well-known actors and actresses. On this occasion he looked at her as she poured him a coffee, wondering whether or not to see how far he could take things. She returned his gaze, put down the coffee, came to him and kissed him gently, then fiercely, forcing her tongue into his mouth.

At two o'clock in the morning an insistent sound woke him. He continued to fumble for the bedside lamp which seemed to have moved, until he remembered that he wasn't in his own bed. He sat up and was just able to see the lamp by the light of the street lamps outside. He turned it on, revealing Lucinda's barely covered naked form beside him. It excited him as suddenly as if someone had touched a switch. She drowsily opened an eye, smiled, and made a move to get hold of him. Harry Timberlake avoided her hand without making a production of it, slid out of the bed, found his jacket, dug out his bleeper and switched it off.

He called Terrace Vale from the bedside telephone, and was patched through to Darren Webb on a car radio. 'Guv, there's been another one.' He gave the location.

By the time Timberlake got there one of the tents that are used for outdoor examinations of crime scenes was already in place. Brilliant lights inside it threw strange distorted shadows of the SOCOs on the walls, giving the whole scene the surreal air of an early German black and white film. Darren Webb and Dr Pratt came up to him.

'Much the same as the others, but more economical,' said Dr Pratt with determined cheerfulness. Timberlake gritted his teeth and gave the smile of a father whose young child has proudly announced that he can write: he has just written his name on the side of Daddy's car with his new penknife. He waited for Pratt's punchline. 'Just the one blow to the heart this time.'

'Death instantaneous?'

'Almost certainly. There's very little blood, and it doesn't look as if she moved around after she was stabbed.'

'How long has she been dead, d'you think?'

'About three hours, give or take an hour. That puts it between, say, half past nine and half past eleven.' In real life doctors don't say, 'He was killed between five to and five past ten...' Unless, of course, the victim was blown up in an explosion everyone heard, or the town hall clock fell on him with its hands stopped at 10.02.

There was movement among some SOCOs at the back of the Volvo. Lights were moved to a low level to shine along the ground, and photoflashes went off. One of the scientific officers was on his knees doing something at the roadside. 'What are they up to?' Timberlake asked Webb as he approached. He indicated a couple of men and a woman SOCOs searching the roadway and verges. From time to time they picked up something and put the object, whatever it was, into a plastic envelope with a label.

'They're collecting French letters. Condoms,' he added, as if Timberlake hadn't heard the expression before. 'One might be from whoever she was with. I mean, I shouldn't think she came down here to pick cabbages, or someone walked off with it in his pocket.'

140

Sergeant Burt Johnson, the chief SOCO, joined the group. 'As soon as the pathologist comes and does his stuff, we'll take the car off for examination.'

'Any identification on the body?'

'Nothing in her pockets, and there's no handbag. The car's registered to a Mrs Mary Cotter, a Terrace Vale address.'

Timberlake turned to Webb. 'Darren, give the nick a call and have them send someone round to tell the husband, or family, whoever it is.'

'Right, guv.'

'Any interesting tyre tracks?' Timberlake asked Johnson.

'I think so. A car came up behind the Volvo and parked about ten yards away, then moved off. The second car's tracks were made after the Volvo's.'

'Do they tell you anything else?'

'Oh, yes,' Johnson said with satisfaction. 'It was a Rolls or a Bentley. The tyres are unmistakable. We've also got a couple of good footprints of the driver.'

'Somebody with a Roller coming down here for a bonk?' Dr Pratt said with astonishment. 'Well, I hope he was gentleman enough to do it in his own car.'

'More room in the back of the Volvo with the seats down,' Sergeant Johnson said matter-of-factly. 'It's the modern passion wagon.'

Sarah Lewis left the house early the next morning. A girl of about fifteen, accompanied by a large mongrel who looked as if he had eaten an entire sheep for breakfast and was now ready for seconds, was stuffing her *Guardian* through the letterbox.

'Hello,' Sarah said brightly. The dog gave an unfriendly growl. 'Jason off sick?'

'Who?' asked the girl.

'Jason – Jason Horlock. He usually delivers my papers.'

'Oh, him,' the girl replied. 'He hasn't done it for a couple of months. He packed it in.'

She turned and walked off. The dog followed, stopped for a moment, looked back and regarded Sarah regretfully. But Sarah wasn't looking. She was wondering, What the hell . . .?

*

Terrace Vale nick was now turning into something like Heathrow departure lounge in high summer when Continental air traffic controllers have gone on strike. More bodies were drafted in from other areas, and another detective superintendent was sent in from Scotland Yard. Harkness was still in overall command of the four murder investigations, while Harry Timberlake was the senior detective on what the Press were calling the Screwdriver Murders.

The car registration computer gave Mary Cotter's address as Palmerston Crescent, a street of houses as diverse as squares on a patchwork quilt. Some of the buildings were silk, in a manner of speaking, others were worn cotton. To continue the image, No. 37, Mrs Cotter's house, was a pleasing, good-quality worsted.

The PC and WPC who had been sent round to break the news of her death reported that a next-door neighbour, roused by their knocking, rattily informed them she lived alone. Another neighbour, a woman who had seen the minor commotion outside No. 37, came out into the street in a nightdress that seemed to be made of a pre-war material called Thermogene, made to put on delicate chests suffering from bronchitis and colds. Over this she wore an RAF officer's old greatcoat. As the police officers were in shirt-sleeve order, this seemed rather excessive. She said she 'did' for Mrs Cotter, who had entrusted her with a set of keys.

Before entering the two uniformed officers wisely waited until Timberlake and Webb arrived.

Like the homes of Brenda Hardie and Jacqueline Clayton, Mary Cotter's home showed no signs of a robbery.

The testimony of her neighbours on Mary Cotter agreed on all major points. Before she was married she was a legal secretary. She gave up working when she was married, but had recently started work again after divorcing her husband. He had gone off to live with a computer operator employed at the pottery manufacturer's of which he was a partner. The operator was named Hector. Since her divorce Mary Cotter was famous for flinging up her heels – while lying on her back – with a number of men. There was more than a hint of envy in some of the accounts.

Mary got the house, the Volvo and a fat alimony settlement. She said she loved getting the regular cheques from her husband, while he apparently found forking out as pleasant as – to use a Ted Greening expression – as pissing hot coals.

It was as good a motive for murder as the AMIP team had heard for a long time. Harry Timberlake and Darren Webb rushed off to see Mr Randolph Cotter at his home in Ealing. Sadly for them he had a perfect alibi. At the time of the murder he was in a cell in the local nick. When stopped driving his Citroen Deux-Chevaux and asked to blow into the bag he practically melted it. At the station the doctor said he could have used his urine for anti-freeze.

So the detectives began checking on everyone in Mary Cotter's address book and diary. Timberlake had a small brainwave. 'Run all the names through the computer to see if anyone is a registered owner of a Roller, or works for a car hire firm or garage – you know the sort of thing.'

It was a bright idea.

But it didn't produce anything.

Although the manner of Mary Cotter's murder apparently was the same as the other two, Harry Timberlake decided to go to her post-mortem just in case something emerged that everyone had missed before. It didn't occur to him that he was being intellectually arrogant.

Dr Goodpasture – no relation of the late celebrated American virologist – performed the autopsy since Professor Mortimer was away lecturing. He was about forty-five and looked rather like a navvy, but he was deft and precise, almost delicate, in his work.

With none of Professor Mortimer's didactic delivery Goodpasture summarized his findings. 'In life she was healthy, with a history of an appendicectomy at the age of about twenty, a termination of a pregnancy five or so years later and a broken tibia ten to fifteen years ago. Death was almost instantaneous from the single blow to the heart.'

Not much help.

Sarah Lewis came out of the supermarket near the end of her road with some tins of food and passed in front of a rather superior toy and model shop. She stopped dead and returned to look hard in the window before going inside. She eventually managed to attract the attention of one of the assistants, who was talking and giggling with a colleague. Sarah achieved this by standing between the two young men and giving one a modified Harry Timberlake stare. His answers to her questions had Sarah leaving the shop with a look of satisfaction.

Next morning she went to Bob Farmer, explained the theory she had formulated the previous evening, and asked permission to apply for a search warrant. His smooth affability dripped away from him.

'Well,' he said dubiously. 'You know the rules these days.'

Sarah did. The Police and Criminal Evidence Act says that a constable applying to a justice of the peace must state (a) the grounds on which he makes the application, (b) the enactment under which the warrant would be issued; and (c) to identify, so far as is practicable, the articles or persons to be sought.

As far as (b) and (c) were concerned, she was on safe ground, and had what Americans would call 'just cause'. (a), however, was sticky. If she were to be honest, her grounds would be perilously close to a hunch, gut feeling or female intuition. There is another condition to be fulfilled in acquiring a search warrant. 'The constable shall answer on oath any question that the justice of peace or judge hearing the application asks him.'

It is, incidentally, a sexist Act. It refers to a constable as 'he' and 'him', without a mention of 'her'.

'Well,' Farmer repeated, 'on the strength of what you've just told me, I can't back you officially, much as I'd like to. I don't see a JP or judge falling for that. If you want to have a go off your own bat,' Farmer said, 'good luck to you. I'd like to see you pull it off.' He gave a smile which signalled that he was aware of the *double entendre.*

'Thanks, guv,' Sarah said. 'I know you would.' Keeping the acid out of her voice was an heroic achievement.

As she turned away, she shouted in her mind, 'And fuck you, Farmer.'

The breakthrough in the Mary Cotter case – and by association, with the Brenda Hardie and Jacqueline Clayton cases – came from the attendant on duty at an all-night petrol station half a mile up the main road from Playing Fields Lane.

Chapter 15

Sarah Lewis was pleasant to Sergeant Rumsden and he allowed her to take WPC Rosie Hall from the uniformed side with her. She planned to make her call at 12.59 p.m. Rosie asked what it was all about, but Sarah told her she'd tell her later. Sarah was feeling rather sick. The elation she had felt when she found the solution – she hoped – to her problem the previous evening had drained away like a drunk's courage in the morning. What she was about to do would cause a human tragedy. Although she was a detective, she was human, too; maybe more human than most.

She picked the time of a minute to one because Derek Horlock shut his shop for lunch at one. Customers wouldn't walk in on them.

Horlock knew something was wrong at once. It wasn't the sight of Rosie Hall's uniform: it was Sarah's face. He had been on the wrong side of the police before and he knew the signs. It was confirmed when Sarah turned the *Open* sign to show the *Closed* to the street. Horlock's mouth was a thin line.

'Hello,' Sarah said heavily. 'I'm sorry about this. D'you mind if I have a look round?'

'There's nothing here. I told you. I've given it up.'

'Then you won't mind my looking.'

'You got a warrant?'

'No. I can send WPC Hall to get one. It'll only take half an hour.' She hoped he didn't know about getting a warrant.

Horlock's shoulders drooped. 'Like I said last time, you lot never let go, do you? Well, go on. Look. I just told you. There's nothing.'

'Not here,' Sarah said. She led the way through the back room of the shop past Horlock's little work area for his clockmaking and repairs, across the yard into the shed. Jason was working on another racing car, a Benetton-Ford. He looked up, and when he saw Sarah with the uniformed WPC he turned pale.

There was only one way to do it, and Sarah hardened her heart. 'Where are they, Jason?' she asked. 'The materials?'

'What are you talking about?' said Horlock from behind her. Sarah ignored him.

'Where, Jason?'

His face turned the colour of dirty snow. He couldn't move or speak.

She watched his eyes and began her search under a workbench. From behind some broken boxes and sacking she dragged out a primus stove and a heavy cast-iron pot. Not far from them was a large biscuit tin. It rattled as she picked it up. Inside were maybe twenty old threepenny pieces. 'Where's the mould, Jason?' He couldn't speak, but once again his eyes betrayed him.

Sarah went to a model of a Jaguar Mark IX saloon. It wasn't like the other hand-made cars: it was a commercial DIY kit sold by model shops. The car was in two parts. She lifted off the roof. The roof section and the car had two halves of moulds of £1 coins.

There was a muted cry of anguish, quickly suppressed, from Derek Horlock. 'All right, Miss Lewis. You've got me.'

'No, Mr Horlock. It was Jason.'

'No, it was me!'

'Where did you pass the coins? Tell me two places where you passed them.' Horlock held his head in his hands. Sarah turned to Jason. 'When did you make them? In the mornings when your dad was at market and you were supposed to be delivering papers?'

He nodded. 'Dad didn't know.' He looked at the tin of threepenny pieces. 'I was going to stop when I'd used up that last lot. I just wanted to be able to go out with my mates and . . .' He couldn't finish. Then, 'How did you know?'

'First, I noticed an outfit for making moulds – toys, model galleons – things like that, in a toy and model shop. It was next to some model cars. Then there was Old Unusual. When you dropped a coin in his collecting box he heard it was a dud. But he thought you were a woman, because he said he smelt nail varnish. Then I remembered I'd smelt something very much like nail varnish in here. Your cellulose.'

'Miss Lewis,' Derek Horlock said pleadingly, but she ignored him. Her voice was unrecognizable when she said, 'Jason Horlock,

I am arresting you . . .' and the rest of the caution.

She knew only too well that two lives were wrecked. Jason would now have a criminal record, the son of a convicted criminal, his future next to hopeless. His father would be inconsolable and racked with remorse he didn't deserve to suffer.

Irrationally, for it was her heart and not her head that was dominating, for the moment Sarah hated herself and the stinking job.

It was two days after the discovery of Mary Cotter's body that Sebastian Mutter called in at Terrace Vale nick, asked for CID and said he might have information about the Rolls Royce that was in Playing Fields Lane. With the first bit of luck he'd had since he was on the Screwdriver Murders, Timberlake happened to be in the building. He rushed down the stairs as fast as if the man from the football pools was waiting there with a cheque.

Sebastian Mutter was twenty-one years old and a student, he informed Timberlake, Darren Webb – and, according to custom, a uniformed PC, presumably there to see fair play. Mutter looked suspiciously at the policemen when he gave his name. He still hadn't come to terms with people making fun of it, and to avoid the obvious would-be funny remark, he spoke in a loud, clear tone as if addressing a conference of hard-of-hearing delegates.

'Interesting, that,' Timberlake said to put the young man at his ease. 'How the traits of your ancestors have persisted in you. The name "Mutter" comes from "Someone who speaks at the moot. A public speaker." Of course, you knew that.'

Sebastian Mutter looked at Timberlake with his eyes wide open behind his granny glasses, his jaw slack. 'Yeah,' he said eventually. He went on to explain that he hadn't come in before because he'd read the police request for any information only that morning. 'I don't see the papers much,' he said, his voice suddenly going quiet in mid-sentence as he remembered the origins of his name.

'I do night duty at the filling station up the main road from Playing Fields Lane. Student grants don't go far. Well, that night a Rolls Royce came in and filled up, and—'

'What time was this?'

'Just after eleven. I was listening to the radio and the eleven o'clock news had started a couple of minutes earlier.'

'Can you describe the driver? Was it a man?'

'I can do better than that. I'll draw him for you. I'm an art student.'

'Get someone to find a sketch pad for Mr Mutter,' Timberlake told Webb. He turned back to Mutter. 'Did he pay cash, or with a credit card?'

Mutter laughed. 'You any idea how much petrol one of those mobile gin palaces take? He paid by credit card. A gold one, of course.'

'With oak leaves and diamonds, no doubt,' said Timberlake. DC Wishart, who was interested in World War II uniforms and decorations, was the only person who knew what his Inspector was talking about.

'Can you remember the name on the card?' Timberlake continued.

'Only his Christian name. Sebastian. And his car had a personalized number. SF something. I always put the car's registration on the slip, in case.'

From then on it was all downhill basic routine. Darren Webb and another detective went to the filling station and went through the counterfoils of credit forms.

They came up with the name of Sebastian Frewin, and a check of the car registration came up with a home address in Greybridge, in the heart of the stockbroker belt. But when they rang his home and his wife gave them his address in town, it made them all think twice. It was at an Inn – not an inn, but an *Inn*.

Sebastian Frewin QC was a highly successful lawyer specializing in commercial cases. Criminals couldn't afford him, unless they were five-star embezzlers who'd manage to salt away millions in Leichtenstein, Luxemburg or the Caymans. Apart from his disgustingly high fees, his 'refreshers' or subsequent daily rates were more than £1,000.

The unlikely appearance of Sebastian Frewin in the frame as the number one suspect, at least for the time being, didn't mean that the squad sat on their hands until he was interviewed. By now they had turned up Mary Cotter's address book and diary, and they had begun interviewing the people in it. Frewin himself didn't figure in either of the books. Whether this was of any significance or not it was too early to tell. Harkness, who had been listening to Timberlake's report, thought for a moment before sending Darren Webb to check on something. Timberlake mentally kicked himself for not thinking of it first.

A few of the people who were in cars parked in Playing Fields Lane at the time came forward, persuaded by the police promise of confidentiality. Inevitably they had seen very little: at the time their attention was understandably on personal matters.

As in the Brenda Hardie case, there was a fairly accurate time for when the murder was committed, so many of the people in the books could provide solid alibis, which at least cut down the follow-up work.

Frewin said he was too busy to see Timberlake in town, but agreed to 'receive' him – Frewin's word – at his home in Greybridge that evening.

When the two detectives were almost due to set off for Greybridge Webb had not reappeared from the job Harkness had given him. He arrived, breathless. 'The super was dead right, guv.' Timberlake's smile looked more like a shark preparing to bite.

Frewin's house was a large stockbroker-Tudor building, with a finely-raked gravel drive and a lawn that looked like green Velcro. A few birds were twittering politely in the chestnut trees. Frewin himself met them at the door. Sebastian's drawing of him turned out to be quite good. He was a man of medium height, large girth and multiple chins. He was wearing a silk smoking jacket. He led them into his study, which could have served as a set for an early Cecil B. de Mille film. He did not offer them anything to drink. Webb decided he didn't like Frewin. Timberlake loathed him. He decided to come out fighting.

He began by touching gloves. 'Mr Frewin, you may have read of the murder of a Mary Cotter in Terrace Vale three nights ago.'

'Yes.'

'Can you tell me why you stopped twelve yards behind her car in your Rolls Royce, registration number SF . . .' – he gave the full number – 'got out, subsequently returned to your own car and drove off, past Mrs Cotter's Volvo?'

Frewin was good. He took a cigar from a humidor, went through a ritual that was positively Japanese, and lit it.

Timberlake was good too. He sat motionless, staring at Frewin.

'On what evidence do you base those allegations?'

'Did you know Mary Cotter?'

'I'm afraid the name doesn't mean anything to me.'

'Odd. She was a secretary in your chambers before you moved from Harcourt Buildings.'

This time there was a tremor from Frewin. 'Of course. I'd forgot-

149

ten her surname. I was always informal with her: I simply called her Mary.' Frewin gave the impression of being as informal as the Grand Chamberlain at Chinese Imperial Court. He was very good. 'You didn't answer my question, Inspector. On what evidence do you base these allegations?'

Timberlake countered with a rhetorical question of his own. 'You will, of course, have no objection to allowing us to take casts of the tyres of your car and of the soles of your shoes?' When Frewin said nothing: 'You are aware, I'm sure, of the procedures in murder cases. The interior of Mrs Cotter's car is being minutely examined at the Metropolitan Police Forensic Science Laboratory' – he rolled out its full title – 'and anyone who was inside the vehicle will have left traces. Oh, yes. We shall ask your permission – to start with – to take away your clothes for examination.'

There was a long, long silence. Frewin got up, walked to the door, opened it and closed it again.

'I shall be frank with you, Inspector.'

'That is always best, sir,' Timberlake replied, with the solicitous tone of the executioner asking if the rope was comfortable.

'You are a man of the world . . .'

'I am a policeman. And I often use the Clapham omnibus.' Webb asked himself what the hell Timberlake was talking about, but the lawyer knew.

'Indeed. I must ask you to keep this confidential, and let it go no further.'

'I can't make such promises, as you well know.'

'No, I suppose not. Very well. I shall have to rely on your goodwill. Mary Cotter was my occasional mistress. We met . . . well, in circumstances like those you know of. It was always difficult for us to find somewhere, and Mary seemed to enjoy the . . . excitement . . . of that sort of encounter.'

'I see. What happened on the night she was killed?'

'She telephoned me at my chambers on my direct line and made a rendezvous with me, for nine-thirty. We had been there before. She was there already. I got into her car and we . . .' He made a vague gesture. 'Afterwards I drove off. When I left her she was alive.'

'Did you pay her?'

'Good heavens, no. I . . . gave her occasional presents. But I didn't *pay*.'

'I'm not asking out of prurient interest,' Timberlake said, again leaving Webb looking puzzled. 'I wanted to know if she was acting as a prostitute.'

'Certainly not with me.'

'One final thing – for the moment, Mr Frewin. Can you tell me where you were on these two evenings?' He gave the dates of the murders of Brenda Hardie and Jacqueline Clayton.

Frewin produced a massive leather-bound diary the size of a mediaeval Bible. 'On the first date I was having dinner with the Westerhams. On the second . . . I was in Birmingham where I had been speaking at a dinner given for a retiring barrister.' Webb noted down the details.

'I shall check, as discreetly as possible,' Timberlake said.

It didn't seem to cheer Frewin up.

'D'you think he did it, guv?'

'Absolutely not. I never did.'

'What? Why not?'

'If he'd killed her, he wouldn't have stopped for petrol half a mile away in that bloody great car, and paid with a credit card. But he had to be checked.' He paused. 'God, can you imagine that overstuffed, pompous pig in the back of a Volvo brake, his trousers round his ankles, puffing and panting as he tries . . .' He shook his head. 'There's no understanding some women.'

'There's no understanding any of them,' Webb said gloomily.

After five minutes' driving Timberlake said, 'Fancy something to eat?'

'I'm starving, guv! I could even manage one of my mother-in-law's shepherd's pies.'

'There's a pub that does decent meals about a mile up.'

'I think I can last that long.'

The pub was quite full and fairly noisy. Timberlake, who had very strong feelings on the subject – as he did on many topics – hoped that the noisiest and most uninhibited of the diners weren't the drivers of the cars in the packed car park.

'Would you like a drink, Darren? I'm going to have a designer water, or something.' As they approached the bar Timberlake thought he recognized a blonde woman with her back to him. She was talking to a good-looking man of about his own height, and making him laugh. When Timberlake was about two paces from her she turned round.

Harry Timberlake almost stopped dead, but recovered quickly enough to make it look as if he had slipped a little.

'Hello, Jenny,' he said in a level voice that surprised him.

'Hello, Harry,' replied Dr Jenny Long. She had done her hair differently from the last time he had seen her, otherwise he would have recognized her instantly, even from the back. All at once he was back in his flat, faced by Jenny and Sarah Lewis, who was wearing only a small towel. Jenny, his mistress of two years, had presented him with a modern-day version of the Judgement of Paris. She had put the front door key he had given her on the table and told him to choose which one of the two women he was going to give it to.

He had chosen Sarah. Now, as he looked at her, he wondered if he had done the right thing. He was a mass of conflicting emotions which left him unable to think of anything to say.

'Are you all right?' she asked.

'Fine.' *No I'm not*, he shouted inside his head. *I don't know how the hell I am.*

'This is a friend of mine, Dr Clennell ... John, this is Harry Timberlake.'

The two men shook hands.

Timberlake introduced Darren Webb.

'Are you going to eat here?' Clennell asked politely. 'Perhaps we could share a table?'

'No thanks. We just stopped in for a quick drink. We have to get back to town.' Webb said nothing. Jenny looked at Timberlake as if she were going to say something, but didn't speak. The two detectives got their drinks and moved away. Timberlake drained his in one go. Webb drank his pint of beer as quickly as he could.

Back in the car he asked, 'What was that about, guv?'

'Nothing,' Timberlake replied in a tone that put the stopper on any more conversation.

The AMIP murder squad's best suspect for the triple murders, Sebastian Frewin, was taken out of the frame when his alibis were confirmed for the nights of the first two murders. All three were obviously done by the same hand, so his elimination from the first two effectively cleared him of the third. They were back to square one, with no obvious line of enquiry to pursue.

Harkness called a meeting of the entire personnel of the three murder squads. First, they reviewed the progress so far, which didn't take very long. So, where did they go from there?

'Superficially there could appear to be some similarities between these murders and the previous multiple murders that took place here a couple of years ago. In fact, they are quite different. The last series were committed in different ways: killing with a motor vehicle, with a crossbow, with a shotgun, and an attempted murder with an explosive device.

'They had nothing in common, but the crimes were solved because Inspector Timberlake discovered what it was all the victims had in common. This time we can be certain that the same person committed the murders.'

No one realized it, but Harkness was wrong.

'What we still have to discover is what these three women had in common. Ideas?'

'All single, – unmarried, divorced, or widowed.'

'All much about the same age.'

'None of them had a steady, ongoing relationship with a man – or woman for that matter,' offered DC Peabody, unfairly known to his colleagues as 'Peabrain'. Harkness and Timberlake both suppressed a mental shudder at his use of the word 'ongoing'.

'Maybe they were all subscribers to a dating agency,' Darren Webb said, surprising himself.

'Well done, Darren,' Harkness said, which was worth more than a Mention in Dispatches. 'You can start on that line today.'

'The murder weapon, the similarities between the women – age, background . . . Is there enough there for a criminal psychologist to give us something of a profile of the criminal?' Timberlake asked.

'I'll arrange for us to have a conference with one tomorrow. Anything else? Right, then. Back to work.'

There was a message on Timberlake's answerphone when he got home. Lucinda Fordham was reminding him that it was Wednesday, and offering him a meal at Chez Fordham, with a mysterious special treat. It took him something like two seconds to make up his mind. Sarah had said she wanted an early night at home, and he didn't want to be on his own. 'I'm on my way,' he told Lucinda, 'just as soon as I phone for a taxi.' He didn't want to worry about having a drink, or two.

It was with more than mild surprise that he saw the inside of her flat when she opened the door to him. The centrepiece of the room was a small table handsomely laid for dinner for two, with white tablecloth, candles and flowers. He was irresistibly reminded of scenes in 1950s movies where the handsome bounder invited the unsuspecting heroine to dinner in his apartment or hotel suite. The roles were reversed this time though. Still, it was the age of female equality.

Lucinda was dressed in a dark silk robe that looked vaguely Japanese. It set off her mid-brown hair and *bleu céleste* eyes to perfection. She looked animated and happy . . . yet she could never lose completely her air of vulnerability and wistfulness.

'I hope you don't mind a cold meal,' she said, 'but I didn't want to cook anything in case you couldn't come.'

'So much the better. It's warm tonight.'

'And the forecast is it's going to get warmer.' Smiling, she added, 'That's not the Met Office's forecast. It's mine.'

The meal astounded him. Oysters – 'They've been in deep freeze since April' – lobster, chicken in aspic and profiteroles. There was a bottle of Möet et Chandon champagne – 'If it was good enough for Toulouse-Lautrec it's good enough for me.' 'But it left him legless.' – and Rémy Martin brandy.

Halfway through the meal Timberlake said worriedly, 'This must have cost you a fortune!'

'Forget it, darling. Yesterday I got a big fat residual cheque.'

'What the hell's that?'

'You'd call it a royalty. It's for overseas transmissions of our show: Australia and New Zealand, Canada no less, Hong Kong, British Forces in Germany, M6 in France . . . Oh, yes, and Malta. I think that came to £3.40.'

Later, as the post coitus tristus began to chill him, he looked at the back of her head as she lay on her side next to him. It could not make him forget another, blonder, head. He knew now why he had accepted the invitation. It was a mistake, a bad mistake. It was like drinking to try to forget you're an alcoholic.

Chapter 16

The criminal psychologist arrived with the modern young psychologist's full kit. He wore a linen jacket, blue shirt and cravat; he had a small beard, a bald spot (an optional extra) and he smoked a pipe, which he regarded from time to time as if it were a crystal ball. He even had a faint middle-European accent. Timberlake suspected it was issued with his diploma.

'I have studied the reports carefully, and I think I can be fairly confident of the murderer's psychological profile, and to some extent, his physical appearance.' He waved a folder containing several typewritten sheets. 'I have made a full report. To save time I shall briefly summarize my conclusions.

'The first significant factor is his choice of the weapon: a long screwdriver, or screwdriver-like instrument. This is clearly phallic. Murders of women with knives and penetrating weapons almost invariably have a strong sexual motivation, conscious or subconscious. In a *series* of murders, all with the same penetrating weapon, the sexual element is absolutely certain.' He seemed fond of the word 'penetrating'.

'Well, they were all women,' Sergeant Bailey said.

'Of course. But there are many motives for killing women, and many methods of doing it,' the psychologist said sharply. 'Now, let us consider the victims themselves. First, they were all of more or less middle age. Second, they were all single, unmarried or divorced. One was an authoritative woman; one was, according to all reports, a woman who had many sexual experiences.

'The conclusion is irresistible: when he kills, this man is killing his mother, who dominated him when he was a child. It is probable that his father was absent from the family home: perhaps he died, or more likely, he deserted his wife and child because of his wife's promiscuity and/or dominating behaviour.

155

'Given the ages of the victims, the man you are looking for is in his thirties; he is a loner, physically insignificant, introverted and timid in public. He has had no real relationships with women, towards whom he has an ambivalent attitude. He despises them, yet at the same time he has sexual feelings for them. Finally, if he has a job it is a menial one.'

'Why did he take their handbags?' asked Webb.

'It is quite common for this kind of criminal to keep something of his victims. The modern "civilized" version of scalping. They most probably have some significance from his early life.'

'What about the fact that all the blows were scientifically delivered to be almost immediately fatal?' Timberlake asked, trying to sound as polite as he could.

'Something he could have learned from a book or books,' the psychologist replied dismissively. 'He could even be a hospital porter, an attendant in a morgue, something of that nature. I'm sorry, gentlemen, I have to go. A lecture at the university. It's all in my report.' He bustled out self-importantly.

Harry Timberlake was doing his paperwork at his desk when the phone rang. It was Newman again.

'I told you not to ring me,' Timberlake said. If anyone in the office was listening they would probably think it was some woman. Sarah, who was sitting at her typewriter, suddenly stopped hitting the keys and stared at the paper in the machine.

'It's important,' Newman said. 'Something's happened.'

'Well, it's nothing to do with me.'

'I'm not going to talk to that *arsch*, that *lèche-cul flagorneur* Farmer. He's not a cop; he's a politician. You coming round, or not?'

'All right. Later.'

Timberlake had his share of the men in Mary Cotter's address book to interview, and he got on with that job before calling on Newman. There wasn't so much as a sniff of a lead from any one of them.

He took his time going to The Sycamores Avenue. He wanted to mull over the business of the women's missing handbags. He wasn't thrilled with the psychologist's explanation but he had none better himself.

Then there was Newman. He couldn't figure out what he was up to. Oh, he probably wants another chance to crow, Timberlake told himself. It didn't seem likely, somehow.

Like all superior detectives Timberlake was sensitive to atmosphere, to vibes. Outwardly Newman was settling into the role of a
well-to-do man of independent means, but although he convincingly
acted the bluff, hospitable host and Carole Pradet looked the lang-
uid voluptuary there was definitely a hidden tension about them.

Timberlake said nothing, allowing the tension to intensify. Eventually Newman said, 'We've been getting threatening phone calls.'

'What sort?'

'A man, obviously disguising his voice.' He paused. 'It *might* be
a woman.'

'What sort of threats? What did he say?'

' "Enjoying it there, are you? Make the most of it. I'm going to
get you, Newman".'

'That's it? Some joker with a warped sense of humour, that's all.'

'He called more than once. And it was no joker. Believe me, he
meant it. To tell you the truth, a couple of times I even thought it
might be you.'

'No. I'm telling you to your face: I'll get you in the end. I'm
surprised at you, Newman. I'm surprised a few nasty telephone calls
can frighten you.'

'I thought you were a good detective. You don't get it, do you? I
can take care of myself. But the calls mean that someone's got a
grudge against me because they expected to get this house. Maybe
they expected to marry Veronica, and that's why she wanted a
divorce; or hoped that she'd leave the place to them.

'*I'm not the only one with a motive for wanting Veronica dead.*'

Timberlake reported the conversation to Harkness, who wasn't
pleased that he had seen Newman. 'Why did he ask to see you, and
not Inspector Farmer?'

Timberlake noticed that Harkness hadn't called him 'Farmer' or
'Bob Farmer'. 'I think it was because I originally had the case. He
doesn't seem to have any empathy with him.'

'Yes. Well, pass it on to Inspector Farmer and make out your
report.' He paused. 'What's your feeling about it?'

'I don't know. I simply don't know.'

Harkness sighed. 'Well, I suppose we'd better start looking for this
mysterious caller. We don't have any better leads at the moment.'

Timberlake managed to keep himself from saying, 'You won't
have. Newman did it.'

*

157

The next morning Timberlake woke early, soon after five, feeling unexpectedly fresh and not uncheerful. He knew he wouldn't be able to get to sleep again so he quietly left Sarah, who was sleeping heavily. He was tempted to wake her gently and perhaps pick up again where they had left off the previous night, but decided against it, reluctantly. He arrived at the nick at 6.30 a.m. and was surprised to find Superintendent Harkness and his bag-carrier, Sergeant Braddock, there already.

'How did you know?' Harkness asked.

'Know what?'

'That there's been another one. Isn't that why you're in early?'

'No. I couldn't sleep, that's all.'

'It came in on the teleprinter and the duty sergeant phoned me. There's been another one. Same stabbing with a screwdriver, same sort of victim, although this one's married. Her name was Helen Strudwick.'

'Oh, God. Where was it?'

'Bexport. In East Sussex. I had a word with the chief super at the Yard' – he was referring to the detective chief superintendent in overall command of all the AMIP teams – 'and he's told them you're coming down to liaise with them. It's their case, of course,' he added warningly. 'A Chief Inspector Galloway is in charge. And, er, the woman was murdered two days ago.'

Timberlake stared at him. 'And we've only just been told?'

Harkness shrugged. 'Minor breakdown in communications, I assume. I've already called your Sergeant Webb. He's on his way in.'

The Bexport main police station was a handsome new building which managed to make Timberlake and Webb feel slightly shabby and wondering whether they'd shaved properly. Chief Inspector Galloway kept them waiting, probably deliberately. The two Terrace Vale men were aware that in provincial forces there was an underlying resentment of officers from the Met. Provincial paranoia, which operates in all walks of life, made the local men feel that Met officers felt themselves superior, cleverer and probably more handsome with it; that they were coming to show the yokel noddies how to do things. Which was not true, of course. At least, not totally.

Galloway was a prematurely white-haired man who looked like someone who had spent all his life in a cellar, eating. He could have

158

played the Abominable Snowman with little makeup, but his dark button eyes were bright and shrewd.

Timberlake was unusually diplomatic and conciliatory. 'It's good of you to let us come down, and we'll be grateful for any help you can give us, Chief Inspector,' he said. Galloway looked at him, and at that moment a uniformed constable came in with three cups of tea.

'Watch out there, Tom,' Galloway said. 'Pile of bullshit in the corner.' He smiled as he said it. 'Plenty of sugar in teas?' He spoke as if words were money and he was mean.

The constable nodded. Timberlake hated sugar in tea, but he swallowed it bravely.

'What we've got so far,' Galloway said. 'Victim a Mrs Helen Strudwick, age fifty-two. Seems she was killed with two blows of screwdriver or similar, in her garage. Apparently got out of her car and closed the garage door, then she was stabbed. The daily found her next morning.'

'In our three cases the handbag was stolen,' Timberlake said.

'Hers still with her, but there's a door from the garage directly into the house.' He paused, waiting for the next question, but Timberlake guessed he already knew what it was. 'Daily said nothing stolen as far as she could tell. Place didn't look as if it'd been turned over.'

'Same pattern as ours. What about the husband? Where was he at the time?'

'In hospital. Well, sort of. Drying out. He'd been there for forty-eight hours. He was sedated, with nurses looking in on him every half hour.'

Galloway coughed, took a great gulp of tea, making a noise like a small lavatory flushing.

'However, we learned last night that the victim was the mistress of Jerome Holworth for the past twenty-five years. Address . . .' He passed a piece of paper to Timberlake.

'That's right near our patch,' Timberlake said, surprised. 'Would you like me to interview him for you?'

'We'll both see him,' Galloway said. 'Day in town for me.' He looked at his watch. 'Post-mortem in an hour. Want to come?'

'I don't think so, thanks,' Timberlake said.

Darren Webb tried to hide his delight. 'See one, see 'em all,' he said inaccurately.

159

'I'd appreciate a copy of the pathologist's report, though.'

'Bring it with me when I come up,' Galloway promised.

'What I should like, if it's possible, Chief Inspector, is to have a look at the woman's home.'

'We've got time.' He made for the door.

The Strudwick home was unexceptional, and not particularly tidy – not unexpectedly, for Galloway explained that Mrs Strudwick had to work and did a job and a half. She worked in an insurance office during the day, and did occasional evening turns as a driver for a women-only minicab service. One of the Strudwicks at least was a high-fi and television enthusiast; there was some quality electronic equipment in the house.

There was a small desk, untidy with papers and letters.

'Been through all that,' Galloway said. But there was something that caught Timberlake's interest, although he kept it to himself. There was an advertising brochure which struck a distant bell. He made a note of the details. These days he was scratching around for anything.

The first thing Timberlake and Webb did on returning to London was to go round to Jerome Holworth's address near Royalty Embankment, the scene of one of Timberlake's more frantic adventures when he was trying to get to a delayed-action bomb before it went off. This time he drove like a little old lady on her way to a jumble sale.

As they turned on to the Embankment, they could see police cars and an ambulance grouped near one of the houses.

'What number is our man?' Timberlake asked.

Webb looked in his pocket book. 'Seven.'

'Must be quite near all that . . .' The two men looked at each other.

'You don't think—' Webb began. But they both did, and were right. The commotion was at Number 7.

They knew that there was a death involved when the ambulance drove away with no passenger in it. Ambulances don't take corpses. Undertakers' cars and vans do that.

Timberlake stopped the car as near to the scene as he could. Before a uniformed constable could tell him to move on he showed his warrant card and introduced himself. 'Who's the body?' he asked.

'A Mr Holworth, I believe, sir.'

'It would be. Who's in charge?'

'Detective Sergeant Troy, sir.'

Timberlake thanked him and, followed by Webb, went into the house to find DS Troy. With exophthalmic eyes caused by a seriously over-active thyroid gland he was a man who looked permanently frightened or astonished. He was as spare as a dry twig and perspiring much more than the temperature warranted. Timberlake explained his interest in Holworth and his link with Helen Strudwick.

'Well, you're too late. He's snuffed it. He's done the Dutch, put out his lights.' In case the other two detectives still hadn't grasped what he meant, Troy added, 'Killed himself.'

'How?'

'In his car. Tube from the exhaust through the top of a window.'

'There's no chance it was arranged?' Webb suggested.

'Very unlikely. Besides, he left a note, handwritten.'

'Does his wife have any idea why?' Timberlake asked.

'She reckons it was because his other woman was killed. The wife's a bit of a hard case, as calm and collected as you like. Not a tear, not a sniff. Well, not surprising, I suppose, if it's as you say, he'd been knocking off the other bit of stuff for donkey's years.'

'Mind if I have a word with Mrs Holworth?'

'For all the good it'll do you. Be my guest.'

The widow could hardly be called 'grieving'. If Ted Greening had been there he would have recognized the type at once: she could have been Mrs Marjorie Greening's sister, tight lips and all. She answered Timberlake's questions economically, without taking the trouble to ask why he wanted to know about her husband. He was sixty-two years old, and an investment counsellor in the City, she said. When it came to cataloguing his movements she was able to give a full timetable over the period of Helen Strudwick's murder, except for when he was at his office. Timberlake was certain that the people he worked with would be able to confirm his alibi – and the next morning he was proved right. Everybody's got a bloody alibi, these days, he grumbled to himself.

Anyway, he didn't believe that Holworth had killed his mistress, but even dead certainties had to be checked and double-checked.

Timberlake promised to let Sergeant Troy have any information he got from Bexport, and forced him to agree to keep him in touch with any developments at this end. He didn't think there would be any. Troy wasn't going to put himself out to dig up any new ones. He had already wrapped this one up in his own mind.

Just before he left Timberlake asked the sergeant one more question. 'If anything else turns up I have to verify, you won't mind if I see Mrs Holworth again?' He made it sound casual and unlikely.

'Guv,' Darren Webb said, 'hadn't we better tell Chief Inspector Galloway not to bother to come up to interview Holworth?'

'No. He wouldn't thank you. He wants his day in town.'

These two new deaths provoked a lot of discussion among the AMIP squads at Terrace Vale. The majority opinion was that Jerome Holworth's suicide was no more than what appeared on the surface: the sad act of a man who killed himself because the woman he loved was dead. The fact that she was a Screwdriver Murder victim was merely one of those coincidences that are sent to make life difficult for the police.

'There's one possibility,' Timberlake suggested. 'This fourth murder wasn't committed by the same person who did the others. It was a deliberate copycat murder done that way to put us off line.'

'Or,' Webb said diffidently. 'Or . . . No, it's too over the top.'

'Let's hear it,' said Harkness.

'Well, suppose, I mean, supposing the first three murders were simply cover for the real motive and the real victim.'

Nobody dropped a pin. Timberlake said eventually, 'Life copying fiction? Possible . . . After all, the first three were all local, and the fourth in Sussex.' Webb looked relieved. Timberlake went on, 'I think we'd better have another word with Mrs Holworth.'

Timberlake found a closer look at the Holworth home in daylight illuminating. The late Jerome Holworth must have been a good investment counsellor and followed his own advice. The inside of the Royalty Embankment house was as luxurious as any of the upmarket Terrace Vale homes. It made him wonder if money was a common factor in all the murders.

Mrs Matilda Holworth didn't seem to be quite the same woman as the one he had met the other night. Although she was still firm-lipped and self-possessed, she was less daunting a figure. She was a nearly handsome, rather than a nearly beautiful woman, wearing no makeup. She explained that she met her husband when they were both students at Oxford. 'He was up at The House. That's—'

'Christ Church. I know,' Timberlake said.

'I was at Somerville, reading Greats.' She was about to explain what Greats were, but could see that Timberlake knew. She went on about her early life with her husband, then stopped suddenly. 'I'm sorry. This isn't what you came to see me about. Unfortunately this . . . situation is inclined to make one garrulous and nostalgic. I suppose you want to know whether I was aware of my husband's relationship with Helen Strudwick. Oh, yes. He admitted it – boasted – when I learned of it. He was quite cruel – mentally, not physically. *Proprium humani ingenii est odisse quem laeseris.*'

'Yes. "It's human nature to hate the man – or woman – you have wronged",' Timberlake agreed. 'So why didn't you ask for a divorce?'

'I had a comfortable life, and I didn't have to put up with my husband's gross sexual fumblings.' She stared directly at Timberlake and then at Webb, who looked away uncomfortably. 'And I wasn't going to let his strumpet take my place here. Now, you'll want to know where I was on the night the Strudwick woman was murdered.' She gave him a piece of paper. 'That's the local GP. I was cramming his daughter.'

Webb looked puzzled. 'Cramming?'

'Intensive coaching for an exam,' Timberlake told him.

'We could do with some of that,' Webb said.

The two detectives were writing their reports when Timberlake stopped and said, 'I'd nearly forgotten.' He got out his pocketbook. 'There was a brochure on the Strudwick woman's desk: Diana Huntress Ltd. It rang a bell.'

'Yes, guv. That was the travel agency where Brenda Hardie booked for herself and her woman friend Sandra Something. Diana Huntress Ltd.'

'Diana Huntress?' came a voice from across the room. PC Pegg was approaching them. 'That's the agency where there was a blagging about three weeks ago.'

'What was taken?' Timberlake asked, suddenly alert.

'That's the funny thing. Nothing. We had it down as a burglary, but I suppose it was breaking and entering, really.'

'The agency links Brenda Hardie, Helen Strudwick and a burglary . . . Peggy, you're a jewel!' said Timberlake.

'Could be a coincidence, guv,' Webb said cautiously.

'I don't believe in coincidences.' This was a blatant lie, and Timberlake knew it, for every intelligent man is aware that in life there can be absolutely extraordinary coincidences.

'What else have we got? Come on, Darren. We're going to meet the Huntress woman.'

Diana Huntress's real name was Hunter, but she insisted on the female version to underline the classical connection. She looked about forty years old, but had spent a great deal of money to erase ten years from her appearance. In a film she would be played by a young Joan Crawford, only six inches taller.

She was something between a *Vogue* and a *Cosmopolitan* model of the efficient woman executive; her short hair had obviously been cut by someone extremely expensive. In view of the average age of her clients, she seemed to have overlooked that Diana was a goddess of, among other things, all very young things.

She led them into her private office. She probably didn't want men cluttering up the place where women clients would see them. The Diana Huntress agency, she explained, specialized in planned trips – she would have been aghast at the use of the expression 'package tours' – mainly for women on their own, although not exclusively so.

'There are women who are not looking for short-time adventures' – she made it sound quite repulsive – 'and want to be able to travel with a group of congenial women without being badgered and pestered by men.' Timberlake couldn't imagine many men being rash enough to importune Ms Huntress. 'There are also financial advantages for such groups,' she pressed on. 'Hotels appreciate that women do not get drunk, disturb other guests, break things and leave disgusting messes behind them, and fix their prices accordingly.'

'Very interesting,' Timberlake said when Ms Huntress paused for breath. 'I understand you had a break-in recently, and—'

'Oh, God, not *that* again. I explained everything at the time—'

Timberlake knew he had to be ruthless. He interrupted. 'I'm told that nothing was taken.'

'That's not quite true. Some computer discs were taken, but that's all. I didn't think the matter was worth pursuing.'

'What was on them?' asked Darren Webb, who was feeling rather left out of things.

'Names and addresses of clients, with details of the trips they had taken, and their accounts.'

'That must have caused you a great deal of inconvenience,' Timberlake observed disingenuously.

Ms Huntress laughed musically, like steel tubes being hit. 'My dear Inspector, do you think that we don't keep backup discs? There was a set here, in the office, in a stationery cupboard, and another set at my home.'

'I should have realized,' Timberlake said with false humility. 'Then will you run these names through your computer and tell me if they were clients of your agency?' He handed her the list. It was clear she recognized the names.

She looked at him shrewdly. 'Oh, so this is what it's all about. One moment.' She sat down at the computer terminal on her desk and set to work. In a matter of moments she said, 'All three were on a long weekend trip to Paris last month. They left on Saturday the twenty-eight and returned on the thirty-first.'

'How many were on the tour – the trip?'

'Twelve. All women.'

'Will you give me a printout of the names and addresses, please?'

Diana Huntress looked long and hard at him before operating the computer. A printer whirred and buzzed briefly and produced a sheet of paper.

'Thank you,' he said. 'I must ask you to keep this absolutely confidential.'

'If you think I'm going to shout out that clients of my agency are being murdered—'

'Quite. Er, did you accompany them on the trip?'

'No.' Anyone would think she had been asked if she went to bingo.

'You got your sodding murderer yet?' Ted Greening said as Harry Timberlake and Darren Webb returned to the Terrace Vale nick. 'This place is like a bloody madhouse with all these gendarmes from outside milling around, and that AMIP joker of a superintendent nicking all our detectives so we're not getting any work done . . .'

This was rich from Greening, who had raised lead-swinging and gold-bricking to a high art form. Ballets could be staged of Greening's work evasion. He could have dodged work in a Siberian salt mine.

'I'm lucky; I'm out all the time,' Timberlake replied with a perfectly straight face. 'I don't know how you put up with it.'

Greening gave him a blurry look and decided to take the remark at face value.

As soon as Timberlake and Webb reported to Harkness the

superintendent called a meeting of all the murder squad detectives working on the Screwdriver Murders who were in the building. Those who knew him took long, last draws on their cigarettes before they went into the conference room.

Timberlake gave a quick briefing of what they had learned from the agency.

'Any ideas?' Harkness asked.

Percy Howard, a ferret-like detective from Southington spoke up. 'Perhaps the four murdered women left the main group either separately or together and saw something, or did something which made them targets.'

'That assumes the murderer knew the names and addresses of that particular four of the group,' Sergeant Webb said.

'If he was the one who nicked the computer discs he'd have all the names and addresses,' Howard said defensively.

'He'd got twelve names and addresses, but didn't necessarily know who was who,' Timberlake pointed out.

'I'm inclined to agree with Inspector Timberlake,' Harkness said. 'I'm not ruling out DC Howard's suggestion, but we may have something even more serious on our hands.'

'The murderer intends to kill them all.' Timberlake's voice sounded like the tolling of a bell.

At first they found it hard to believe that someone planned to kill *twelve* women, then realized these days anything was possible in criminal circles.

Harkness gave Harry Timberlake and Darren Webb four names each of the remaining members of the group on the Paris trip. 'You've had experience of this sort of situation before, so you know you'll have to tread very warily indeed not to frighten them unnecessarily. You will have to tell them to be on their guard, however. You'd both better take a woman officer with you,' he added. 'It may be less intimidating for them.'

There were only two woman detectives in the room: WPC Rosie Hall, who was a temporary CID aide, and Sarah Lewis.

'Lewis, you go with Inspector Timberlake, and Hall, you with Sergeant Webb.' Timberlake looked at Harkness, and wondered if he'd guessed anything. The man was sharper than a serpent's tooth, although not as nasty.

'We'll take my car,' Timberlake said, as he and Sarah set off for the worst moments in both their lives.

Chapter 17

The first woman on Harry Timberlake's list was a Mrs Violet Jenkin, a widow who lived in a semi-detached house in Terrace Vale's middle-stratum area. She opened the front door with a pair of vicious-looking shears in her hand. She was dressed like a Chinese peasant, if there are any Chinese peasant women who wear green wellies, expensive perfume and are made up as if they are ready for the catwalk.

'Ooops! Sorry about these!' she said, brandishing the shears dangerously. 'I was doing a little gardening.'

She removed the wellies and invited them into a room with chrome, leather and glass furniture that could have been stolen from a set of *Star Trek*. The two detectives managed to work out which pieces were chairs and sat down gingerly.

Mrs Jenkin said she had read about the murders, but it hadn't occurred to her the victims were members of her group. 'We were all on first-name terms, you see.' She read one of the weightier journals that cut fripperies like photographs to a minimum.

No, she didn't remember any of the women going off on expeditions of their own. The party stayed together throughout the trip.

Sarah gently warned her to be careful of strangers for the time being, which translated meant 'until the murderer was caught'.

Next was a Miss Jill Bender, a spinster living in a block of mansion flats. She irresistibly reminded Timberlake of the Mouse, Piers Aubusson's PA and would-be slave, only older. Like Mrs Jenkin, she too was barely aware who the murdered women were, until Timberlake explained. No, they all stuck together during the tour, she declared. Abruptly she leapt up and scurried from the room as if Harry Timberlake and Sarah Lewis were about to produce screwdrivers.

She returned with a paper wallet of colour photographs.

'Which ones were they?' she asked, handing over a group photograph. Timberlake indicated the four victims. Miss Bender clucked and tutted sympathetically. Timberlake looked intently at the photograph and said sharply, 'Who took the photo? You're all here, all twelve of you.'

'I took it. My camera has a delayed-action thing.'

The two detectives studied the other photographs one by one, desperately trying to find a clue among the set of typically dull holiday snaps. Miss Bender had never had such attentive viewers of her photographs, although they would soon acquire notoriety among her morbid neighbours.

Timberlake sat up sharply. 'See that?' he said to Sarah. 'Who's that there with the camcorder?' he asked Miss Bender.

'Anthea ... something. I can't remember her surname.'

The third name on their list was Miss Anthea Reddish, of Church Road.

When Timberlake pulled up outside the house he was unaware that the driver of a five-year-old Mercedes 220 automatic parked across the road was watching the house. Timberlake and Sarah Lewis could not have suspected that they were within twenty yards of a murderer.

Anthea Reddish was not at home, but the agency list had her daytime work address and telephone number. To their surprise they found she was a local solicitor, who presumably did no criminal work otherwise they would have known her. Despite her name she was a sort of pale pre-Raphaelite woman, whose appearance belied her authoritative manner.

Timberlake did not beat about the bush. He explained the situation tersely. Anthea Reddish gave no sign of emotion, although she permitted her eyebrows to rise at his last sentences. 'You had a camcorder with you on the Paris trip. We'd like to see the material you shot, urgently.'

'Why?'

'There may – just may – be something on the tape which will give us a lead to the murderer ... and prevent further killings.'

When Timberlake arrived with the two women back at the house in Church Road his heart was beating slightly faster than normal, and he felt a strange tingling in the whole of his body, as if a small electric current was running through it. All his instincts

168

were telling him that he was closing on his quarry.

Miss Reddish searched through a stack of cassettes, found one and put it into the VTR machine.

It was a typical holiday recording, a sort of animated version of Miss Bender's photographs: members of the tour party, Parisian landmarks, seascapes and a shot of a Hovercraft overtaking their ferry. Timberlake and Sarah watched the tape closely, twice, occasionally using rewind and stop frame. There was nothing in the whole ninety minutes that meant anything to them.

Anthea Reddish brought them cups of tea during the viewing. 'Nothing?' she asked when the tape came to the end for the second time.

Timberlake had seldom felt more wretched. 'I'm afraid not,' he said.

'Perhaps you'll have better luck with the other one,' she said brightly. 'I did two.'

'Please God,' he said audibly.

After the first seconds of electronic snow and zigzags on the tape it had the tour party preparing to mount the gangplank of the ferry at Dover. Many of the women smiled or waved, others struck exaggerated poses. One or two women were photographing Anthea Reddish as she filmed. Then suddenly, as the camera panned:

'Stop!' Harry shouted, leaping to his feet and sending his cup of tea flying unheeded.

In the background, seen between two women, staring out at him from the screen, was the figure of Carl-Heinz Rohmer, a.k.a. Henry Newman. He was standing beside a sign which gave the date, Saturday 27th, and the time of sailing, 9.30 a.m. From his expression it was clear he had seen he was being filmed.

'Newman! I told you! I told you!' Timberlake shouted.

'I don't believe it,' Sarah murmured. But she did.

Everything now fell into place with a thunderous clang. To keep his alibi watertight Newman couldn't allow a recording to exist of himself in England on the morning after his wife's and his mother-in-law's murders. Nor could he risk any of the party remembering him if there were any further publicity about the murders. It was a well-known legal maxim that an alibi proved to be fabricated was almost as good as a confession. He had to eliminate them . . . all of them.

169

Timberlake ejected the cassette from the VTR and broke off the safety tab on the case so that nothing could be recorded over it.

'Miss Reddish, I want you to take this tape to Terrace Vale Police Station. Give it to Detective Superintendent Harkness or Detective Sergeant Webb, and *no one else.* Explain what's on it and tell him WDC Lewis and I have gone to arrest Newman. We'll need a van. Do you think you can remember all that?'

'Of course,' she said equably and repeated almost verbatim what he had said. She behaved as if this was an everyday occurrence like drawing up a will or conveyancing a lock-up garage.

Timberlake was lightheaded with euphoria and a burning desire for personal revenge: revenge against Newman for sneering at him and almost openly defying him to prove he'd killed his wife and mother-in-law; to the back-sniggerers who had said he was obsessive and wrong about Newman he wanted to say – to shout – in effect, 'I told you so.' He wanted to restore his reputation . . . Justice came into it somewhere, too.

It was an overwhelmingly heady mixture for a man totally unaccustomed to this degree of subjective emotion, and he was temporarily bordering on the psychotic. For the first time in his life his judgement had failed devastatingly like a computer hit by a massive overload of power. The result would be catastrophic. To entrust vital evidence to anyone but a trusted police officer was madness.

Sarah was pleased that he had won against all the odds – or was going to – but because her involvement with the case was minimal and impersonal, her own reactions were less violent.

'Come on, let's get moving,' he said impatiently.

'Hadn't we better wait for the backup?'

'It'll take too long.'

Sarah hesitated, but Timberlake was already on his way to the door.

Once in the car Sarah glanced sideways at him to see if he was calming down, but he was as keyed up as ever. She was scared. She considered snatching the key from the ignition to make him stop and think, but Harry Timberlake was no ordinary detective, and it made her hesitate. She decided to stay with him and try to act as a brake on his impetuosity.

Newman himself opened the door to Timberlake's knock. 'Ah, Harry,' he said with his usual false bonhomie. 'Hmm, I like your new assistant. Come in.' They went into the main sitting room.

'Your girlfriend not here?' Timberlake asked.

'She's gone on an errand. She won't be long.'

It was Timberlake's great moment. 'Carl-Heinz Rohmer, also known as Charles Henry Newman, I am arresting you for the murders of Ann Pascoe and Veronica Newman on the night of the twenty-sixth to twenty-seventh of last month. Do you wish to say anything? You are not obliged to say anything unless you wish to but whatever you say will be taken down in writing and may be given in evidence.' Despite his excitement he got the caution word perfect. 'I shall also be charging Carole Pradet with conspiracy to murder.'

'You've gone off your head, Harry. What brought this on?'

Timberlake answered formally. 'I am in possession of a TV recording which shows you in England on the morning of Saturday the twenty-seventh.'

There was a long silence. Eventually Newman sighed and said wryly, 'I suppose I'd better get some things together.' He walked calmly into the next room. Harry Timberlake was still euphoric enough to be careless. He didn't wake up to the possible dangers until Newman returned to the room with a .32 Walther PPK automatic. Newman quickly stepped to Sarah's side and pointed the gun at her head. 'You try anything, Harry, and she dies first.' He smiled, but it was worse than a menacing scowl. 'Killing one more won't make any difference now. Behave yourself and you'll both live.'

A burning rage seized Timberlake: a rage against himself for his stupidity.

'Sit over there,' Newman told him, indicating a low couch which was difficult to get out of in a hurry. Timberlake looked at Newman. His gun was rock steady, pointed at Sarah. Although her face was white she had herself under control. Her voice was steady when she spoke.

'Is it all right for me to sit down?' she said.

'OK. Just there, next to me.' He addressed Timberlake. 'Congratulations. I didn't think you'd ever break my alibi. If it hadn't been for those women ... I underestimated you. Less than you underestimated me, though.'

Timberlake thought that if he could keep Newman talking long enough they would all be there when the backup van arrived. Newman would be armed, but at least the odds would be better.

171

'How did you get all those people to swear you were in Marseille that night? You couldn't have bribed them all.'

'Carole and I made a long tape-recording of a row. She moved back and forth in front of the blind while the tape was running. She's nearly as tall as me and everyone was convinced they'd seen both of us.'

'How did you get into England without a passport?' Sarah asked. She guessed what Harry Timberlake was doing and was doing her part.

'Good question. A couple of months before Veronica chucked me out, I got a travel document at a local post office in Southend. I went to a cemetery, found the name of a man born about the same time as me, applied for a birth certificate, and faked a form from a doctor saying he'd known me for years. It was too easy.'

'You started planning it that long ago?'

'Sure. I suppose you guessed why I came to see her a couple of days before I killed her?'

Timberlake nodded. 'So if we found any traces of you in the house you had an explanation.'

'Afterwards I made sure I hadn't left any hairs in the bed ... or on her.' The implications of that remark revolted the two detectives.

'Why did—?' Sarah began.

'Why did I screw her? Why not? She wanted it. I did her a favour, really. What's a better way to go than after a good screwing?' He grinned.

'Did you have to be so brutal?' Timberlake said.

'Yes. For lots of reasons.' He grinned again.

Until now neither of them had fully realized just how much of a psychopath Newman really was.

'And her mother?'

'Oh, she was easy. She always slept heavily after her regular nightcap. I smothered her with a pillow so she wouldn't hear me and Veronica and kick up a fuss. You know, Harry, you did me a favour. That time you talked to me about Sod's – what was it?'

'The Sod's Law effect, the random factor, the unpredictable element that even the cleverest criminal can't foresee.'

'Yeah. You got me thinking. At Dover I'd noticed that mob of silly bitches with their cameras and the stickers on their luggage: Diana Huntress Ltd. So to be on the safe side, I broke into

172

the agency – that was easy – and got the computer discs with the addresses.'

'I know. That's what put me on the right track.'

'For all the good it's done you. Carole and I checked on their movements to find the best time to eliminate them, and then search their homes. I didn't leave any obvious signs: I'm an expert.'

'Why kill them with a screwdriver?' Sarah asked.

'Quick, silent and almost no blood. We had a couple of killings like that in Dortmund when I was there.' The gun was still pointing at Sarah's head as if locked on by radar.

'Were you going to kill *all* the women?' Sarah asked again.

'Sure. Listen, when you've killed once, it gets easier each time. And my first one was a long time ago.'

There was the sound of the front door opening. Sarah sighed with relief.

'Your lot haven't got a key,' Newman said with another leer that made Timberlake want to smash his face in.

Carole Pradet entered the room. She was dressed conventionally in what Sarah recognized as an Armani suit, and carried a croco-dile-skin handbag. She stopped dead in the doorway, her eyes widening.

'Everything's under control,' Newman said in French. 'And you?'

She replied in Flemish, or German. Newman nodded with sat-isfaction.

'You'll never get away,' Timberlake told Newman. Even at a time like this he avoided the full cliché, 'You'll never get away with it.' 'They know all about you at the nick. Even if the backup doesn't get here before you leave, they'll—'

Newman nodded to Carole. 'In French,' he instructed her.

'I got her at the traffic lights.' She took two things from her hand-bag and threw them on the table, out of reach of both Timberlake and Sarah. The first was a plastic bag containing a bloodstained screwdriver. The blood went all the way up to the handle.

The second object was a cassette. Timberlake's heart felt like lead.

'The random factor, the unpredictable element,' Newman said. 'It works both ways. Carole was watching the house when you two arrived. We watched the houses one by one to find the best times to deal with the women. Carole phoned me on the car

173

phone, and I told her to wait and see what happened. Later, when Anthea What's-her-name drove off in her own car Carole followed her. People trust a good-looking woman driving a Merc.' He gave a great gust of laughter. 'So now nobody knows where you are and what you've got on us.' He laughed again.

Harry Timberlake and Sarah didn't feel like laughing.

'Now, get out your car keys, finger and thumb, and put them on the table beside you. Slowly.'

Timberlake had no alternative.

'Carole, get the other gun and my belt, and put the cases in the Mercedes,' Newman told her in French. 'Bring it right up to the house. Take his car and hide it round the back of number twenty-three. They're away at the moment.'

'Be careful of my car!' Harry Timberlake said, before his lack of a sense of proportion struck him.

Carole returned with a money belt and another Walther PPK. She kept Sarah covered while Newman put on both money belt and gun and then went out.

'As I said, your warning did me a good turn,' Newman went on. 'I've been liquidating as much of Veronica's money as possible – cash, bearer bonds and the rest. It's in one of those cases and this.' He slapped the heavy money belt.

Timberlake managed to keep his voice steady. 'What do you intend to do with us?' He knew it was a foolish question.

'Well, that depends. If you don't try any silly heroics, you'll be all right. Cold and uncomfortable, maybe, but OK. Veronica was loaded, really loaded. She had a cabin cruiser, did you know?'

Timberlake shook his head.

'Me and Carole, we're going to the Continent – which country doesn't matter to you. We'll take you with us, and somewhere midway in the Channel or North Sea we'll put you in the dinghy. By the time you're picked up in the night, we'll have disappeared.'

Timberlake knew he was lying, and he guessed Sarah knew it too.

The Sycamores Avenue being the sort of place it was the garages had connecting doors into the houses. Getting Timberlake and Sarah into the car was easy enough with the threat of the guns. Timberlake sat in the front passenger's seat while Newman drove. Carole Pradet stayed on Sarah's right hand side, holding the gun in her ribs. Timberlake knew something of the gun. Although it was not a very powerful weapon, at close range it would be deadly. High-powered guns can often do less damage than low-powered ones. A high-powered bullet can go straight through a body, while a low-powered one can tumble over and ricochet inside, causing far more damage.

Newman gave Carole Pradet strict orders: if Timberlake tried anything, or either of them tried anything, she was to shoot Sarah. 'And don't think she won't. She killed one of the others herself,' Newman warned.

It not only hamstrung Timberlake, it put him in a straitjacket as well. He might have risked his own skin, but he couldn't – wouldn't – take a chance with Sarah's life while there was the faintest hope of their getting out of this mess.

It was a maxim in wartime that if you were taken prisoner, the best time to try to escape was as soon after being captured as possible. The longer you were in captivity, the slimmer the chances of evasion became. Timberlake was observing, thinking hard and trying to come up with a plan. His mind was a tumultuous blank.

'Where is this boat?' he asked as they drove south-east across London.

'Hastings.'

'That's a long way out of town,' Timberlake said, trying to sound casual and relatively relaxed to make Newman think he trusted his promise to let them live. He wondered whether Newman would imagine him to be so naïve. The man was so arrogant he possibly might just believe in his own ability to take them in. 'You'd think she'd have kept it at Brighton, or somewhere convenient to town,' Timberlake went on.

'She used to, before she decided Brighton was too vulgar.' Newman laughed.

By the time they got to Tunbridge Wells Timberlake still hadn't the glimmer of a plan. After they passed through the town and arrived in open country again Sarah spoke up.

'I've got to pee,' she said. 'Can we stop somewhere?'

'Forget it,' Newman said.

'I've *got* to,' she complained.

'Do as you're told and shut up!' Newman said tensely.

Slowly Timberlake turned round to look at her. 'Do as you're told!' he said loudly, looking her directly in the eyes. He hoped she could read his thoughts. Newman was watching her through

175

the rear-view mirror. She remained expressionless.

Newman was becoming increasingly edgy. Timberlake was certain that he was planning to do something soon. He could see a big TV aerial mast ahead, and he knew they were approaching Bedgebury Forest. There it would be easy for Newman to take them into the woods, shoot them and hide their bodies in bushes or undergrowth. By the time they were found Newman and the Pradet woman would be far away. His suspicions were confirmed when Newman turned off into an empty side road and speeded up the car.

'Stop fidgeting,' Timberlake said to Sarah, 'and *do what you're told*!'

He started easing himself more comfortably into his own seat with his hands down by his side. Newman was jumpy:he looked at him suspiciously. Timberlake gave no sign of noticing. He was concentrating on preparing for a triple manoeuvre which he simply *had* to get right first time. He was like a competition diver on a springboard about to perform a complicated dive, rehearsing his movements, making the dive in his head before actually jumping.

'*Duck*!' he roared.

At the same time he pressed the release catch of Newman's safety belt.

He put his left foot up against the dashboard and swung his right at the automatic gear lever.

And missed.

He had a weird sensation as if time had suddenly slipped a cog. Everything became dream-like and appeared to go into slow motion, even his own actions, as if they were moving under water. He hoped to God that Sarah had understood and ducked down behind his seat.

It was an age before he managed to make his muscles respond and make another lunge at the lever.

This time Timberlake connected, and he smashed it from Drive through Neutral and Reverse into Park, breaking the safety catches with the strength of sheer panic.

The noise from the transmission and engine was awful: it was the death scream of some metal monster. The car stopped as if it had run into buffers.

Beside him Newman described a graceful parabola and hit the windscreen with his head. The bizarre slow-motion effect persisted and Timberlake saw the windscreen balloon outwards before Newman went through it, slithered across the car's bonnet and on to the ground, where he lay, stunned.

At the same time Timberlake felt a thump in the back of his well-padded seat and knew that Sarah had reacted to his shout and had ducked down to safety. Carole Pradet flew upwards and forward faster than Newman because she had no steering wheel to hold on to. Her face hit the back of his head, crushing her nose, before she bounced up and hit the roof of the car. The gun she was holding flew out of her hand somewhere. She screamed, then began to moan quietly as she lapsed into unconsciousness.

Timberlake was winded and he ached where the safety belt had bitten into his body. He grunted out to Sarah, 'You all right?'

'I think so,' she said.

'Find the gun, get her out and into the recovery position, and tie her hands behind her back.'

'What with?'

He pulled off his tie. 'That.' He forced himself to move out of the car.

In front of the car Newman was getting to his feet. He looked terrifying, his face a crimson mask twisted with rage and some other emotion Timberlake could not fathom. He struggled to his feet, dragging at the gun inside his jacket. Sarah looked up and saw him almost at the same moment that she noticed Carole's gun on the floor of the car. She snatched it up, screeching 'Harry!'

Sarah threw the gun to Timberlake. He grabbed for it, but dropped it and it fell. As he bent down to pick it up a bullet from Newman's gun smashed into the side of the car a foot above his head.

'Drop it!' Timberlake shouted, pointing his gun at Newman.

The blood-soaked man fired at Timberlake again. The bullet hit a bumper and whined off into the air. At the best of times it's harder to hit someone with an automatic than most people think. And Newman was unsteady and badly shaken after his accident. Timberlake marvelled at the man's strength to be able to get up at all after what he had experienced.

Timberlake fired, well above Newman's head. Somehow he couldn't bring himself to shoot another man, even under threat from him. Newman had no such inhibition. He fired once more.

Timberlake was thrown back against the Mercedes as if some-

one had hit him with a sledgehammer. He slid to the ground, and
the gun fell from his hand. Blood spurted from his jacket. Sarah
screamed. Newman took a deep breath, held his gun in both hands
and levelled it at Timberlake's torso from ten yards.

There was a deafening sound from beside Timberlake. Sarah
had snatched up the gun and fired at Newman. He felt the wind
of the bullet as it whistled past his head. Newman hesitated for a
moment, wondering which one of them to shoot at first. It nearly
cost him his life, for Sarah loosed off another shot, which missed
him by as little as the first.

Newman cursed in German, turned, and ran off in an unsteady
lope across a field, away from the main road. He gave neither a
glance nor a thought for Carole, lying half in, half out the car.

Sarah turned to Timberlake. 'Harry!' she shouted.

'I'm all right. Shoulder.' He levered himself up by the side of
the car and took the gun from Sarah's hand. He began to move
after Newman.

Sarah held him back. 'You'll lose too much blood.'

'See if there's a first-aid box in the car.'

There was one in the glove compartment. Sarah found a large
pad, quickly ripped open Timberlake's blood-soaked shirt and tied
it tightly against the wound. He nodded his thanks, then began an
unsteady jog after Newman.

'Let him go,' Sarah said. 'He can't get away now. He'll be
picked up.'

'*I'm* going to have him,' Timberlake said. He suddenly looked
like a stranger. He pushed her aside and started after Newman.

After no more than twenty yards his chest felt as if it was
trapped in a massive iron vice and his head swam. He fought
against a terrible temptation to abandon the chase by telling himself that Newman probably felt even worse than he did. Once he
fell flat on his face as his foot caught in a grass tussock and the
dull ache in his shoulder turned into a sharp pain. He deliberately
conjured up images of Veronica Newman, of Mary Cotter, dead
in the back of the Volvo, and others, to stiffen his determination.
Somehow he managed to keep going.

In front of him Newman fired again, but he was too far away
for the shot to be effective, and his aim was wild. The two men,
pursuer and pursued, lurched onwards like two drunks. Newman
led the chase towards where the ground began to rise. It was odd:

people running away always tended to run uphill, Timberlake remembered. He kept putting one foot in front of the other mechanically, like a marathon runner with only a couple of miles to go. His shoulder and upper chest felt warm and sticky, and he knew that the bleeding had started again.

Way ahead of him Newman came to a faltering halt at a line of trees. Timberlake didn't think it was fatigue, but rather because of something he had seen. Newman took another couple of paces . . . and disappeared.

Somehow Timberlake managed to increase his speed, but even so his progress was almost pitiful. He plodded on, his breath rasping in his throat, the sound of his madly beating heart sounding in his ears. And then he saw it.

The ground fell away steeply to a deep railway cutting. Newman, covered in earth and twigs, was at the bottom. Wearily he picked himself up and started to reel along the track. Timberlake took a deep breath and started to slide down the slope on his back. He hit the bottom with a thump that knocked the last breath out of him. It seemed an age before he could drag himself to his feet again. It couldn't have been that long for Newman was not far away.

As Timberlake half-walked, half-staggered after him he became aware that it was only a single track, probably a local shuttle service. Dizzily he noticed there were three rails, one at the side slightly raised above the others: the live electric rail. He kept to the other side of the track, away from it.

He stumbled on, caught his toes on a sleeper and pitched sideways. He stretched out his arms to save himself. To his horror he saw that he was falling straight towards the live rail. He reached as far forward as he could, and managed to land with his hands on the far side of the rail, his body arched above it. He despaired of finding the strength to raise himself up. His heart was drumming madly in his ears. Timberlake took a deep breath, and gingerly put one hand on the ordinary rail . . . and then the other. From all fours he managed to drag himself back on to his feet again. Although the granite chippings between the sleepers cut deeply into his knees and hands he was hardly aware of the pain.

Simultaneously with the sound of a gunshot a bullet hit a rail beside him and caromed off somewhere. Timberlake was only too aware that he was a stationary target and tried to get to his feet again. A second bullet ploughed into the granite chippings, scattering them in a sharp-pointed shower.

'That's six,' Timberlake told himself. The magazine of a Walther PPK holds seven cartridges. At the same time he realized that he had dropped his own gun somewhere.

The chase, which would have been ludicrous had it not been deadly, started again.

The cutting curved and Newman disappeared from view. As Timberlake rounded the bend he saw there was a tunnel. Newman was nowhere in sight. The sides of the cutting were too steep for him to attempt to climb, so he had to be inside. Timberlake approached cautiously, aware that Newman still had a gun.

He paused at the entrance, keeping as far to one side as possible. He listened, and could hear Newman's uncertain footsteps up ahead.

The tunnel was old, dating back to the early days of the railways. It was narrow, with the walls perilously close to the rails. Gloomy amber lights showed up small recesses in the tunnel walls at about thirty-yard intervals, where men working on the rails could stand when a train passed.

A small oval of light indicated the far end of the tunnel. From time to time the feeble amber lights gave a glimpse of Newman's tottering form. Timberlake was finally gaining on him when he heard a terrifying noise.

A train's whistle sounded as it rounded a bend at the far end and then blocked out the light at the end of the tunnel. Newman was silhouetted against the powerful lights on the locomotive. It bore down on the two men remorselessly. The driver was sounding his whistle in pointless, urgent blasts. A new noise reverberated unbearably in the tunnel: the banshee screech of brakes bearing on the train's steel wheels.

Timberlake could see in a flash that Newman was caught midway between two recesses, and he would never get to one before the train was on him.

All too soon Timberlake was aware of his own deadly danger. For the first time in his life he was aware of his own mortality. His first instinct was to turn and run back to a recess, but an almost instantaneous appraisal of the situation told him his best chance was to race the train to the next recess ahead of him. Newman had started to run for the same recess, although he must

180

have known it was hopeless. He fired his remaining bullet at Timberlake almost aimlessly. The bullet ricocheted away down the tunnel adding to the intolerable cacophony that was beating on Timberlake's ears.

The whole situation had lasted only seconds, but it seemed a lifetime before it ended in extraordinary drama.

At last Newman knew that he was beyond hope. He stopped running, stood foursquare in the centre of the track, pulled himself up to his full height and deliberately raised his arm in a salute, or maybe a farewell, to Timberlake. The train hurtled on, and Newman was gone.

He was a cold, calculating murderer, a thoroughly evil man. Yet he died with style.

Now the locomotive was bearing down on Timberlake. He believed he would be safe in five paces, if he could make them.

Five ... four ... three ... two ... He was level with the recess and a pace from safety when everything went black.

Chapter 18

The first thing he was aware of was an ache; a dull, numbing ache in his left shoulder and upper arm. He tried to open his eyes, but the lids were like lead. He managed it at last, then closed them again as a hard white light made his head spin. Somebody very far away was saying something, but he couldn't understand what it was.

Cautiously he made the effort to open his eyes once more. He was in a plain room with white ceiling and white walls. Away to one side he thought he could make out something that might be curtains. It dawned on him he was lying down. He tried to sit up, but his body refused to obey his instructions, and his shoulder hurt abominably.

'Guv, you all right?' The voice was quite close now, and at last he recognized it. It was Darren Webb, sitting at his bedside.

'Where am I?' Timberlake asked. Even in his barely conscious state he was annoyed with himself for his predictable cliché.

'Hospital,' said a woman's voice at the moment that Timberlake realized it himself. 'East Sussex.'

He turned his head. A nurse was at the side of his bed taking his pulse on his injured side. 'You're going to be all right, Inspector. There's no serious damage.'

'How you feeling, guv?' Webb said.

He licked dry lips. 'Like I've been hit by a train.' And then he remembered, and came out in a cold sweat.

'What happened?' Timberlake asked at last.

'Well, we got most of the story from Sarah Lewis and the train driver and—'

'Is she all right?'

'Fine, guv, fine.' He paused. 'Newman's dead, and the Pradet woman's under arrest. She's coughed the lot. Sarah Lewis tied her up with a tie, would you believe?'

'Fancy,' Timberlake said, feeling better by the moment. 'How is Sarah?'

'Fine. They soon patched her up.' Before Timberlake could ask him what was wrong with her, Webb went on, 'The train driver was pretty shaken for a while, and—'

'*He* was shaken!'

'He was able to say the train didn't hit you, but you passed out as you got into the gap in the tunnel wall. The doctors here said it was probably shock and loss of blood, and you hit your head when you fell.'

'We gave you three pints of blood,' the nurse said proudly, as if most of it was hers.

'What's wrong with me?'

'Nothing that won't mend,' she said. 'The consultant will be in soon to give you all the details. You had a bullet in your shoulder,' she added with awe.

'There's half Fleet Street and the BBC and ITV outside wanting to see you,' Webb told him.

'Don't worry,' the nurse said darkly. 'We won't let them bother you till you're ready.' Horatius declaring that he would keep Lars Porsena and the Etruscans off the bridge could not have sounded more determined.

Timberlake was seized by a moment of panic. 'What's happened to my car?' he asked.

'It's OK, guv. I went and picked it up myself. It's in the garage at the nick, not a scratch on it,' Webb reassured him.

'Thanks, Darren.'

'Couple more points, guv. That Holworth character who committed suicide in the garage: it was nothing to do with his woman friend being killed. He'd embezzled his clients out of a couple of million.' He waited for a moment, then said with a touch of embarrassment, 'There's a lot of red faces back at the nick, guv. You must be quite chuffed, proving you were right after all.'

'Not really,' Timberlake said sombrely. 'Four more innocent women were killed.'

'There'd have been a lot more if it hadn't been for you.'

'It's no compensation.'

'At least Newman paid for it.'

183

Timberlake nodded without speaking. Unusually for a policeman, he wasn't in favour of capital punishment.

Webb grinned wryly. 'Remember the psychologist's profile of the killer, guv?'

It hurt Timberlake's shoulder to laugh so much.

'I think that's long enough, Sergeant,' the nurse said. 'There are other people wanting to see the patient, and we don't want to tire him out, do we?'

Darren Webb rose. 'I'm really glad you're all right,' he said, with more emotion than Timberlake had ever heard before. 'Well done, guv. Bloody well done.' He went out quickly.

A few minutes later the door opened and someone came in. The nurse said, 'I'll leave you two alone.' To the visitor she said sternly, 'Not too long, now, and don't excite him.' She went out.

'Hello, Harry,' Sarah said quietly. She leant over him and kissed him.

The kiss sent a tremor through Timberlake. It was like no other kiss she had ever given him. He looked up at her. Her left arm was in a sling, and the side of her face was bruised and swollen.

'What's wrong? What happened?'

'I broke a bone in my arm, and caught my face on something in the car. I didn't realize it until it was all over and I began to hurt.'

'Are you all right? You sure?'

'Definitely. Anyway, I've got seven days' sick leave.'

'You didn't drive down here like that?' he said, worried. 'Did Darren Webb give you a lift?'

'No. A friend.'

She left it at that. It was like cold water in Timberlake's face. That's all he needed: the strange kiss and 'A friend,' with no explanation. Timberlake understood at once. It said more than a long speech. To be fair, Sarah hadn't meant to break the news to him while he was still ill, but her lack of natural duplicity betrayed her.

Conflicting emotions swept through him. At first he was depressed that it was over between them. It took some moments for him to admit to himself it had been over for some time. To his astonishment, he began to feel something like relief. At first he couldn't believe it, but the feeling persisted and grew.

'It's been great,' he said.

It ended like that, without discussions, rows, accusations, recriminations or tears.

Neither of them knew quite how to say goodbye. They were spared awkward farewells by the sound of women arguing in the corridor. The door burst open, and Lucinda Fordham made an entrance. She did not come in, she Made an Entrance, shutting the door in the angry face of the nurse.

She was dressed in black as if Timberlake was already dead, and carried an enormous bouquet of flowers. Putting the flowers on a table, she rushed to his bedside, ignoring Sarah. For one moment he was afraid she was going to throw herself on top of him.

In the tragic tones of Lady Anne beside the corpse of her father-in-law in *Richard III* she cried 'Harry, *darling*! Oh, God, I'm so *relieved* you're all right!' It could have served for a passage in a Verdi opera. Timberlake wondered how she would have behaved if he'd been killed.

And then it hit him. She was *acting*. Her whole life was a series of acts: the shy fragile young woman, the lover with her moans and cries in bed, the homebody sophisticate with the dinner she had fixed for him at her flat which was straight out of a 1930s von Sternberg film . . . They were all role-playing. He couldn't believe how naïve he had been. It was chastening.

The over-the-top performance was interrupted by the nurse.

'That's enough!' she said. 'Everybody out, now. The consultant wants to see the patient.'

Lucinda Fordham gathered herself up and Made an Exit, looking soulfully over her shoulder. Timberlake reckoned she would have forgotten him before she got out of the hospital grounds.

Harry Timberlake and Sarah Lewis looked at each other for a long, long moment. They said nothing: there was nothing to say. She went out.

The consultant approached the bed. 'Hello, Harry,' she said. It was Jenny Long. 'How do you feel?'

'Confused,' he said. 'And relieved, I think.'

'Uhuh.' She picked up his chart. 'Yes, you're coming along quite well.'

'How are you, Jenny?' he asked quietly.

She shrugged. 'Oh, you know,' she said noncommittally. For once she seemed ill at ease.

For a man who had faced up to an armed murderer intent on killing him, Harry Timberlake was timidly indecisive. Jenny Long wasn't going out of her way to help him.

Finally, he cleared his throat and said rather too loudly, 'I missed you.' He thought it was true, more or less.

Jenny Long considered this statement for a long moment. 'It was your choice.'

'Yes,' he said miserably. 'I suppose I thought it was right at the time.'

She paused even longer. 'I suppose I missed you, too.'

The silence was painful.

'Jenny, would you like your key to my place again?'

She looked him straight in the eye and just said two words.